Praise for Peter L.

"Peter LaSalle has worked his way deep into the storytelling place. Serious, anomalous, his narratives are set into motion by the obsessions and perturbations of living. There is no model, no recipe—each world is uniquely known and irresistibly defined."
—**Sven Birkerts**, author of *Changing the Subject: Art and Attention in the Internet Age* and editor of *AGNI*

"I've always believed that as a short story writer Peter LaSalle has been in the same class as Donald Barthelme and Joyce Carol Oates. . . . His style now flows with such masterly ease that he can be said to be in a class of his own, at the forefront of American creators of original prose." —**Zulfikar Ghose**, author of *The Triple Mirror of the Self*

"LaSalle is one of our finest storytellers."
—**Jay Neugeboren**, author of *Max Baer and the Star of David*

"LaSalle's command of the language is admirable, but even more admirable is his moral vision." —***Dallas Times Herald***

"A major talent." —***Providence Journal***

"Masterful and idiosyncratic stories." —***BOMB Magazine***

"Dreamy stories, deliciously descriptive."
—***Atlanta Journal-Constitution***

"LaSalle's stories are subtle, evocative, haunting—and brilliantly written." —***Kirkus Reviews***

"LaSalle is a master—his writing is so intelligent and thoughtful, so smooth and fluent, its current so strong, and his characters so easy to care about, even to love, that one forgets to look for the stylistic sleights of hand so admired by academics and instead gets caught up in the lives of people who could easily be one's best friend, lover, aunt—or oneself." —***Foreword Reviews***

"A smart and open writer with a restless intellect and infectious passion." —***Publishers Weekly***

SLEEPING
MASK

Also by Peter LaSalle

The Graves of Famous Writers (stories)

Strange Sunlight (a novel)

Hockey Sur Glace (stories)

Tell Borges If You See Him (stories)

Mariposa's Song (a novel)

What I Found Out About Her (stories)

The City at Three P.M. (travel essays)

SLEEPING
MASK

Fictions

PETER LaSALLE

Bellevue Literary Press
NEW YORK

First published in the United States in 2017 by
Bellevue Literary Press, New York

For information, contact:
Bellevue Literary Press
NYU School of Medicine
550 First Avenue
OBV A612
New York, NY 10016

© 2017 by Peter LaSalle

This is a work of fiction. Characters, organizations, events, and places (even those that are actual)
are either products of the author's imagination or are used fictitiously.

These stories have been previously published, sometimes in different form, in the following:
Another Chicago Magazine ("A Day in the Life of the Illness"); *Antioch Review* ("The Absent
Painter" and "Lunch Across the Bridge"); *Boulevard* ("Southern Majestic Zone"); *Hotel Amerika*
("A Short Manual of Mirrors"); *The Literary Review* ("Boys: A New African Fable"); *New England
Review* ("What Can't Not Happen"); *Post Road Magazine* ("E.A.P: A Note"); *Santa Monica
Review* ("The Flight" and "Found Fragment from the Report on the Cadaver Dogs of Northern
Maine, 1962"); *Tin House* ("A Late Afternoon Swim"); and *Western Humanities Review* ("Sleeping
Mask"). "The Flight" also appeared in the anthology *Air Fare: Stories, Poems, and Essays on
Flight* (Sarabande Books, 2004), and "Lunch Across the Bridge" in the anthology *Best of the West*
(University of Texas Press, 2011). A Portuguese translation by Ian Teixeira of "E.A.P: A Note" was
published in *Livro* (Universidade de São Paulo, São Paulo, Brazil, 2012).The author is grateful to
the editors of all these publications.

Illustration credit, page 167: Jacket design by Cathy Saksa from PORTRAIT OF DELMORE: JOURNALS
AND NOTES OF DELMORE SCHWARTZ 1939–1959 by Delmore Schwartz. Jacket design © 1986 by
Cathy Saksa. Reprinted by permission of Farrar, Straus and Giroux, LLC.

Library of Congress Cataloging-in-Publication Data
is available from the publisher upon request

All rights reserved. No part of this publication may be reproduced or transmitted in any form
or by any means, electronic or mechanical, including photocopy, recording, or any information
storage and retrieval system now known or to be invented, without permission in writing from
the publisher, except by a reviewer who wishes to quote brief passages in connection with a print,
online, or broadcast review.

Bellevue Literary Press would like to thank all its generous donors
—individuals and foundations—for their support.

This publication is made possible by the New York State Council
on the Arts with the support of Governor Andrew Cuomo and
the New York State Legislature.

This project is supported in part
by an award from the National
Endowment for the Arts.

Book design and composition by Mulberry Tree Press, Inc.

Manufactured in the United States of America.

First Edition

1 3 5 7 9 8 6 4 2

paperback ISBN: 978-1-942658-18-4
ebook ISBN: 978-1-942658-19-1

for A. Norman and Hope Conroy LaSalle,
in memory

*Dreaming and wakefulness are the pages of a single book,
and to read them in order is to live,
and to leaf through them at random, to dream.*

—Borges

CONTENTS

SLEEPING
MASK

SLEEPING MASK

HERE, TAKE IT, my darling.

Do you like the feel of it? No, don't be afraid. There in your fingers it is so light, isn't it? Such soft black velvet on the inside, the magenta satin on the outside, the ribbon of its band. What? You have never really held one before? You have seen them, or heard of them, in books or in the movies? Well, it is not a matter of seeing one or hearing about one anymore—just take it as you lie here on the bed, feel it.

The soft black velvet on the inside,

The magenta satin, shimmery, on the outside.

The elasticized black ribbon of its band.

And let me help you with it. Relax. I will take the true mane of your golden hair, lift it from your bare back, your sculpted neck, the wings of your shoulder bones so delicate. Let the world of your eyes entirely aqua be gone at least for a while, and, yes, place it to your fragile face like that, let me lift the pound or more of that wonderful hair as you ease back to the pillow, let me loop the band over your head. Does it feel comfortable? Is the moonlight bright behind the long drapes here gone at last, is there just the darkness and more than that—the Essence of Darkness. Fold your arms over your breasts, stretch out your bare legs. Relax. Of course, it is really dark, and, of course, you are *really* somewhere else. And don't worry if you were scared as a girl there in the low mountains of your *grand-mère's* village in the faraway province that you would rather not think about right now, the big darkness of your feeling your way home along the hedgerows of a rutted road in winter when the stars themselves were too absolutely scared to show their faces. Or the big darkness when your *cousine* Valérie took you to the cellar of the farm's fieldstone barn in the evening. She told you it would be a most secret club, the two of you alone down there below the cows knock-knocking against the worn boards above, the dizzying stink of the damp hay in their stalls, the distorted silhouettes of two little girls (ten, maybe eleven) in a cellar moving along the damp mortar-and-granite walls by candlelight, as the pair of you walked slowly, very slowly, to the farthest corner. But once, you made the mistake of letting Valérie get too far ahead of you; she suddenly pinched the candle's flame and refused to make the slightest sound, move even the metaphor of a muscle, and you screamed to her in the big, big darkness to please say something, to please, really *please,* never do that to you again, and light the candle now, immediately—*please!*

It was worse than the dirty-faced boys at the *école* taunting the girls in the courtyard of cobbles, shoving, taunting, shoving some more. Until one of the girls fell, a scraped knee or a gashed elbow, for the terrible blood that was, in truth, all that boys of that ilk (little tormentors, little beasts) wanted, then they lost interest. Valérie said that she and you would have the place where nobody could ever find you, and dark-eyed, elfin-nosed petite Valérie instructed you to sit on the dirt across from her, in that supposed club in the farthest corner of the cellar of the barn, where, true, nobody up there above—the boys at the *école,* or the ghosts of the farmers and the ghosts of the farmers' wives, even the ghost of your beloved *grand-mère*—could ever get at you, the two of you finally settled, hidden alone there. Valérie always asked you to tell her a secret that you would never dare to tell anybody else, and Valérie promised that next she would do the same, the candle flickering—though she never did. She always just let your own confession spill out in nervous whispers, before, inevitably, her turn came and she flatly proclaimed it was time to go, or she quickly changed the subject, telling you, "Shhh, I think I hear somebody." And in your innocence you strained to listen for the boots of drunken, limping Oncle Étienne above, and Étienne, needless to add, was never there. Still, the boys in the courtyard, Valérie tricking you again into making a confession—none of that amounted to anything compared to that one time you let her get ahead of you (did she maybe *try* to get ahead of you?), and she kept walking and walking toward the corner far back in the cellar, where the two of you had set up a cider barrel as your table, so with the chipped blue vase placed on top of the barrel, that was enough to define it as your private domain: the two of you had a club.

But then she had to snuff the candle; she had to let you panic in the black of it all.

She let you scream that you would kill her if you ever made it out of there, but right then you thought you would never get out of there, escape, and there was only the dark, and there was only you swallowed by it, and there was . . .

Relax.

Here, let me adjust the mask for you myself. Let me push the few vagrant strands of hair from your forehead, and let me spread out the long golden tresses on the pillow. And you are not alone now, not lost. I am with you,

You have put on the sleeping mask I have handed to you.

The soft black velvet on the inside, the magenta satin on the outside.

The black ribbon of its band.

What do you say?

You ask what do you look like now? At this very moment lying on the large bed? Darling, my eternal love, what you look like now is this:

There is a world. There is a famous city in that world. In that city there are *arrondissements*, there are *rues* and there are tree-lined *grands boulevards*; a Métro rumbles underneath it all, and there are blue-enameled signs with white letters, square-shaped street signs, bolted to the sides of the yellow-stone buildings. In one old frilled building on one particular street in a neighborhood of no real consequence, there is a room on the *deuxième étage* behind closed drapes. In this bedroom there are the shadows of hopelessly dated tortoiseshell furniture, then the swirled baroque trim along the ceiling's molding atop the walls; the walls show cracks, the ceiling shows cracks. On the edge of the bed sits a man, and let us say that man is someone like me, an alleged member of the esteemed diplomatic corps. The bed itself is actually a massive contraption with a warped tortoiseshell-veneer headboard; there is a quilt pushed aside in a lumpy pile, also the wrinkled linen for the mattress and the long, bolster-style pillows. That linen may be the sole clue that the man and the woman in the room, even the city, are not in some other time altogether. Or perhaps another era, because the sheets are white with a big patterning of black asterisks and exclamation points, splashed too loudly, the kind of linen bought, surely, during a *solde* at one of the large *magasins* on Rue de Rivoli or over by the Place de l'Opéra—in the designer's mind the whole idea of the fabric was probably comical and campy, not at all serious. But that effect is lost now in the high-ceilinged room of moonlight behind the tall windows' drawn drapes, a room where the mussed sheets showing a pattern of exaggerated punctuation indeed also suddenly take on the seriousness of everything else at the moment. Here, as I said, a man sits on the edge of the bed, the man is looking down at the woman, who reclines on her back. The woman is willowy, very tall, or so it seems, to observe her in this supine position and from this angle of viewing. She is entirely naked, and there is her pale white skin, with a faint sprinkling of cinnamon freckles on the shoulder tops; there are her long arms folded across the rise of her chest, the spring roses of the tips of her breasts covered that way; there is the xylophone of her rib cage, then the ginger tuft between her curving thighs, the knots of her knees and the long, fine calves; her feet are somewhat mossy at the roughened toes from wearing sandals all the time now that the warm weather is here. On the pillow with asterisks and exclamation points rests her head, and it seems that this woman, someone like you, has had the fullness of her hair arranged by the man—again, someone like me—around her head, so that the divided strands of the golden mass spread out on the bolster in tapering flames. The woman is wearing a sleeping mask. It is an object that in its basic oddity, or maybe its basic defining concept, is somehow only a pairing of absolute opposites.

It is familiar yet strange. It is decadent yet heavenly. It is . . . But you know how that goes.

And, my darling, it appears that with the moonlight quite strong behind the drapes, and with the noise of a baby Renault or Citroën going through its gears on the narrow street below—louder and louder, until there is silence again, just the low melody of fragile breathing again—it seems, my darling, that suddenly I am more certain of the whole scene, sure of what I am witnessing. And the man is I, and the woman is you. And I say to you, "Relax."

As I lie down beside you. As you ask me what I am doing, and I say—whisper, really—I say one more time for you to do just that: relax. I say I am simply reclining, lying down beside you. I know you are more than relaxed, however, and you say something about how my story of the man sitting on the edge of the bed with a woman lying down wearing a sleeping mask has made you lusciously tired. Then you drift into some soft talk about a spotted leopard that comes up to you in a jungle to warmly, wetly, lick your hand as if the beast were a gentle kitten, a scenario out of a dream that seems to have nothing to do with anything but certainly has everything to do with that more important Realm of Nothing. And next you talk about another scene altogether. You are in a wheat field, where children have made lovely kites out of newspaper, the kites dance in the blowing blue air above the yellow undulations of the wheat, dance in darts and dives, and the silvery strings leading up to them in long arcs tighten and slacken and tighten, the bow-tie tails shivering—and you are happily watching the children flying those kites, you are thinking about . . .

As your voice, slower, stops in midsentence. You let your arms slacken, and they slip to your sides. You are asleep. And even if it hurt you so for me to confess that I lied to you about not having as much as phoned my ex-wife, let alone spent several nights with her, during that strangest of all dreams that somehow took on the texture of my ten-day trip as an envoy to Manhattan the month before, even if you cried and confronted me with other things, too, especially my insulting frankness with broken-down Thompson when I was drunk at the Czech embassy's formal reception, as I shouted at you as well there and behaved very badly, to say the least, it has nothing to do with this moment in the bedroom—*now*.Because we have made love, long and passionate and crazily devouring love that becomes that much sadder when it involves a young woman and—in the standard vernacular—"a man of a certain age"; but there was no sadness, no comedy whatsoever, in your whimpers of pleasure, your cries, also in my own declaration, strong and resolved and spoken at the exact instant when we released each other from the sweaty wrestling, completely spent after the building and building and utter building savagery of our lips locked in such kisses, I looked right into your aqua eyes, the two of us evanescing, and I said to you, more sure of myself than ever before: "I don't *ever* want to die."

Then, for some reason, I was holding a sleeping mask. And in my own dream (I still see you crouching in the jungle of big emerald ferns and big scarlet trumpet flowers, down on one knee while the gentle leopard puts his wet tongue to your lovely alabaster fingers to lick away at them; I still see the children in the yellow wheat field with their homemade kites fashioned from newspaper, your standing there and marveling at the little ballet of their druggingly wonderful play—those are your dreams that truly do speak of your tenderness, your specialness), and, yes, in my own dream I sit next to you on a bed after the lovemaking, and I hold out the mask for you to take. While you ask me, "What is it?" Or, as you say, "Is it really a sleeping mask?" Propping yourself up to your elbows, you confess to me that, of course, you have heard of such a thing, but you have never actually seen one before. But I tell you softly to simply relax, just ease yourself back to the bed, your head on the elongated bolster of a pillow with huge asterisks and exclamation points.

I hand the mask to you.

o o o

THE SOFT BLACK VELVET on the inside.

The magenta satin, that effect called watermarked, on the outside, and the dangling loop of the black ribbon of its band.

Do you like the very feel of it? Here, don't be afraid, just relax and let me help you with it. Do you like its soft feel?

Well, *do* you?

BOYS:
A NEW AFRICAN FABLE

BUMA SAID IT WAS CRAZY. But for once, the Boy told himself, Buma did not know. Because the Boy knew it would be easy to steal into the school at night. The Portuguese saint ladies who ran the school would be sleeping, and the girls themselves would be dreaming, maybe of boys like these, the rebels in the bush.

o o o

THEY WERE STRONG, brave boys, he knew. And they were fighting against the aristocracy people of the government and the man named Dihidjo who called himself president. Dihidjo was a thief, and surely the Portuguese saint ladies realized that. Dihidjo lived the life of a king in the whiter-than-white palace in the Other City, and Dihidjo had so many Mercedes-Benz automobiles, even some Rolls-Royce automobiles, that nobody could count just how many anymore, it was said. Dihidjo's soldiers in their green camouflage uniforms were called Crocodiles by the boys, and like those vicious, big-toothed beasts, they fed on the flesh of the people, with Dihidjo himself maybe demanding a golden goblet of the warm spilled blood now and then. The Boy had once actually seen Dihidjo deliver a speech to a crowd in the central square of the Other City. Dihidjo was not a very big man, and he wore a sport shirt, slacks, *and* sunglasses. It was said that nobody had ever seen Dihidjo without those sunglasses; the Boy could believe the story that he always wore them, because to peel them away from his mahogany face would be to observe just two deep holes underneath—Dihidjo had no eyes in his face, and to have eyes, even for a thief like Dihidjo, would mean to have to openly witness and therefore admit to his own greed, as well as that of his military officers and government ministers, the aristocracy people. A man with no eyes was for all intents and purposes a dead man, a talking skull, as far as the Boy was concerned. Dihidjo and his aristocracy people would soon be defeated, and the nationland would have freedom at last. Field Lieutenant M. promised that. But at last wasn't now. And the Boy believed that as good fighters, he and his rebel brothers needed to have girls for companionship in the camp where they lived among themselves, Field Lieutenant M. showing up only occasionally. The Boy had always listened to Buma, and he had always known Buma was the brightest of all of them.

But this time the Boy knew better about the girls. Buma was wrong.

○ ○ ○

IN THE CAMP ONE EVENING, the subject came up again.

It was a beautiful night. The stars were flames; the sky was bulging purple; the breeze from the baobabs carried the magic of the rare spices once transported along the ancient trade routes in this part of the world. It was the kind of night that a boy would wish to have a family, but, again, he was too old for that now, so it was a night that a boy needed a girl. The Boy was twelve, the others about the same age.

"With the Portuguese saint ladies," Buma said, "it is a different thing. They are not like the soldiers, and they are not lazy or easily frightened. They will come after us if we take their girls."

All the leader boys lay around the red dirt there.

The Boy. Buma. Jabo. And the twins, Hakee and Ned.

The twins were not as strong as the other leader boys, needless to say. But simply by being twins they wielded a certain power that demanded respect. Twins were like that, special in their own way. The Boy remembered a scene one idle afternoon. In the heat, Hakee walked around aimlessly on the red dirt of the encampment, shirtless and shoeless, his hands jammed in the pockets of his ragged khaki schoolboy shorts. Meanwhile, under a tree, Ned slept entirely soundly, shirtless and shoeless, too, in the same kind of shorts. They were skinny, toothy boys. The Boy wondered if Ned sleeping that way in the tree's green shade was dreaming Hakee walking around like that, and so his twin was really himself. Or, to reverse it, if the one walking there, Hakee idly kicking up tiny clouds of dust that puffed like magician's smoke, if Hakee was awake but also letting himself snooze to be ready for an attack, any emergency, so that Ned sleeping there was actually himself. Yes, twins were very special.

"Soldiers are one thing," Buma said, "Portuguese saint ladies another thing."

"And this is the most important thing," Jabo said. "Maybe I take this thing and put it under the long dress of one of those Portuguese saint ladies, and then what do you think she will say?"

He sat cross-legged now, a gruff boy with a barrel chest.

He patted the blue snout of the AK-47 on his lap. The twins laughed and Jabo smiled.

Jabo was the bravest of the boys, and Jabo never hesitated. It was Jabo who took it upon himself to sneak into villages at night and punish anybody who might be rumored to have been supplying information to the Crocodiles about the movement of the boys. Jabo had done the same thing to exactly six people. With a chrome-bladed knife, serrated and intended for cleaning river fish, he carved off the lips of the first informer as neatly as stripping a peel from a banana, and when he was praised for such by Field Lieutenant M. on one of his visits, Jabo did the same to five others suspected of similar behavior. All ages and both sexes. So that it was not unusual lately to spot somebody with merely unevenly healed scars around a mouth straining to spit out syllables at the North Crossroads marketplace. That served as a good warning to anybody else who might entertain plans of consorting with the Crocodiles. Jabo patted his gun again now.

The twins laughed some more. Buma tried to talk seriously of the Portuguese saint ladies. He tried to get the Boy to enter into an argument with him, to reply to his, Buma's, charges of the craziness of this scheme to capture the girls from the school. But the Boy realized this wasn't the moment to argue; he stood up and shuffled over to his blanket to sleep.

o o o

SLEEP AS HE DID OTHER NIGHTS, before and after that. The sky purple, the stars like flames indeed.

○ ○ ○

ONE THING BUMA DID EVENTUALLY AGREE ON was Jabo's belief that the old uncle was causing the real trouble. For a while now there had been suspicions that news of the movements of the boys on attacks or stealing supplies was reaching the Crocodiles very far ahead of time. The Crocodiles seemed to know where the boys had been scouting, where they might be taking action next. This wasn't just the usual whispering by some casual informer who had observed them and told what he or she knew when the green-uniformed thugs showed and started asking around a village, and this informing was certainly more organized and ongoing. Jabo was convinced from the start that the betrayer was the old uncle, the aging man on the creaking blue bicycle.

"Where does he go all the time on that bicycle?" Jabo asked. "He leaves in the morning and then he doesn't return until just before the sun is behind the hills. He is the one. He goes to the Other City and he talks."

"It could be a lorry driver who does it, the talk to the Crocodiles," Buma said, weighing the argument himself. "A lorry driver moves faster than an old man on a bicycle."

"The lorry drivers don't care," Jabo said, "the lorry drivers do not live here and they do not know any news to carry. And the only thing they ever know about in these villages is where to find the diseased whores, and the only thing they really carry away from the villages is the disease itself. Besides, don't the lorry drivers give us what we ask of them from their loads most of the time? No, they don't care at all. It has to be the old uncle."

"You could be right," Buma conceded. But obviously he remained unconvinced.

Until there came a terrible skirmish beside the scummed-over Divisional Reservoir Pond. Two of their boys were killed, younger ones, and the Crocodiles were lying in wait for the pack of them going to fetch water that day. The Crocodiles *must* have had information, and the uncle *must* be taken care of.

There was a week of storms, loud thunder and hosing rain-fall at the end of every scorching afternoon. During that time even the old uncle didn't risk going anywhere on his bicycle. The boys waited for him every afternoon by the Big Curve on the crumbling two-lane asphalt road built by the colonizers, but he never came. Then after the following full week of weather especially hot and achingly dry, they had their chance at last to intercept him. Buma and the Boy had positioned themselves as lookouts on a flat-topped hill above the Big Curve. The twins were hiding below, one of them in a gully on each side of the road. Their job would be to trip the old uncle. They had covered a sturdy braided nylon rope with gravel on the grayed asphalt and they would tug it up, taut, when he was upon them, with Jabo himself hiding and ready to pitch in to do the kind of work he unquestionably did better than any of the rest of them.

The Boy watched the old uncle approaching.

A white-haired man of just bones and wrinkled black skin, he wore baggy flour-sack trousers and a torn golf shirt. The red flip-flop sandals loose on his feet seemed to make the pedaling more difficult, and the blue bicycle was truly ancient, probably sal-vaged from a trash heap and the tires rotting and half flat. What the Boy would remember was the sprocket's creaking—it grew louder and louder as he approached: first no more than a bird's chirp in the distance, then almost a dog's rhythmic yelping. From that vantage point, the Boy could see the twins crouched low on either side of the road; Jabo was there beside Ned, directing the whole operation. The old uncle looked hot, and the golf shirt, yellow, was darkened with perspiration. Nevertheless, the way that he pedaled and pedaled in that constant squeaking, you might have wagered that he had come all the way from one end of the earth and, if he had to, he would venture all the way to the other end of it. A sack hung from the rusted handlebars, and one second he was lumpily moving along . . . and the next second he had tumbled over completely against the nylon rope pulled flat across the front tire, the boys on him and the uncle reduced to but an animal snagged in a net. At first the man tried to fight the trio of attackers; he wildly flailed with more energy than you would have expected to come from such a pathetic specimen, though before long he lost heart. They dragged him to the gully at the far side of the two-lane; the Boy appreciated his own distance, and when the others below moved behind a cluster of brush, the Boy was relieved that he would not have to witness what was about to transpire at the hands of Jabo. Of course, Jabo had with him the long serrated knife, the mirroring chrome blade of which he polished endlessly with a rag while in the camp, and before long the old uncle's wailing began. It was interrupted only by one of the twins—Ned or Hakee, and sometimes the Boy really couldn't tell the difference—coming out to fetch the blue bicycle from the road. The Boy thought that even while Jabo was lost in his savage work, and even if Jabo often seemed outright crazed, Jabo definitely was the sole one among the three of them down there who had the sense in the course of this to advise that somebody should go out and retrieve the bicycle—the sight of it would cause a passing lorry driver (there were seldom automobiles on this route) to stop and start looking around. Buma and the Boy remained on the hill.

The yelling of the old man was so loud. And it continued on when the blackened slabs of clouds moved in and started emptying from the sky a wall of hissing blue rain again, the thunder detonating.

"This is not good," Buma said to the Boy.

The Boy did not answer.

Then it was over. Jabo, his teeth like broken shells in his grinning, emerged first from behind the bushes in the gully. He had the bloodied knife in one hand, and in the other hand, held over his head in triumph, was the foot of the old uncle, which had been sawed off several inches above the ankle.

The rain poured. Jabo pumped the thing into the air a few more times, the worn red rubber sandal still dangling from it. The twins emerged from the gully on all fours to make the climb. They were also smiling.

If Buma didn't relish the brutality of it, the Boy knew, Buma did finally admit that he had been wrong and Jabo had been right—no doubt the old uncle had been the problem, and the old uncle would no longer be pedaling anywhere on the creaking blue bicycle. And, true, their raids on the occasional lorry driver for supplies after that, plus the one direct encounter with the Crocodiles, a prolonged shooting skirmish, went well and nothing like the earlier mess when two of the younger boys had been shot at the Divisional Reservoir Pond.

o o o

"IT WAS A NICE THING," Buma said about the incident he had often told the Boy of before. "Very nice."

"Tell me the story again," the Boy said. "I like to hear it so many times."

They were stretched out in their filthy blankets at night. The other boys in the camp were dozing. The Boy and Buma were talking idly.

Buma began the narration. It was his favorite story, and somehow it became the Boy's favorite story, too. This was about Buma when he had been a child, not a rebel and a dedicated fighter as he was now. He had a family then, and like most of these orphan boys, he had lived with his family in the Other City. (Field Lieutenant M., the rebel chief, insisted that they call it such now; they were never to refer to it by the old name given to the capital by the colonizers, which Dihidjo and his set used so readily and without any qualms.) Buma had four sisters. Dressed up on Sundays, when their own parents were relaxing with relatives or possibly taking a nap late in the day, the children liked to walk over to the embassy club of the European King Country. There was a chain-link fence surrounding the grounds, and the grounds were as watered and green and perfectly well groomed as anything in a picture magazine—such lush vegetation in a region of dryness (except for this annual shower season) always smelled of sweet, refreshing chlorophyll. The embassy club of the European King Country had white buildings with red-tiled roofs; it had three tennis courts and a small rectangular pool, a shimmering electric-blue oasis that in itself was magical.

"We would just watch, my sisters and I," Buma said. "And it was all beautiful. As I told you before, my sisters were very pretty, and they wore fine Sunday frocks. Sometimes we stood by the fence and looked at the people swimming, and they dove from a high diving plank and, better, they had this special way of swimming on their backs sometimes, almost as if they were doing it while fast asleep. Or we stood beside the fence over at the tennis courts, which I liked more than even the swimming pool. They wore white clothes and white shoes, and they slapped the bright yellow ball, a furry thing, back and forth and back and forth, like it was happy work they had to do. When finished, they looped towels around their necks and they sat out on the back verandah, drinking from glasses such a clear, clear liquid that it was no liquid at all, a slice of lime on each glass. They looked like antelopes, it is true, the way that all white persons do look like long-faced antelopes. Still, sitting around like that, laughing and talking and drinking, they were very happy antelopes, even if they did, I am sure, miss their real homes far away back in the European King Country."

"Tell me about that one day," the Boy said, because that was the best part of this tale every time Buma recounted it. "Tell me about that one day when one came right up to the bunch of you standing at the fence."

"The tea party?"

"Yes, there was no clear liquid that day, it was a tea party," the Boy said.

As they lay there, the blankets to their chins, Buma told him once more how one of the white women had invited them to come around to the front gate, then onto that back veranda.

There Buma sat with his sisters, who showed good manners in handling the tiny china cups with the milky tea when it was offered to them. There were other women in tennis clothes, and they agreed how "adorable" the girls were; the woman who had invited them offered them all biscuits with cherries on top. Buma had always been proud of how wonderfully his sisters handled the whole thing, how with no prompting they proved to be real ladies themselves.

The Boy thought this was the time to try to win Buma's support on the plan of taking the girls from the school run by the Portuguese saint ladies. But when he mentioned that, when he said that sisters were girls, too, and it would be good to have girls as company in this ramshackle camp, Buma became angry.

"Sisters are not girls *that* way," he chided the Boy.

"I know," the Boy answered, low and apologetically.

He knew Buma's sisters had been killed in the Second Tribal War, everybody in his family was gone. None of the boys had families.

However, the Boy detected that Buma was softening on this. And maybe, the Boy thought, Jabo's having been right about the old uncle constantly betraying them was helping the Boy make his case in arguing now—Buma had come around once, so he might do the same again. (Much later did they learn from other villagers that the old uncle on the road was traveling to the Other City every day only to bring his even older mother a proper meal packed in the sack that hung from the rusted handlebars of the blue bicycle; she was in some sort of hospital there, the villagers said.) A few days after the talk about the sisters, Buma announced that the Boy could be right concerning this matter. Jabo and the twins enthusiastically supported the plan—they said they had been behind it since the first suggestion. The boys would have girls at last, from the Portuguese saint ladies' school.

o o o

THE EVENING BEFORE THE RAID, the Boy dreamt he was alone in the Other City, at night. In the dream he had been summoned to Dihidjo's palace, and as he approached the edifice it looked so essentially white that perhaps a crack painting crew gave it a fresh coat every day, had done such work that very morning. He was escorted by several Crocodiles through the courtyard filled with the expensive automobiles he had often heard about, then through the hallways and to the cavernous room where Dihidjo himself sat perched on a throne. There was red marble and frilled gold embellishment everywhere, and Dihidjo wore his usual sport shirt and slacks and the inevitable (perpetual? eternal?) wraparound sunglasses. In the dream the boy approached the throne set very high on a dais, by himself now and without the Crocodiles, and behind the reflecting dark sunglasses Dihidjo waited for him to shakingly come nearer. It was then that the Boy noticed that one of Dihidjo's legs was but a stump below the knee, the foot of it having been severed at the calf, and it was then that the Boy reached into a plastic mesh go-to-marketplace sack he had apparently been carrying all the while. He lifted out of the sack a withered, amber-soled foot, which seemed very much the foot that Jabo had been showing around as a trophy for the past couple of weeks. The Boy held out the foot in both palms like an offering; he started slowly up the red marble steps to give it to Dihidjo, who was as small as he looked that one time that the Boy, when younger, had heard him give a speech in the central square. Dihidjo waited for him. And then Dihidjo appeared so moved by the gesture that he suddenly wasn't the Dihidjo of the many Rolls-Royce automobiles and Mercedes-Benz automobiles, Dihidjo of the thieving aristocracy people and Dihidjo who enjoyed an occasional sip from a golden goblet of the blood of the masses of those murdered in the nationland over the years. He was only a little man thankful that his foot was being returned to him. He was weeping, in fact, dabbing at his own eyes, and the tears streamed below the sunglasses, which is when Dihidjo slowly started to peel them away from his face, and . . . and the Boy woke from the dream with a start.

o o o

THE BOY WASN'T SO SURE ANYMORE of the idea of attacking the school to capture the girls.

o o o

THOSE THEY CALLED THE PORTUGUESE SAINT LADIES were, of course, the nuns who ran the institution for orphan girls at the edge of the attempt at a suburb in the Other City. What became the infamous raid all went smoothly—too smoothly, maybe—the night they snuck into the school.

The school was a compound of yellow stuccoed buildings. The older girls, who were the boys' age, slept in a separate dormitory house. The boys were amazed at how the girls themselves there amid the rows of steel-framed cots were entirely complaisant, giggling when first awakened in the darkness and soon quite understanding that the guns meant this was serious and they'd best behave. They were told to take whatever they needed, because they would be gone for a long while, but a tall girl with pink eyes wasn't so complaisant. And when she flatly ordered out of the dormitory Jabo and the twins and three of the younger boys—the contingent in charge of rounding up the girls—the Boy looked from where he was again keeping watch, this time in the corridor; the Boy was surprised to see the always brutal Jabo cower, even stutter a little in agreement with her. The tall girl said they needed some privacy to dress properly. Jabo nodded some more. The other girls—most stuffing clothing into matching orange athletic duffel bags probably given to the school by a sport shop, seeing that the school had produced so many female long-distance runners, with one girl now casually puffing up her hair before a single tarnished mirror at the end of the big screened-in room—the other girls stopped what they were doing almost in unison at this turn of events. It was as if they couldn't believe that this looming brute of a boy in his ragged khaki shorts and khaki shirt, Jabo, had taken seriously the suggestion of the pink-eyed girl.

"Jabo," one of the boys who wasn't even a leader boy, a younger boy, called to him, warning, "Jabo!"

Jabo wasn't fazed. He was for once at a loss for a plan of action—Jabo was totally unsure of himself, brave Jabo. The Boy knew that he couldn't let the situation stand, if only for the fact that he realized, above all, it was never wise to let one of the regular boys have to tell a leader boy how to behave.

The Boy entered the room from the corridor. The Boy had enough sense to suspect that this bossy tall girl, with those very pink eyes, was the type who would like to herd the whole bunch of these boys back out of the dormitory room, so she could quickly slam the door, lock it, and dispatch somebody to climb out a window and run over to the huge shadowy house where the Portuguese saint ladies lived.

"We will stay," the Boy said to Jabo. Jabo was still lost, no idea as to how to respond, and this wasn't a matter of the usual informer who would lose his lips to Jabo's fishing knife, or a matter of a worthless old uncle—these were *girls*. "Come on, now," the Boy said with military harshness, making his voice loud and firm in addressing the girls, "get yourselves ready."

The girl who had been arranging her hair at the mirror smiled. She was skinny, very pretty, and she had managed to smear her lips with a touch of scarlet lipstick that she must have kept hidden where the strict Portuguese saint ladies had never discovered it. She showed deep dimples when she smiled, her eyes giant as a doll's. She stood in flimsy green gym shorts and a flimsier child's white camisole shirt; a little satin bow studded the neck of the camisole shirt, the Boy noticed. She looked right at the Boy.

"What's your name?" she asked him, tilting her head to one side.

"Just keep packing," the Boy growled. Or, he tried to growl, and he wasn't sure if his breath powering the words came out right. "Come *on*."

"But what's your name, boy?" she asked again. She continued to smile.

The Boy waved his AK-47, a genuine Soviet Kalashnikov with a steel rather than a wooden stock; he looped it as if to rope in the entire mess of strewn clothes and schoolbooks, white sheets shoved to the tile floor during the commotion of the supposed raid.

"I said, let's *go*," the Boy told her, firmer.

Jabo and the twins made much theater out of poking around with their own AK-47's, the younger boys following suit. They all exuded only brusqueness now, and they directed the girls into the deserted corridor, more of the cold tile flooring, and out into the schoolyard. The frames of the two soccer goals glowed bright white in the moonlight; dew sparkled like diamonds.

The Boy was glad that Buma had stationed himself as a lookout by the house where the Portuguese saint ladies lived. The Boy was glad that Buma had not been on hand to see the sorry performance of everybody concerned back in the dormitory. But that was nothing compared to the sorrier performance surrounding what followed. It seemed that when they were finally out of the suburban neighborhood, Jabo noticed that the twins were missing. Hearing that news, Buma volunteered to go back; he was willing to risk everything to return on his own to rescue his beloved comrades from whatever danger they had encountered. He left on his own to search. As it turned out, Ned and Hakee had lingered in order to break into the school offices to hunt for a treasure that one of the girls had told them was hidden on a high shelf behind the Sister Superior's desk: boxes and boxes of candy bars, kept by the Portuguese saint ladies to reward a girl for good behavior—a class assignment well done or a race well run, and the like. Buma, in time, brought the twins back with him, and while he seemed angry with them, nobody else did. Soon the twins were magnanimously passing out the candy bars to everybody, gooey chocolate-and-coconut things in lurid blue-and-orange wrappers, and the Boy knew that Buma had been right to initially doubt the worth of the raid. The idea of taking the girls was indeed a crazy one from the start, crazier if you actually saw the giddy procession disappearing into the darkness of the bush, over the red-dirt paths that only the boys knew about and that led to their camp. Absolutely crazy.

In truth, the so-called Portuguese saint ladies were *not* to be deterred as easily as the Crocodiles. If the Crocodiles didn't particularly care about what happened to any orphan girls, the Portuguese saint ladies did; according to later statements, they were the ones who convinced the foreign television reporter with his camera team to look into it, dispatched from—in the boys' parlance—the "European King Country."

○ ○ ○

ON THE PATH TO THE CAMP THAT NIGHT, the girl with the smeared lipstick kept close to the Boy. She kept asking him his name, her dimples deep that way when she smiled.

"You must have a name. Every boy has a name."

But the Boy didn't answer. He wasn't quite himself. None of the boys were themselves, and it wasn't simply Jabo being tongue-tied earlier or the Boy being, well, a little baffled at the moment about why his stomach felt like a fluttering of roused birds, how the whole confused episode had somehow metamorphosed into a true party. The twins didn't even have their AKs combat-ready, but kept them slung over the shoulder like arrow quivers; they were too busy handing out more candy bars to anybody who asked for another of the heat-softened things. Each carried a large box of them.

"What's your name, boy?" the girl said again.

"Shush," the Boy said, embarrassed.

Scared as well. *And why did the Boy have to remember now the images from that dream of the villain Dihidjo crying behind his sunglasses? That scene of the Boy approaching the man on his throne?* The Boy had no idea what it meant.

"Give me one more of the candy," Buma said to one of the twins, Hakee.

"Here you go," Ned responded, taking one from his own supply. "Another for Buma."

"That boy is a pig boy," the pink-eyed girl laughed, "he eats too many candy bars."

There was general laughter. Laughter from Buma, too.

The skinny girl continued to keep in step with the Boy.

"Everybody has to have a name," she said.

The Boy tried to ignore her. He tried to avoid thoughts of the dream. Instead, he strained to entertain himself with the variety of minor incongruities that had formerly entertained him, fascinated him, such as Buma asking one twin for a candy bar and then the other twin producing it, as if the pair were one and the same all along. But it wasn't working.

The Boy bit from his candy bar.

o o o

THE BOY COULDN'T FALL INTO SLEEP THAT NIGHT. He was excited at last, happy. He lay on his back and stared at the stars, inhaled the spicily fragrant air blowing gently from behind those baobabs. (Two weeks afterward, with the foreign television crew in tow, the nuns in their simple coarse-cloth habits followed the trail of crumpled blue-and-orange candy bar wrappers. That is how they found the secret camp that the boys had always managed to keep well hidden, completely cut off from any access by the Crocodiles. A few of the girls returned to the Other City with the nuns, but most chose to stay, and three weeks after that the nuns admitted their mistake and took it upon themselves to file formal complaints with the international agencies—not against the boys, but against the government of the self-proclaimed President for Life, Iko Kor Dihidjo. Apparently, once the TV crew discovered the camp, Dihidjo sent in troops to slaughter anybody found living there, girls included with the boys; the bodies were heaped into a mass grave layered with quicklime. Meanwhile, smooth Dihidjo, lying, publicly declared that the mission had started as a humanitarian one before fighting broke out, an attempt to bring the frail orphans of the Second Tribal War back to the capital for rehabilitation and rescue from their strange life in the bush. When Field Lieutenant M. was contacted for comment, he denied any knowledge of the boys, and by that point rumors were already circulating that Field Lieutenant M. had decided to abandon his rebellion and take a post in the capital as one of the president's important ministers, a joining of forces, so to speak. The international agencies and other outside authorities approved of such a peace wholeheartedly, so an investigation never came.) The Boy rolled one way in the blanket. Then he rolled the other way. He thought of the girls, especially the pretty one who had tagged after him on the path, and he thought of how Buma himself, a boy of such constant pondering and such constant worry, had seemed happy for once in his life. The Boy still couldn't sleep.

The Boy heard a noise. He heard somebody moving. He tensed, thrust his arm out of the blanket to reach for his Kalashnikov, then relaxed again when he saw it was only Jabo strutting around. Jabo was a silhouette, and the Boy could see that Jabo was playing not with the foot but with his other prize—the string of dried lips. He twirled it around on one finger, the hardened dead flesh clicking, and he whistled low some tune, surely not wanting to disturb anybody. You couldn't blame Jabo, the Boy thought, and Jabo was just Jabo. The Boy suspected that Jabo was also happier than he had ever been.

o o o

"I WILL SURPRISE HER when I tell her my name tomorrow," the Boy said half aloud, and with that he finally fell asleep.

E.A.P. : A NOTE

I.

AMONG THE LITTLE-KNOWN ODDITIES OF POE'S LIFE, one that scholars seem to eschew, is that he had dreams of two actual books about him from university presses published well over a hundred years after his own death. It is interesting that so many of these scholars, especially contemporary commentators, have chosen to maintain such reticence on this matter, despite the fact that during his lifetime Poe recounted the dreams in detail to several acquaintances. Reports even show that he was highly specific regarding the two volumes in question.[1]

In the first dream, he was sitting at night by the sea, alone, and the landscape he described strikingly resembled that of the sepulchral setting of the poem "Annabel Lee." He spoke of cliffs and waves whispering against rocks very far below. Further, he said there was an oddly intense moonlight, more than enough

---

1. Early biographies do give some attention to this: *Edgar Allan Poe: The Man,* by Mary E. Phillips, 2 vols (Chicago, 1926), and *Poe and the Southern Literary Messenger,* by David K. Jackson (Richmond, 1934). Also, to a lesser degree, there is a brief discussion in the very early, and, in the words of Julian Symons, "the passionate and eccentric" *Edgar Allan Poe and His Critics,* by Sarah Helen Whitman (New York, 1860). A detective novelist, Symons himself wrote a popular biography of Poe, *The Tell-Tale Heart* (New York, 1978).

to read by, though at that stage in his life he was constantly complaining of oil lamplight (and certainly candlelight) never being bright enough for his eyes: they had strained so long in the years of not only working on his own stories and poems but the seemingly ceaseless reading of, and writing on, the works of others—the continual hack labor of book reviewing that often supported him. The dream, according to the sources, was quite literal, almost as predictable as anything else in the everyday, except that sitting there on the cliff's edge in the moonlight, probably in his usual black boots and very black frock coat, he was reading from a book that, as said, wouldn't be published until long after his own death. He was specific indeed about the title and other publication particulars in his recounting of the dream as provided to Rufus Wilmot Griswold, his literary executor, and then Maria Clemm, his mother-in-law. He said the title was *Edgar Allan Poe: sa vie et ses ouvrages* (i.e., *his life and his works*) by Charles Baudelaire, the essay translated and with critical commentary by W. T. Bandy for this annotated scholarly edition, and it appeared as number 22 in the Romance Studies Series, University of Toronto Press; as stated by Griswold, Poe went on in his talk to mention the cities and year of publication as Toronto and Buffalo, 1973. He also described the physical book itself in considerable detail. Poe marveled at its sturdy blue-and-black marbleized cloth binding and the quality of the thick creamy paper, the strong black of the Palatino type. Griswold, who would later become known as the perpetrator of more or less a cottage industry in his writing sensationalistically about Poe, spreading exaggerated stories of the writer's debauchery, even madness, can in this case be found as very reliable, because the description of the book, related to him by Poe, is uncannily accurate, a perfect representation of the volume eventually published. Griswold reported how Poe noted that judging from the book, he, Poe, had become quite famous posthumously, and to a large measure the fame apparently could be attributed to a keen interest in France in his work; that interest came after the translation of his tales and poems into French by a certain Charles Baudelaire, who would himself prove, in time, very recognized, too. Poe told Griswold that according to Bandy's critical commentary in the book, there appeared to have evolved a genuine controversy in subsequent years on whether Baudelaire had possibly plagiarized the bulk of his long essay on Poe—which first came out in a Paris newspaper—from biographical and critical journal articles back in the United States, with Baudelaire allegedly doing little more than translating such material, sometimes line by line, for much of his piece. The essay proper, "Edgar Allan Poe: sa vie et ses ouvrages," is reprinted in its original French alongside an English translation in this University of Toronto Press volume, and that constitutes approximately half the book; the editor Bandy's lengthy introduction and prolific footnoting comprises the remainder of its 126 pages. In addition to citing Poe's mention of the book's physical makeup, Griswold said how Poe was intrigued by that question of possible plagiarism but little else. Therefore, one may conclude that Griswold didn't capitalize to a greater degree on the exchange with more of his own exaggeration about Poe, if only because he probably considered this particular dream altogether too esoteric—meaning, it could be that Griswold merely dismissed it as a far-fetched alcohol- or drug-induced somnambulistic vision that wasn't worth touting, even for a scoundrel such as himself who had initially met Poe when he, Griswold, was a decidedly profit-minded journalist and poetry anthologist, Griswold eventually working his early influence to gain a large measure of control as legal executor of Poe's literary oeuvre. Maria Clemm's account of the dream as related to her by Poe had many similarities, though other than notation of the title, author, and publisher, she was not as exact in talk of Poe's physical description of the book; she made no mention of his opinion on the text of the Baudelaire essay either, its arguments. But she did provide valuable information, a personal response from Poe of the variety that might be expected to have been given to her as his mother-in-law and immediate-family member, somebody intimate. Clemm stated that in the dream Poe was basically struck by the scholar W. T. Bandy's dedication page for this book from the University of Toronto Press: *"In memory of Alice."* And she emphasized that Poe didn't seem in the least fazed by the incredibility of Bandy's project, a volume that was a study of an essay on Poe by a then little-known Frenchman who would be largely responsible later for the widespread recognition that Poe never received in his own lifetime.

Poe simply told Clemm, maybe in his whispery, gentleman's voice that has been documented so well,[2] "Alice, a lovely name, isn't it? I wonder if Bandy loved her truly."

---

2.   While there has been much discussion of the acknowledged "handsomeness" of Poe's speaking voice, the best treatment of this occurs in *The Histrionic Mr. Poe*, by N. Bryllion Fagin (Baltimore, 1949). Fagin immerses himself in the topic, with his basic argument holding that Poe's being the consummate actor in life and also in his works was to be expected, seeing that he was descended from theater people on both sides.

II.

FOR INFORMATION ON THE SECOND DREAM, we have only a single source to rely on, but in the recounting, this source is so precise and vivid that the material offers a fullness that appears lacking in the combined accounts of the first dream from Griswold and Clemm. (Concerning the second dream, we do have significant supporting corroboration, yet there are no names; nevertheless, a number of persons were reportedly baffled during Poe's lifetime when he referred to this dream several times in the course of public lectures, for Poe the delivering of such lectures often a task easily as distasteful as that of his literary journalism.[3]) John Sartain, the Philadelphia engraver and editor, a longtime loyal friend of Poe, gave the information outright. Poe told him that in this dream he was locked in a cavern, darkened, that maybe metamorphosed into a mansion, equally darkened; and he was reading by flickering candlelight, wishing the dim illumination were better—understandably so, because this was a book that consisted chiefly of illustrations. Once more Poe was exact on the title and physical detail, to Sartain, anyway, if not in the public lectures. The book was *The Portraits and Daguerreotypes of Edgar Allan Poe,* by Michael J. Deas; it was published by the University of

---

3. Any documentation as to the content of the lectures themselves becomes difficult to establish; the talks were never titled, merely headlined as "An Evening with Mr. Edgar Allan Poe," or the like. Jackson (op. cit.) in his brief mention of this dream, however, does maintain how, indeed, attendees in those auditoriums had themselves reported hearing Poe speak of this particular dream.

Virginia Press (Charlottesville, Virginia) in 1989.[4] Poe spoke in even more complimentary terms this time of the large folio-size format and the brown cloth binding with lettering in fine raised black and gold—for the title, author, and publisher—along the spine. And in his dream of that darkened space,[5] Poe sat at an ornately carved mahogany desk that somehow seemed

---

4.   It is understandable that Poe failed to link the place of publication with the very university he had attended for the tumultuous academic year 1826–1827, the period of such legendary gambling and sizable debt: for Poe, the press's official name given on the title page—University of Virginia Press—would have been somewhat oblique, considering that when he was enrolled, the university itself was known to most students, colloquially and routinely, as "Mr. Jefferson's University."

5.   This coincides with his constant use of contained, claustrophobic spaces in the tales. Surely an interesting assessment of this issue is Princess Marie Bonaparte's *The Life and Works of Edgar Allan Poe* (London, 1933), complete with its famous introduction by Freud for this ultra-Freudian reading. Bonaparte's study, while rigid and markedly dated as to its unflagging psychoanalytical tenets, is still very valuable in establishing basic themes concerning Poe's obvious sexual impotence, his idealization of his dear mother who died so young, and hence his obsession to constantly return to a tomb-like/womblike environment with her or any other deceased female, a space symbolized by the wine cellar in "The Cask of Amontillado" or the enclosed mansion in "The Fall of the House of Usher." Bonaparte tells us: "That Poe was a potential sado-necrophilist is something all his work shows, and only his most purely literary devotees would deny it." Her analysis of *Pym* is most fascinating in terms of this remembered and longed-for realm of darkness, the substitute for a more normal sexual gratification, as the hero there encounters islanders who are black, simply, and logically, because the whole world would appear black if seen from inside the womb, according to her argument; the fact, too, that the islanders in that tale have specifically black teeth "represents a displacement upward to the mouth of qualities appropriate to the real or, rather, *cloacal* vagina, with, for instance, its darkness and the imagined presence of *teeth*." Which in itself astutely suggests that the impotent man often envisions teeth as anatomically part of, and therefore ominously "guarding," the female sex organ.

to have been provided for his study of the book; he flipped through the large pages in which Deas—to repeat, well over a hundred years after the death of Poe—had gathered (and dutifully annotated with information on the circumstances surrounding the creation and production of) all existing sketches, oils, etchings, and daguerreotypes that Poe posed for at different stages in his life. (Deas even goes as far as to carefully list "Rejected Depictions," those that hucksters claimed, in the full thrust of Poe's later notoriety, to be genuine but were obviously sham, and "Lost Depictions," those that have turned up in reproductions over the years, but for which the originals are not to be found in any library or private collection.) It would seem surprising that Poe was not struck once more by the very truth that the book testified to his eventual literary importance to this degree, how his reputation would be such that a whole volume would one day in the future be devoted to cataloging these images of himself, as he sat there in the dream and examined the book and as, let's say, a raven called outside or perhaps a huge antique clock ticked and echoingly ticked away the mortal hours, the kind of "things" that were always transpiring in Poe's tales (or, as the contemporary poet Richard Wilbur tells us: read "dreams" for "tales"). Poe spoke at length to Sartain of the dream, what the audience members also recall Poe relating in his public lectures. With respect to the famous "Ultima Thule" daguerreotype that has provided us the baggy-eyed, dark-haired, mustached Poe that is the most common image today,[6] Poe remarked that it was

---

6. Poe was clean-shaven on the upper lip until the last few years of his life, strangely enough.

true: "I looked at it, and I thought to myself, He does seem to have gotten the mouth right"—the "he" referring to Edward H. Manchester, the daguerreotypist who produced the plate at his studio on Weybosset Street in Providence, Rhode Island, in 1848.[7] None of the remaining contents appeared to greatly interest Poe (Deas's extensive commentary or even the reproductions themselves) except for what Poe considered, after reading at least some of the book's text, Deas's excellent and concise explanation of the daguerreotype process itself in an appendix; it is a process that probably requires explanation to modern readers, and apparently it wasn't always entirely clear to somebody in Poe's era either, a time when daguerreotypes, newly invented, were extremely popular. In fact, Deas's prose in the book is remarkable for its clarity here: "Exposures— which ranged anywhere from a few seconds to up to a half minute—were made by uncapping the lens. The plate bearing the latent image was then removed from the camera, developed over a tray of heated mercury, and stabilized in a bath of sodium trisulfate. The completed image was usually matted and framed in a leather-bound miniature set lined with satin or velvet. Because no negative was used in the process, each plate was essentially irreplaceable."

Poe's comment to the Philadelphian Sartain, a part-time daguerreotypist himself by trade, proved as absolutely intriguing as his being very fascinated—and as he had told Maria

---

7. Manchester's establishment was, according to city directories of the time, on Weybosset Street and not Westminster Street, as so often has been erroneously reported in relation to the "Ultima Thule" daguerreotype.

Clemm—with the dedication page of the other book he dreamed about.

Poe said to Sartain: "That daguerreotyping, it's all really quite simple in terms of chemicals and precise procedure involved, once somebody does explain it to you. Nothing magical about it whatsoever, old chap, when you think of it."

A DAY IN THE LIFE
OF THE ILLNESS

Oh, to awake from dreaming!
—Virginia Woolf

THE ILLNESS HAS COME to have a certain affinity with windows. Sometimes the Illness will simply stare out a window for moments that aren't moments at all, and this can happen in any of number of places. It can happen in the morning, let's say, after showering and putting on a white terry robe before applying makeup (just a touch of lipstick) in the upstairs bathroom, where the window looking down to the neighbor's backyard is a twelve-paned, wood-frame one; it is late winter. The snow has melted some in the last few days, leaving patches of bare lawn somehow yellow. There are three snow shovels, arranged in order of descending size, set upright on their handles against the dark-planked fence, the paddle on the smallest bright red, as if trying to cry for attention amid the bigger slabs beside it; the couple of yews seem almost too green in the morning sunshine, glossy and the limbs not having been given a final buzz with the hedge trimmer the September before, so they look a little every which way and out of control, nicely so. The Illness thinks that there is a Stevens poem about this time of year, Stevens's Connecticut not all that far from this Boston, of course, but the Illness can't be certain.

The Illness stares—there must be a Stevens poem about this, such late winter sunshine being very special, struggling but sure of itself.

○ ○ ○

BUT TODAY THERE IS NO TIME to linger.

There are two classes to teach, a lecture in the morning then the seminar in the afternoon, and there is, maybe strangely, the man to have dinner with who works in a law firm down-town; in the course of a rather awkward telephone call, a date was arranged for Cambridge this evening. Yes, strange, even if friends had been trying to pair the two for months, all claim-ing they would be *perfect* for each other, Susan adding, "Don't be put off by the lawyer thing, take my word. He's just one of the legions who logged into law school at a point in his life when he probably didn't know what to do next. He reads, and he reads a lot, and I knew him way back when we both were in college together, up there in the tundra of old Colgate. He wrote poetry in college, believe it or not, and did it not just for the usual easy B in a creative writing course. The sad truth of the matter is that for a male to write poetry on his own back then in Hamilton, New York, where the hockey thugs in their flashy maroon uniforms, they were the ones who really ruled the place, well, that was more a miracle than anything else. You'll like him. You *are* the right kind of woman for him, and the two of you really have *so much* in common."

o o o

THERE IS BREAKFAST OF COFFEE and orange juice and buttered toast with blueberry jam. There is the ride on the "T" out to the university in the fine old Boston suburb. An antique, probably only put into service in a crunch, the car is one of those rattling green clunkers, snub-nosed and with riveted sides, more like an authentic trolley than the newer squared-off, bus-style models, and it is near empty at this time of the morning, after the commuter rush. The Illness, however, isn't really concentrating on reviewing the notes scrawled on a yellow legal pad for the Virginia Woolf seminar in the afternoon. This week the discussion is on a later novel, *The Waves*, which admittedly maybe doesn't rank in reputation with the two very best-known ones, *Mrs. Dalloway* and *To the Lighthouse*. Still, nobody can deny its utter lyrical daring; there is the whole innovative concept of staging the entire lifetimes of several close friends—male and female, from childhood to old age—against the intervening italicized sections that document the progressive advance of a single day as seen on a deserted beach, the low aqua phalanxes of waves rolling toward shore, repeatedly, endlessly, to spread in such lovely fan patterns on the smooth amber sand. Or, if the Illness for now is going along with the reviewing of notes on the pad, the tearing of tiny triangles from another blank yellow sheet to mark passages in the hardbound edition there on the cracked brown leatherette seat beside the carefully packed briefcase that sits open, true, if the Illness is accepting this, it is also doing what it has to do too often lately, raising doubts about so many things. The Illness knows full well that while the large lecture class in the morning, a survey of American lit, will go smoothly enough, the Woolf seminar could turn complicated.

Recently the university has received a good deal of media attention, not in the least bit complimentary. An old Jesuit institution that for years was content to operate more as a commuter school than anything else, accommodating bright Catholic boys from the Boston area, it has transformed itself into a major seat of research, and, going coeducational, it now attracts a student body from across the country. A former nun who taught women's studies made it a policy not to admit male undergraduates to any of her classes specifically on women's studies; this was challenged in court the year before by a male undergraduate, and when the few Jesuits remaining on the faculty tried to quietly dodge the impasse by holding her to some mandatory retirement provision in her contract, the situation worsened. Though the woman herself, quite old, was never confrontational (she calmly explained that she simply had her beliefs), and while she didn't stand up loudly to any of it on her own, protest arose from an organized group of female students on campus; suddenly the place with its routine mock-Georgian spires and very routine football weekends was being talked about, first in the *Globe,* then, nationally, on those evening programs that were all imitations of *60-Minutes,* the so-called news magazines—Ted Koppel on ABC devoted a full session of *Nightline* to it. The noise finally quieted down, maybe because the elderly professor didn't appear to ever want *any* part of it, but it passed not without changing the atmosphere on campus, so that even a seminar on Woolf for select master's students has the potential of degenerating to nothing but back-and-forth political argument. And the Illness isn't about to overlook the possibility of exactly that happening this afternoon.

The old car clanks around the final curves at the small station, the electric connection atop its swaying pole igniting in startling blue flashes. The pad and the book are tucked into the briefcase again, which is then zipped firmly shut.

o o o

THE LECTURE HALL IS IN A NEW BUILDING, but still has that feel of a big teacup, the pockets of empty seats seeming even more the vivid royal blue of their twill upholstery because of the whiteness of everything else surrounding them: the walls, the ceiling, the raised podium itself encased in a bright white vinyl veneer. The microphone needs adjusting now and then to compensate for occasional feedback squeal, something the kids have become used to by now, the third week of the second month of the semester. The talk is delivered almost entirely without notes, on Henry James's *Daisy Miller*, the "poor" rich girl who in her typically American vivaciousness, even overromantic dreaminess, wants too much in life. (One attraction of a job at this particular university, originally coming here after a Ph.D. at Harvard a half dozen years earlier, is not only that it does keep you in Boston but also there is less specialization than at the acknowledged elite schools—so, even if one's field is twentieth-century British, there is always room to teach something more general, such as an American literature survey, if only to refresh your own memory about American literature.) The students seem interested, there in their sweaters and heavy hiking boots, they scribble notes, and it is at times like this—and especially with so much recent talk of complete remission—that the Illness becomes rather envious, almost insists on complicating everything, asserting its independence, trying to lose itself in what it itself, the Illness, knows.

The Illness knows, for instance, all about CT scans and MRIs, quite different, actually. And it is not just that one photographs the full supine body with X-rays and the other reproduces it through magnetic impulses, to re-create what it registers with electronic imaging. Which is but a basic understanding of the difference, nothing more than that and having little to do with what the Illness really knows.

For the CT scan you have to change into a johnny in a little cubicle. And no matter how many times you think you understand the setup of the flimsy gown, printed with pallid octagons or pallid pin dots, it is a contraption you have to figure out all over again each time you do find yourself in that closet of a changing cubicle, the marbleized gray linoleum cold on your feet despite your also remembering to wear thick wool socks, because at least you can keep wearing socks during the test. For the CT scan there is an intravenous iodine feed, administered by a technician, and there is the grouchy radiology nurse who, for some reason, you imagine might have been through a recent divorce, still relatively young, with altogether too much makeup for a nurse and longish chestnut hair in a functional twist—she seems bitter about that divorce, or *something* in her life; she will make sure you are laid out correctly on the crisp paper atop the slab, and she explains again how the procedure works, what you already know from prior visits. She will go behind the wall with the observation window, speaking to you through the microphone; she will repeatedly tell you when to inhale deep, holding your breath, and she will tell you when you can exhale again. The big cone around you examines slowly down the length of your body, she speaks, and if you do look at your arm you can see the brilliant iodine flowing through the intravenous tube, or if you do look up to the buff-painted wall you can see her face, ghostly, behind that glass insert so thick that it reminds you of a convenience-store booth where the cashier asks you to place your money into the tray below the bulletproof shield, yet this glass probably has some lead in it to protect her, day after day. You are the patient, but, nevertheless, you would like to reach out to her somehow, to use your hand to touch clear past the glass and place your own fingers tenderly to her rouged cheek, tell her to appreciate life, to rid herself of whatever the sadness is that gives her the gruff demeanor, which in time she will realize there is no reason for, because such sadness, like so much else, is only minor, as insubstantial as, yes, that very sight of her through the glass that reflects the glaring fluorescent lights—her image so *very* ghostly.

For the MRI everything is different. The MRI lab isn't even in the city, but is in sort of a strip mall, a single-story, low-slung redwood building surrounded by fresh landscaping and tasteful boutiques. The staff there doesn't seem as much a part of the medical profession as a gymnastics team, maybe, in white trousers and matching purple polo shirts showing the little embroidered logo of the health services company on the front pocket. The girl who checks you in at the desk in the small waiting room is gracious and most friendly, and the same two guys who always escort you back to the rear examination rooms both look like they lift weights, strong young men who are licensed paramedics—apparently, the largest complication of an MRI is coping with the fits of claustrophobia many experience while lying down on that pallet to be chugged into the tight, white-lit cylinder, as the rattling knocks of the imaging machine start slow, speed up, then go slow again; the men are required to be on hand for any such emergencies, it seems. They always remember you; they know you have no trouble with the claustrophobia, and for this examination there's not even a need to get undressed, put on one of those hopelessly flimsy—demeaning?—hospital johnnies. Together, the two of them ask you again to make sure that you remove everything metal from your pockets, and they provide you with the key to the little gray-enameled locker in which to put your purse and anything that might contain metal; the reading of the page to you asking if you ever had any metallic splinters lodged anywhere in your body, also if you ever worked a machine-shop job where that might have happened, is all a cheery routine. The two men like the way you can even smile with them a little as you stand there with the plastic-topped brass key for the locker in your hand, asking them why, if you are supposed to have *no* metal, did they just give you this key? One takes it from you, smiling, the other, smiling, escorts you into the large room with a box of stuffed toys in one corner (how heartbreaking to think of the fear of a child during this), and, working in tandem again, they adjust you on the pallet, measuring the exact center with a thumb on your thorax. Meanwhile, a pretty young Hispanic woman in loose white hospital trousers and a purple polo, the nurse technologist who is also familiar, sits in one corner and looks at her monitoring screen, dismissing the men when they have you positioned just right. She says she will tell you through the machine's built-in speaker when each new set of imaging is about to begin, and with foam earplugs installed, you lie with your arms folded across your chest and wait for the loud clicking, sometimes like slow castanets, sometimes faster and like the drummer's lead-in to an old Go-Gos' song you suddenly, and oddly, remember from your own girlhood and those summers at the family's vacation place in Stonington, more than carefree. Of course, what the Illness knows is that, ultimately, it probably isn't just simple claustrophobia for patients who seem to panic when brought into this room, slid into this cylinder that is very close against your elbows, your hips—it surely is more a matter of what a perfect representation of a coffin the machine is, the long hollow pod of it a trim encasement, as when a coffin's lid is shut, the white-lit plastic all around you making an eerie translucent equivalent of the pleated cream-colored satin with which they inevitably line all coffins, and . . .

"Does the seven pages for the first term paper mean seven pages of like, you know, any size font?"

It is the five minutes of questions, a set-aside period at the end of the lecture, and the inquiry comes from a skinny girl with round horn-rimmed glasses; it draws snickering from some of those scattered in the other seats, chiefly a few of the more oafish guys. As it is explained to her that the font should be normal size, twelve points, with normal-size margins, one inch, that explanation triggers the thought that, no doubt, it is time to get more up-to-date and start giving length-of-paper requirements in word count, easily calculated on a computer, and also the thought of how wonderfully naïve a class of freshmen and sophomores like this is—you spend an entire forty-five of the fifty minutes allowed trying to set that scene of young Daisy in the mossily dank Colosseum with her handsome young Italian suitor by such drugging moonlight, a place a proper young lady really shouldn't be and where she will contract the malaria that will bring her to an early death, and, true, after forty-five minutes spent on that, the pressing question raised by a student involves how long, precisely, the paper should be.

The lecture notes are gathered up at the podium, and maybe a good idea would be a quick check at the office before going to lunch with some colleagues at the faculty dining room. The Illness follows the campus's criss-crossing walks, almost an argyle patterning, and the chimes from the carillon play an unidentifiable between-classes song, watery bells echoing. With the remaining few shoveled piles of snow from the last storm quickly melting, there is a sweet smell of earth to the day, rich and undeniably heady; several more days of this weather and some yellow springtime crocuses might actually bloom, totally confused.

o o o

"I'M GLAD I CAUGHT YOU," he says on the phone. "The secretary at the main number told me that you sometimes stop by your office before lunch on your teaching days to see if any students are looking for you. So I guess you're not one of those elusive profs who keeps an office merely as a front, never comes anywhere near the place, which was the old trick too many of them had when I was in law school."

His voice on the phone is relaxed, more casual than when the date was first arranged with his call in the evening the week before. He says that rather than simply meeting in Harvard Square later, as had been arranged, he could perhaps drive out to the suburban campus and pick her up, while he listens to the explanation that so much extra driving would would be ridiculous, especially with the heavy traffic at that time of day—plus, there are some errands to do in Harvard Square, or not exactly errands but just poking around in the bookshops, browsing.

"I envy you," he says, "a life where you immerse yourself in books? Why don't we trade places, like tomorrow."

Which elicits polite laughter. He asks what the seminar is on that afternoon, and when told, he responds that he should read more, not just the books on politics and history he does read: he should read important literature, somebody like Virginia Woolf, whom he admits he only knows about from the play—or, more so, the old black-and-white movie of the play with Virginia Woolf's name in the title, starring disheveled Richard Burton and, back then, still mysteriously beautiful Liz Taylor. And now he laughs, saying that with his having seen the movie, it means he *really* knows what academic life is about, though he adds that he only remembers—clearly, anyway—the movie's opening scene, when Burton, a professor, and Taylor, his wife, both heavy boozers, shuffle around their living room in a big old house in a university town, hurrying to clean up before the younger new professor and his very wide-eyed wife arrive for the evening.

"It was great," he says. "They were madly picking up strewn newspapers and dumping ashtrays into drawers of end tables there in the living room, things like that. Do you remember the scene, both of them puffing away on cigarettes, probably unfiltered Camels?"

When he is told it was filmed at Smith College out in Northampton, he says he never knew that, but it sounds right, "Everything had that look, come to think of it."

The chat continues.

"Then seven o'clock in Cambridge it shall be," he finally says, "downstairs there at the Casablanca Bar. And I warn you, I'm absurdly punctual."

But there is no chance to leave the office immediately, head to lunch. Erin Halligan from the graduate seminar knocks, and when Erin enters, it is as if the Illness itself now looks up from the desk. Erin has been the somewhat noisy leader of the occasional disruption in the seminar on Virginia Woolf, and while an undergraduate, she had been a student of the women's studies professor who had barred males from her class. In a way, it is not difficult to understand Erin's outlook. From an Irish-Catholic background in Pawtucket, Rhode Island—a place one can easily picture if never having been there just from its reputation as another grimly run-down textile-mill city, like Lowell or Lawrence, maybe—Erin seems to have to compensated for such a background with a rare hunger for education and things cultural in general. She is an eager, clear-complexioned girl with her glossy dark hair cut functionally short, strikingly green eyes; she tends to wear only black, her outfit today black jeans and a bulky black turtleneck sweater. She sits down on he chair across from the large desk. She explains how she has been troubled with her reading of the Woolf novel, and she says she is glad that she can now talk about it some before the session later that afternoon. She reaches into her book bag and takes out a paperback copy that is the new Harcourt edition of *The Waves*. The book has a cover that is maybe based on the original woodcut cover done by Vanessa, Virginia Woolf's sister, for the first edition published by the Hogarth Press, which would have been well after the company moved on from operating out of the Woolfs' own home, Monk's House; this updated version uses a pattern of bright blue, yellow, and white to show several shells floating on undulating waves, and inside the largest central shell, a young woman, naked and long-haired, is snuggled on her side, eyes closed and curled up with knees cocked and one arm under her head, definitely dreaming. It is a beautiful cover; the design captures perfectly the spirit of the book, very dreamlike as it presents the assorted voices of the friends spoken throughout life in counterpoint with that continual soft breaking of waves on an empty beach.

Erin keeps speaking:

"No, and it has nothing to do with any preconceptions. In fact, Virginia Woolf has always been one of my heroes, ever since I read her long essay 'A Room of One's Own' way back in high school. I mean, she's always been the prototypical— or maybe the word is *ultimate*—voice of the woman writer, in asserting her independence, in taking a stand on that sort of thing so long before it was popular to take a stand on it. But it's her political opinion, the really blatant condescension throughout this novel for the lower classes, the common people, or just her ignoring them, that bothers me. There's always the assumed position of privilege for these characters who she gives us in the book talking of their lives, as if the boys at posh boarding school or at Oxford or whatever, their vainly dreaming about their eventual distinguished careers, or the girls' going on about flowers or how men see them at parties—because there's way too much obsession with their appearance, how the girls think they look—amounts to much in the larger scheme of things. I also heard something else, but I don't know if it's true or only a story. I heard that when Joyce was searching for a publisher for *Ulysses*, the manuscript got sent to Woolf and her husband, that they were willing to consider it for publication by their Hogarth Press, but they finally turned it down, with some remark from Virginia to a friend, something along the lines of Joyce's work just being the product of a rather common young Irishman having been given too much education and showing off with it. I mean, that's a complete put-down, really snobby elitism, too."

Her little tirade over, Erin sits very upright and listens to some explanation conceding that what she says about the Woolfs turning down *Ulysses* for their press was the case, yet it most likely had to do with Virginia being offended, even shocked, by the sexual frankness of Joyce's manuscript. Joyce's was a world that Virginia Woolf couldn't have been expected to have had any exposure to. And while there is no denying her considerable literary daring, going into stylistic territories that even Joyce might have found challenging, such as the untethered voices in *The Waves*, Woolf was the product of a staid Victorian society, both in sexual mores and—more importantly with respect to this novel—in an instilled and very distinct class pecking order: she came from a stuffy, well-to-do family, albeit an accomplished one, with her father a university don and famous philosophy scholar, her siblings all extremely intellectual. Then an anecdote is offered to Erin about the French Marxist critic who once said the reason why he truly hated Jane Austen was that she wrote so well, that she was just too convincing in the way she put words themselves together to weave her story in any of the books; he didn't like to admit it, but while reading her he forgot about his social agenda completely, that Marxism, and for the several hours immersed in a Jane Austen novel he was an absolute believer in the fact that marrying well *is* defined by its leading to the enjoyment of inherited wealth with a suitable spouse; in other words, the critic actually cared very much whether or not each of the girls in the books—Elizabeth in *Pride and Prejudice* probably the best example—was by the final chapter going to make a good marriage, one based on primarily materialistic grounds. Yes, the critic said he intensely hated Jane Austen for that, making him forget his convictions, and Erin listens to the suggestion offered that possibly the case is the same with Virginia Woolf—she writes so well she is beyond mere politics.

But a light laugh accompanying the observation elicits only a frown from Erin, who puts the book back into her bag, as if removing Exhibit A from the judge's bench. Erin leaves the office with a simple "OK, then," adding that she will explain her thoughts better at the seminar meeting. Which, when she is gone, the Illness knows, can only suggest without a doubt that what awaits in that seminar room later, from 1:30 to 3:00, is going to be anything but the celebration of the stylistic daring, the sheer visionary magic of words, alluded to a few minutes before in trying to win over Erin Halligan.

And it is ten till one now, and there is—or was?—the meeting with Father Normandy and the others for lunch at noon. John Normandy, the Dean of Liberal Arts, is a Jesuit, and when he called the other day he said it had simply been far too long since "our star younger colleague" had joined "our little table of ragged thinkers" at the faculty dining room.

o   o   o

. . . true, the soft white light inside the arch above you for the MRI like a coffin's shimmering pleated white satin, or the way that for the CT scan the rouge-cheeked nurse looks at you, ghostly, from the inset glass window across the room . . .

o   o   o

AT FIVE PAST, THE OTHER PROFESSORS ARE GONE, and Father Normandy is the only member of the group left. There will be time for a quick sandwich. He nods when the apology is given for being late, about having first stopped by at the office and that leading to a ringing phone to be answered and then a student showing up. Erect, sharp-featured, elegantly silver-haired, Father Normandy is in his late sixties, and he, as dean, was the administrator who led an effort to try to keep things reasonably smooth during the publicized protest concerning the women's studies professor.

Also, the Illness realizes that Father Normandy was the sole colleague officially notified at the time of the initial diagnosis and then the treatment. It was explained to him that one would rather keep mention of it to a minimum if only because that was the way one wanted it, to avoid any pity or stares or just having to constantly explain, especially at a time when tenure had been worked hard for and recently received while still very young for a scholar—and then to *suddenly* have gotten the diagnosis like that. In his discreet, unobtrusive way, Father Normandy handled such wishes well, kept strict confidentiality; meanwhile, the Illness does relish that the priest knows, that there is at least *somebody* on campus who knows. Father Normandy, now in Roman collar and well-tailored black suit, has a national reputation, not only for his respected book on Hopkins's poetry but also for the many years he was in New York City; he was based at Fordham then but worked out of midtown Manhattan most of the week as the editor of the established Jesuit magazine *America,* for which he recruited some of the best younger Catholic scholars and Ph.D. students from around the country to do book reviews and cultural pieces. In fact, that was how contact was first made with him and how even before the Ph.D. in literature was finished at Harvard, his encouragement came in a suggestion to apply for the position at this Jesuit university in the suburb.

After complimenting on appearance and also on so many good reports about how much the students appreciate at last an *interesting* lower-level humanities class, the American literature survey, he mentions that the decision has been made to finally do away with this faculty dining room. It is small talk that goes into some meandering discourse that the Illness really doesn't listen to very closely (there is that upcoming seminar in a half hour or so), talk concerning how fine the food was in another faculty dining room when Father Normandy taught for a year at a new campus of the Université de Paris, west of the city and beside the "skyscraper theme park" of the La Défense district; he says students weren't allowed to as much as peek into, never mind enter, that particular dining room.

"For a long while, my first months there, it seemed that it was but an attempt by the French administrators to keep students very far away from professors, except for the mandatory few hours a week professors had to actually show up and lecture. I'd already learned that there were no individual offices for professors. There was just a shared cloakroom, certainly because no French professor would think of meeting with a student individually, and in Paris one wouldn't even think of calling oneself a professor, but rather liked to be billed as an 'intellectual.' The food in the faculty dining room was exquisite, even if it was served by those whom we over here would call cafeteria ladies, I suppose. One day it would be *truite grillée,* another day *lapin aux herbes,* better than what you might find in any famous upscale French restaurant in the West Fifties."

His French is perfect, the rolling *r*'s in the *"truite grillée"* and the silky elision of the syllables in *"lapin aux herbes,"* too. He says that he himself thought that having such special faculty cuisine was more elitism, the professors dining magnificently while the students broke simple bread on the other side of the wall in their own scruffy dining hall, until he discovered that the very same fare could be purchased by students as well, prepared in the same kitchen, on the aforementioned other side of that high dividing wall—and, better, the use of government-subsidized chits let the students do it for *half* the price for the *identical* meal. He chuckles, saying he is not sure if the lesson to be learned is not to trust preconceptions or maybe the larger truth that it is more than a fact—you really can't get a bad meal anywhere in France.

The very word he used earlier, *elitism,* only reminds of Virginia Woolf, the upcoming seminar.

He offers another compliment about looking wonderful, though the Illness wants to say that applying makeup before the mirror early that morning somehow didn't confirm that. Next, more as a priest than a colleague and dean, he inquires if a full social life is being led, as is befitting somebody he calls "a lovely, intelligent young woman," and in reply—a seemingly automatic reaction, which maybe the Illness doesn't like to hear—mention is made of the upcoming dinner with a lawyer, "a friend of friends," later that evening. A glance at the functional Timex on the wrist shows that it will take some hurrying to get to the seminar room on time, and a rather quick departure is made, the foolishness of referring to what must have sounded like "a big date" lingering in the mind.

o o o

"I DON'T KNOW, BUT LIKE I SAID, it worried me all weekend," Erin Halligan says in the seminar room, richly oak-paneled, in one of the original spired, mock-gothic university halls. "I mean, it really did."

"Just relax, girl," Danny Wilbourne says to her, across the table. "How many times do I have to tell you—let the words speak for themselves, let all these wild voices of all these characters in the novel take you through what is the long march of the years—or sort of more like the march of the waves, I guess, is what I want to say. You've got to just read—read and relax."

And with that, Danny furrows his brow and wags his finger at her, a put-on scold.

"All right, all right, I get the idea, Danny," Erin says.

Danny is African American, handsome and with an easygoing way about him. No question about it, he is the brightest in the bunch, recruited for the graduate school from his small Catholic college (Salesian Fathers?) in Florida and maybe not long for literature study; he wants to write his own fiction, and he belongs in a top-notch M.F.A. program, a writers' workshop that will let him do just that somewhere else (while intense scholarship has always been an accepted commodity at Catholic institutions, creativity—which might be seen as frivolous—often has not). Erin makes a sophomoric joke about how Danny should be one to talk about relaxing, and how can she, across the table from him, have any *chance* of relaxing with his sitting in the chair there wearing that bright-red V-neck sweater, the thing loud enough to be literally shouting at her. Everybody around the table laughs, and the laughter announces the final sputtering out of what Erin probably saw as her own agenda for the day in the seminar, something she had to do, considering that she had become so politicized during the women's studies debates, though it seems she doesn't always fully believe in all of it. She admits outright now that she loves Virginia Woolf's beautiful sentences, always has and always will.

After that, the session goes smoothly, almost too quickly in the excitement of what turns out to be a group celebration of the book, *The Waves,* as they listen to the passages marked earlier while riding out to the university on the "T" now being slowly read aloud by their professor, and then the larger point made: Granted, the voices of Woolf's characters speaking, the bunch of them taking turns talking, might all sound the same, might all share the same lyrical intensity even if the concerns of each character are very different, but that is no flaw—Woolf lets the heart, or hearts, speak as if beyond the confines of an individual's personal language, has the voices enter an alternate airy realm (a perfect sunlit green valley? the beach with those waves on the glistening blue sea at balmy noontime?) and float into the world of bona fide poetry; there, the truths of the heart are spoken in a universal way, how they never *can* be expressed in the simple everyday of things. The students keep listening.

The seminar runs a quarter hour over the usual time slot, it goes *extremely* well, and afterward Danny Wilbourne comes up to talk about how he just thought of something. He says that Faulkner also does the same thing—has the voices of the poor Mississippi tenant farmers in his *As I Lay Dying* assume a definite shared lyricism that is the true language of the heart, despite how it doesn't always reflect a diction within those characters' verbal ability. All the way to Harvard Square on the "T," a fine feeling from the session remains, and how very insightful Danny was to link Woolf and Faulkner as he had, an observation quite fresh; the best part about teaching is always that it is a two-way street, which is to say, the professor also learns as much, or more, in the entire process.

o o o

HARVARD SQUARE SPREADS—is there any other word for it?—*resplendent* in the afternoon sunshine of the February day.

Margaret Barrington (it seems the first time all day she is

inside herself again, has her very name) waits for the WALK signal there at Massachusetts Avenue in front of the old Coop that's currently a Barnes & Noble (it also seems, at last, that she is back in the active voice, as if she is actually *doing* things for the first time all day, like now contentedly waiting for the light, and the world isn't but a blur of everything transpiring in the passive, what those comically correct computer grammar checkers that her undergrads depend on for word processing would love to admonish against, to the point that the check would have to be turned off repeatedly—disabled, even—there would have been so many warning beeps throughout a day like the one she has presently experienced), and she continues to wait for the WALK signal. The ornate news kiosk there where Mass Avenue and Kennedy converge is a busy little exotic island in itself, the stand with its copper roof corroded lime green, people picking up and flipping through the pages of magazines at the outside racks; the modern concrete-and-glass block of Holyoke Center rises high behind it on one side, to the other side is the profusion of ancient rose brick of Harvard Yard, the students with scarves and ski caps, their down parkas looking clownishly inflated, hurrying this way and that.

A big silver-and-yellow "T" bus passes in a puff of black fumes that suggests a benevolence as well, the aroma reminding her of the streets of Paris—Margaret Barrington's simple Paris, and certainly not John Normandy's sophisticated Paris with its *lapin aux herbes* and, she is sure, the very delectable *truite grillée*. A faraway jet up in the too-blueness above leaves a delicate trail, as if whispering something, a message most necessary that Margaret almost, but not quite, does seem to understand.

Margaret crosses the street. She thinks she might browse in the Grolier Poetry Bookshop, a favorite of hers over on Plympton, check Schoenhofs' Foreign Books, too, before backtracking to the Casablanca (no longer the old grimy cavelike Casablanca, where she had spent considerable pleasant time with friends as a grad student, but now a more recently refurbished incarnation of the downstairs bar/lounge that's still a reasonable facsimile of the original) to be there on time to meet her date, who, she laughs to herself, *warned* her of his "absurd punctuality." He said they could decide on a restaurant while having a drink.

o   o   o

TWO HOURS AFTER THEY ARRIVED HERE they are still seated at the small Spanish restaurant—by this point the elderly waiter seems not in the least surprised anymore that this tall, prematurely gray-haired Rob MacLaren speaks fluent Spanish, how he more than held his own in ordering the paella for two and the rare-vintage *rioja*; he even made the guy feel good about the fact that, sad to say, as the waiter confessed, he wasn't actually from Spain but only Guatemala—and, indeed, a full two hours later Margaret and her date are still talking.

What is surprising is how honest it got, so quickly. Not only talk of their own vulnerabilities (he knew about her year of treatment, said their friend Susan had assured him the latest diagnosis was good, and Margaret knew about his painful divorce from his wife of twelve years, the daughter he wished he could see more) but also talk of the important things that can arise out of an ordinary day, as Margaret maybe goes on too long in trying to describe how the potential disaster of that afternoon's seminar turned into a little party in the end, totally unexpected, therefore better *and* sweeter because of that. He repeats what he said earlier, how lucky she is to have the career that she does, one that unites vocation with avocation, and he says he used his secretary's computer terminal that afternoon to check Amazon.com to see that she is "famous," her two books listed there. "Princeton University Press, no less," he says. But she assures him that, first, having a book on Amazon.com is no accomplishment, there probably isn't a book in America, and maybe most of the world, including stapled-together, vanity-press pamphlets, not at least *listed* there, so that doesn't mean anybody is buying or even aware of the books; and, secondly, she wouldn't recommend either of her books, saying they are little more than a perpetual grad student's nose-to-the-grindstone fare, though she does hope to at some point write something meaningful, work that isn't just for the academic research and theory world, but something that matters. She wants to write the kind of book that's more a pure appreciation of literature, to capture the state of mind she seems to be approaching sometimes when she is interacting with students in class, caught up in the flow, and her ideas begin to wonderfully—maybe magically—mesh, as in the seminar earlier. However, she catches herself now, knows she *is* talking too much about herself, granting that he seems to encourage it, and she at last prompts him to talk more of his own work. And he does, again with such honesty:

"When I first got out of Columbia Law, I didn't care that I wasn't one of the stars, law review and the rest of it. I accepted the fact that I wouldn't be snatched up by a large Manhattan firm or land a clerkship with some name federal judge in Washington either. I was content to simply sign on with the attorney general's office back here in hometown Boston, doing consumer protection, which I liked. The utilities division, you know, and all it took was one big, well-publicized case where I nailed the old NYNEX crew good for overcharging, perpetrating deceptive billing for years, then after that three firms who specialized in representing the utilities sector came head-hunting for me. And, man, was I easily wooed, with a family then and buried under bills, needless to say. After a half dozen years with a firm, I joined up with a couple of other guys in the same end of the racket and went out on my own, and now the firm, my firm, I guess, keeps getting bigger and bigger, mostly product liability lately. Black & Decker is our major client—or what Black & Decker has to defend itself on when some poor idiot who didn't read the instructions right cuts his finger off using one of their more idiotic power saws. There's gold in them thar tools, if you know what I mean. Fool's gold, I suppose."

"Susan told me you wrote poetry in college," Margaret says.

He winces. He is athletic and *decidedly* good-looking in early middle age—the tallness, also the eyes very special; they are eyes eerily pale blue and the way that eyes used to appear, she thinks, in those old Civil War daguerreotypes of the soldiers, before development chemicals became more sophisticated and could pick up lighter hues.

He says:

"She told you that, huh?"

"Yes," she says.

"Susan always was a big mouth."

They both laugh.

When they walk to his car, parked next to a stubby silver meter on Holyoke Street, it turns out to be an expensive black Porsche coupe, a sleek little bullet, really, with the polished metal hubs gleaming in the streetlight, the taillights looking like giant carved rubies; it is a car not of a man who has just been speaking of realigning his life, perhaps even trying to get back to the social concern he'd known when he first worked in the attorney general's office, but more the car of a high-rolling bachelor, meant to impress shampoo-fragrant girls in tight sheaths and wobbly heels a dozen years younger than him, probably met in the dating bars on Newbury Street.

"This is your *car*?" Margaret says.

"I know, I know," he says, acknowledging the seeming indulgence of it, unlocking the passenger-side door for her. "Hey, why don't we just forget the car and get back to that poetry I wrote in college."

Margaret likes the way he deflects the teasing about the Porsche; it's funny.

Before he drops her off there in her newly gentrified Dorchester neighborhood, they kiss lightly. He says he'll call her in the morning, and she says OK.

o o o

IT HAS BEEN A LONG DAY, and to sit on the bed's edge is to feel a bit of a headache from the wine, then untie the belt of the terry robe and remove it before slipping under the down comforter; the silver-painted radiator, a steam system, clanks before it trails off in a fading staccato.

Then to get up again in pajamas, go into the living room and set the thermostat for a nighttime sixty-two.

There is moonlight, and back in the bedroom the Illness stares out the twelve-paned window to the backyard, which is bathed in bluish-silver now, the glow of it strong. There are still the three snow shovels propped upright against the neighbor's wood-planked fence, the shaggy yews.

"What was that all about?" the Illness asks.

But there is no answer.

"Come on, I think we need to talk about this, I mean, this date, this man that you're still thinking about, his eyes, his voice, his easy laughter. Aren't you forgetting something?"

Still nothing. The moonlight seems to pulsate; the bare limbs of a maple are like massive upturned claws against the large sky.

"Well?" It presses with the question; the tone is chiding, close to threatening. *"Well?"*

But just then the radiator seems to give the only necessary answer, its sudden hiss more like a "Shhh." A whisper to be quiet, and, yes, "Just sh-shhh."

o o o

IN BED THE COMFORTER is very warm.

There is some thought of the ride on the ancient "T" trolley car that morning, what indeed could have been years, not hours, ago.

There are other things. There is Father Normandy's Roman collar, crisply starched, and there is Erin Halligan's copy of *The Waves,* the new Harcourt edition with the long-haired young woman asleep in the cocoon of a shell on the cover; there are all those people leisurely lifting magazines and newspapers from the racks of the Out of Town News kiosk at the very epicenter of Harvard Square, a lovely late-winter painting in itself, and . . . and. . . and—yes, this is it—and there is also the Wallace Stevens poem about this time of year, its title now remembered, "The Poem of Our Climate," or perhaps "The Poems of Our Climate," that title plural. And what a lovely, lovely poem it is, with a central image of flowers in a cut-glass vase on a table in fragile February, sunlight streaming in through a window and the dust motes themselves there indoors suspended to the point of significant stillness, and . . .

And soon there will be dreaming, too.

THE FLIGHT

I.

HERE IT IS STRAIGHT:

I finished soaping my hands in the lavatory's little sink. I took one of the heavy white paper towels and dried them, soon confused the way I always am about where exactly you're supposed to stuff the thing. Sure, on the wall was a red diagonal slash across the symbol of the toilet to say that they're not allowed to be put there, but there came that moment of complete confusion—lostness?—as to where the push flap on spring hinges was to toss trash into. The noise of the jet's engines was pretty loud back there by the tail, and I crumpled the towel in a ball and put it on the formica counter. I took out my pocket comb and passed it through my hair a couple of times, and I thought that maybe the brownish mirrors that the airlines used did lie to a certain degree, making my hair seem thicker than it actually was at my age and making my complexion seem to hold more of a hue than it actually did, too. But that was OK. The cubicle smelled of the minty miniature bars of soap, and after unlatching the bolt on the polished metal door, I twisted the knob and halfway out remembered that I hadn't done anything more with the balled paper towel. I kept going anyway. I planted my loafers solid the way you do on the carpet of the aisle to maintain some sense of balance, on my way to my seat again, 12-D in coach.

It could have been United or American. It could have been Northwest that had recently merged with a European company (Lufthansa? KLM?), or it could have been perpetually bankrupt Continental, which appeared to stave off any complete collapse by constantly changing its logo colors, as the old red-orange-and-yellow combo had now become a more simple gray and blue, I think. (Though possibly Continental was out of the sucking eddy of Chapter Eleven, hadn't I read somewhere, or had it even folded as a company completely?) Actually, it didn't matter, and it had been a long while since I had cared about what airline I was booked on once I told the cabdriver where to drop me off at the terminal; my travel agent knew that he would remain my travel agent only as long as he worked his computer with at least the minimal effort needed to come up with the best fare with the fewest restrictions for the dates I needed. I have never been one of those people who cared about frequent-flyer miles or that sort of thing.

Never.

II.

I GRIPPED THE LAST HIGH-BACK UPHOLSTERED SEAT to steady myself, then I touched the one in the second row from the rear on the other side to steady myself as well. I continued along the aisle, and while I seemed to remember a heavy, bearded guy with a laptop computer in a row by himself far back, and also an old woman with white hair like fiberglass insulation and sitting under a pink afghan in another one of the rows by herself, neither seemed to be there now. In fact, I kept moving up the aisle, and if the plane had been about half full, I was certain, when I went to the lavatory minutes before, it was now completely *empty*. And it wasn't simply a situation of my thinking I remembered the bearded guy (I could still see his fat fingers poking away at a keyboard that was too small for the very bulk of him, in his cheap polyester dress shirt and splashy flowered tie, almost a bear performing a circus trick), or thinking I remembered an old woman with that afghan tucked like a bib right up to the baggy skin of her neck. It wasn't just those specifics. Because now in that flying plane there wasn't the usual legion of self-satisfied lawyers with briefcases filled with lies; teenage mothers balancing screaming three-month-old babies; college kids with ears plugged into music; tanned vacationing couples coming back from some sunny island, the male member of the duo in his resort garb constantly standing up again to unlatch the compartment above him, at the female's urging, and check that whatever they had bought as a souvenir, inevitably made of wicker, was still safe and not getting crushed up there. There weren't even the jutting-jawed older stewardesses, those who have kept their jobs well past their or anybody else's prime due to a succession of lawsuits by their union against the company, or the young, lithe ones with translucent skin, lips like bruised plums, and wispy hair kept ever so neat in a French twist, the lookers they always assign to first class. As I said, there was *nobody* there. I glanced to make sure I was at 12-D, an aisle seat. I picked up the gray seat belt with its heavy chrome buckle, and I slid back into my place, reaching down with both hands to find the two ends of the belt and tighten it over my lap.

I reached up to fiddle with the air nozzle above for my seat, and I adjusted it so the flow was aimed smack at me.

III.

I LOOKED OUT THE WINDOW, its plexiglass scratched, to see the bright sunlight and the fine daytime blue above the billowing clouds, yet I suppose it was really night out there, the stars blinking in the blackness of it all. A stewardess (but I definitely must remember to say "attendant" nowadays) had earlier come down the aisle with a stack of magazines, holding them in front of her ample chest like a high school girl with her books after class and letting the passengers see the titles marked in easy-to-read black on the white spines of the binders; naturally, there hadn't been much of a selection by the time she reached me, though I wasn't far back. Those in the seats ahead of me had made short work of anything good like *Time* or *Sports Illustrated,* even *Esquire* or *The Atlantic* or *Harper's,* and I had felt that little shred of rage that everybody must experience as you witness somebody ahead of you like that cavalierly lift three or four issues off the stack for ready future reference, while you and the rest later on will be left with what amounts to less than the usual crumbs. When she had stopped beside my seat, I took a personal investment magazine that I had no interest in, and it was either that or a golf magazine. Still, I wanted to maintain some integrity, not admit that I had been defeated, or as much as slightly bothered, by the sheer greed of others, not only in this plane but also in the entire vicious world, I suppose. To repeat, it was a routine. The last thing I had on my mind was personal investment or money in general. I had found out long ago that if you worked reasonably well enough to keep a job (like my largely meaningless one somewhere halfway up, wobblingly, the reported "corporate ladder"), there would always be money, and if anything beyond that was to be observed it was that for me more money had always had the predictable effect of needlessly complicating life (even if I didn't like to overpay on a plane ticket); maybe around college age, when I worked all sorts of truly odd jobs in the summers, I learned that there was no magic about money, and what a do-nothing uncle once told me was probably the best advice: "Cash your paycheck on Friday and then look at those green bills, boy. Look straight at Hamilton and Jackson and even Honest Abe. And you tell me, boy, if right there on that green salad they're not smiling at your stupidity, every one of them with a quiet grin, dead as they are now and knowing at last the Big Joke that's at the heart of what you're holding in your mitts." No, I didn't think of the personal investment magazine now, but instead lifted from the upholstered pocket on the back of the seat in front of me, below the folded-up plastic tray, the latest issue of the airline's in-flight magazine. The articles in those things are usually pure junk, stories on cities and on food, telling you nothing worthwhile and all written with an upbeat, vaguely nauseating Chamber of Commerce tone that you already have had your fill of by the time the morning network TV news shows sign off the air. On the other hand, I never tired of flipping fast past the ads for indestructible suitcases and Franklin Mint miniatures (does anybody *buy* that crap?) in the

back to get to the maps. So I studied the map of the hub terminals in various cities, and admitting that I wasn't sure what city
I would be landing in or if I did have to make a connection, I
liked to feel that if dropped in Memphis or Detroit or Atlanta,
anywhere, I would know my way around the place. How I could
work my way from a gate way out on the arm of Concourse B,
let's say, clear to the other arm (the dotted blue line indicted
either an escalator or stairs) of Concourse A, way out there, too,
at Gate 37. Such a plan, the preparation, would be necessary if
I had, let's also say, only twenty-two minutes between flights,
right? I carefully memorized them one by one for a while, then
I went to the two-page spread with a map of the United States;
arcing red lines fanning out from the cities, especially the hubs,
showed the airline's numerous routes, and I noticed the kind
of thing that you always notice in looking at a map like that.
"Man, Maine is way up there, isn't it, deep into Canada, actually." And, "It's kind of amazing the way that the huge green
fertile plain of the East, solid as it is without the markings for
state boundaries, gives way to the nearly twice-as-huge slab of
the High Plains and Mountains, all golden brown on the map,
of the American West indeed." Other lines running off the page
edges indicated that there was a whole world beyond, not only
Paris and London but also Frankfurt, where I most likely never
would go and didn't care to visit, anyway, and, far south, Buenos Aires, where I surely never would go either. But it was good
to think that by this hour in Buenos Aires the lavender dusk
had come and gone in a flutter of pigeons around the national
monuments, the bright buses chugged past ornately frilled white
buildings behind fine black ironwork gates and well-groomed

young couples strolled on the wide, tree-lined boulevards chatting in sweet Spanish, surrounded by the sound of airily soft guitar music drifting from somewhere, but, as they say, who knows *exactly* where. Again, I would never go to Buenos Aires. And right then that fact rose like a major failure in my life, the kind of omission that causes you to turn away from looking at your pathetic self in a color group snapshot somebody shows you from a backyard Sunday afternoon barbecue party you were once at, as you admit to yourself that you never had the guts for much of anything daring, not even fudging it a bit on your income tax forms, never mind going to Buenos Aires. The plane engines whispered away. Outside, at the tapering end of the wing in what was very much night, a red light blinked on and off, on and off, on and off—rhythmically.

I stared up from the magazine. I tossed it to the seat beside me. I stood and looked around again. Hell, it was true: I had somehow left a half-full flight and gone into the lavatory, and I had come out again five minutes later to find nobody there. I panicked. *What was I doing thumbing through a magazine in a situation like this! What was I doing dreaming about fucking Buenos Aires!*

IV.

OF COURSE, THERE MIGHT HAVE BEEN OTHER THINGS. And there might have been something about my two sons, Jack and Freddy, from my busted marriage. I should see them more. The older, Jack, who tries to keep a brave face through it all, acts more sophisticated than his fourteen years old when I visit. The last time I was with him and his brother for a weekend I took them to a chain Italian restaurant. We three sat at the table, and Jack must have caught me ogling a college-age blonde with a snub nose and big made-up eyes, wearing tight shorts and cork-soled canvas wedges, candy-striped, plus a daringly skimpy halter top, as she swayed across the room; Jack said to me with a put-on knowing smile, an equally knowing voice that was maybe his own way of confirming the propaganda with which his mother had pumped him, "Man, who can blame you for acting the way you do, with stuff like that on the loose nowadays." He shook his head histrionically, as if to cool himself in his feigned rising Fahrenheit after seeing the girl: "Whewww." And I bought Freddy a baseball glove, gave it to him during another weekend visit. I suggested we all head out to the municipal park for a little catch. Freddy sat in the backseat, saying nothing and staring at the glove. It was a massive black leather contraption with silver lettering touting its many high-tech features endorsed by the famous major league player whose stamped autograph under the pocket was affixed like a signature on a rare art treasure—about the best glove money could buy, costing me over a hundred bucks. And then when Jack and Freddy and I started tossing the rawhide around there amid the park's azaleas and May trees dripping their lime-green spangles in the year's first suggestion of genuine warmth, I could tell something was wrong. Freddy had never wielded Jack's bravado; and Freddy was now moping, had moped the whole day, I guess. Until later, when he was alone with me and finally said, with his head hung low and Freddy so heartbreakingly shy, so heartbreakingly *fragile,* "I don't know, D-Dad"—the poor kid stuttered terribly when nervous, his teachers routinely reported—"it's kind of embarrassing. I m-mean, if I had to play with other kids, a glove like this that costs so much would be kind of st-stupid." I wanted to hug him as hard as I could right then and there, the scared ten-year-old flesh of my flesh, but I knew that would only make matters worse. Or there could have been something else altogether, like when I said to my father just before he died something that I had no right to say to him while he lay there hooked up to tubes and tanks, the EKG monitor beep-beeping at the foot of his cranked-up hospital bed. And how often in dreams I have attempted to stealthily return to that hospital room, tiptoe in and watch him sleeping there; I want to wait for him to wake, to tell him that that wasn't what I had *meant* to say, or that he had *misunderstood* what I'd meant to say—but, of course and as said, I never had the chance, because he died that night after I spoke it, when I walked the corridor's beige linoleum, passed the nurses' station by the chiming elevator and returned to my own apartment to log the several tossing and turning hours of what I pretended was sleep. Sure, there could have been a lot of other things, but for the moment there was just that ridiculous in-flight magazine on the middle seat in my row, the loosened end of the belt on my seat next to it.

I was still standing in the aisle.

V.

I CONSIDERED RETURNING TO THE LAVATORY. I wondered if I could start this over again. And maybe by coming *out* of the lavatory again it would all be different, and then I would simply walk through the door there and into the half-full cabin and it would be the way I had left it before I went *into* the lavatory. (I pictured now that crumpled paper towel on the formica counter beside the tiny oval of the sink. I knew I shouldn't have left it there, more gutlessness on my part and somebody else having to face a mess I couldn't solve.) But at heart (*heart*, what a word, huh?) I thought that deep down (much better phrasing) I already knew that nothing would be different. So instead of heading back toward the tail, I headed up toward the cockpit.

I passed the curtain that led to first class, abandoned, too. I saw an orange oxygen mask that one of the stewardesses must have left on the work counter after her demonstration at the beginning of the flight; also piled on the counter were the remnants of the first-class meal already served, plastic champagne glasses and plastic plates that were gilt-edged and supposed to look like authentic china. It was certainly true that they had enjoyed a real meal of, apparently, sliced leg of lamb and steamed asparagus spears and new potatoes sprinkled with tongue-tingling herbs, not simply the quarter of a wheat-bread cheese submarine sandwich, tastelessly limp, that they had doled out to us in coach, the single cookie in cellophane and the diminutive red apple at least keeping with the theme that the stewardess had announced straightforwardly to us, that of "Snack." I looked at the first-class seats the way I always looked at first-class seats when given a minute to linger and assess them, rather than just sneak a peek in the process of being hurried in and out of the plane when on the tarmac—it was impressive how wide they were, with soft glove leather fit for a limousine, intricately rolled and padded, and not the grungy twill found in coach; they offered enough legroom (particularly important for me at six four) to accommodate not just somebody tall but perhaps one of those fairy-tale giants who wander benevolently the dark, dark woods with a big, big silver-bladed lumberman's ax on the shoulder, searching to help someone in dire need—if that makes any sense. Really spacious seats, all right. I looked at the closed door to the pilot's cockpit, the black slab, and I didn't hesitate. And, understandably, I knew what the deal was, figured beforehand what I would find on the other side. So without even knocking I just opened it in a quick yank; I saw the seats for the pilot and copilot as empty as anything else, with the minor triumph of my saying to myself, "Aha, I told you so!" The dashboard was a splattering of instrumentation: monitoring lights, dozens of gauges and a couple of glowing-dialed gyroscopes under bulbed glass, all sorts of toggle switches and ridged knobs. It was very much night, dim in there, and attached to the pilot's seat was a side tray with a large mug of coffee on it, so fresh that steam still streamed from the heavily creamed gunk. It was tough standing that way, hunched at my height, and I got a little giddy in anticipation, almost vertiginous, to think that maybe I would sit down in the pilot's seat myself. But to do that, place my body in front of the complicated dashboard and with my loafers close enough to touch the pedals lower down—big cast-aluminum slabs—and with my hands close enough to reach out and grab like a pair of longhorns the twin plastic grips of the yoke, yes, to sit down would be the ultimate transgression, would be to *do* exactly what I *wasn't supposed* to do. I looked around. I looked out the door to the first-class cabin, then coach. Nobody was there, so what did it matter? (Or, as a stranger on a stool beside me in the posh bar of a hotel where I was staying last month on business said, after the two of us had sat there for about an hour and sipped smokily aromatic scotches, never speaking, both of us staring straight ahead at the bottles behind the bar, as he finally said right out of a more-than-proverbial blue, pivoting to face me, "What the hell does any of it matter?" Then he pivoted on the stool to return to his original position, and we both stared straight ahead some more, saying nothing else for probably another hour, before I left.) And what did it matter now if I sat down in that pilot's seat? Which I did—slowly, very slowly, I admit. But once settled there the intensity of my outright fear of doing it evanesced, and I looked out the windshield, ringed with a riveted frame of more aluminum, and I marveled at how with the engines hissing, with the plane being up there eight miles high, speeding at about five hundred miles an hour, it was easy to savor the sensation that there was no movement whatsoever, only stillness. I craned my neck for a better view, and in the sky very black hung the stars very yellow, so bright that they could have been matches flickering. If you could tap into a something you thought you once learned in Scouts, you could maybe pick out positively Gemini the Twins and Orion the Hunter (the angled line of stars denoting his warrior's belt, then the droop of another line of them telling of his mighty sword), the two refreshing Dippers as well. I craned my neck to look out the windshield's side panel, next stretched my entire torso across the copilot's seat to look out the panel on the other side. The setup was quite cramped in there, and you usually never realized when back in the body of the plane that up front the craft tapered, and what could accommodate easily the four or six seats across in coach could barely handle, at this stage of the fuselage's nose, the two side-by-side seats. Before me on a chrome hook was the intercom's mike, square-shaped and with a squiggly black telephone-style cord dangling below. I lifted it off the dash, pressed the green SPEAK button a couple of times; I heard the click of static through the whole system back there in the cabin. I got nervous again, and it wasn't merely the nervousness that so many men (why not women, I wonder) are reported to suffer in public speaking (they say that the lion-hunting, seven-hundred-kilo-bull-dodging Hemingway himself had one utter phobia—having to address an auditorium of people), but a nervousness, maybe, that if I did talk now, at long last and even if there was nobody around, I had to say something worthwhile, announce over the speakers something significant. Like: "It pains me so to think that anybody in the world has to hurt anybody else." Or possibly something deeply personal and to a brutal degree honest: "I hated to go to gym class as a kid, because in shorts and T-shirt and being so goofily gangly, I always knew I looked like a hunched-over sorry bag of bones." Or: "I'll admit it, I've never been able to spell *neccessary* (sp.?) or *seperate* (sp.?), and even in college at the so-called Ivy League university I would look it up in my ancient red-bound *Webster's Collegiate* for a term paper, and then a day later when doing another paper, or just writing a letter, I would have to look it up again." But when I did speak, it came out nothing like that. I pressed the button a couple of more times and heard the crackling static again, proof, again, that the system functioned, and I cleared my throat. I spoke aloud my own name—first, middle, and last—and I could have been hearing it for a first time, the empty syllables, the absurdly long roll of that hopefully ritzy middle name that traced back to my mother's Huguenot ancestry—I could have heard it all and said, "So, what's that supposed to mean?" I hung the mike back on the chrome hook. I rose from the pilot's seat. I left the cockpit and returned to my seat, 12-D in coach.

I sat down, was now for some reason extremely tired. I thought I might take a little snooze.

VI.

BECAUSE, SITTING THERE ALONE, without even a crepe-paper shred of hope as to where I was heading, I wasn't scared whatsoever now. There was nothing I could do about the situation but let it happen. And conceding that, I told myself what I no doubt knew, or seemed to sense, from way, way back, all along in what is commonly labeled a life:

"This is when it starts to get interesting."

The jet, a 737, plowed on through the swallowing sky.

LUNCH ACROSS
THE BRIDGE

THEY WOULDN'T KNOW ABOUT IT until the next day.

Later they would read of it in the paper, eventually hear it on TV. The couple would learn that what happened that day at the restaurant called Arandas was all part of what Nuevo Laredo across the border was at the moment. But, as said, they didn't know that then, when it happened there at Arandas.

It was a fine restaurant just two blocks off the city's main street, a modernistic villa-style setup—pale lavender stucco and tinted glass, walled in for its own little enclave with a courtyard offering gardens of fleshy hibiscus and the stars of oleander, a hissing fountain—and they had simply walked over the international bridge from their hotel in Laredo to have a late lunch.

They didn't say much as the meal was ordered. Closing the big menus, they smiled and thanked the waiter. They smiled at him again when the food was served. They both surely realized they were beyond talking any more about the sadness in their lives right then, losing a child like that. They had driven here from Austin, going south for four hours or so on the interstate—over the dusty flats peppered with mesquite and prickly pear, always a dreamlike landscape, in a way—only because they had often done that when younger and during college years at the university, gone to the border for a weekend to relax. Maybe they now thought that just getting out of Austin for a weekend, being somewhere else, would help.

The restaurant was half full, if that, in midafternoon, the waiters moving around the tables in their black trousers and very white shirts; there was the low buzz of talk and the soft clinking of china and silverware.

If he was thinking anything in the long stretches of silence at the table, it was how beautiful she always looked, even now after what she had been through. He was maybe thinking how that very day, in the lobby of the stately old hotel in Laredo on the Texas side, he had noticed people glancing at her—tall and slim, her auburn hair loose, her dark eyes large. There was something about her beauty at this age, no longer a girl, that made her quite striking, the look of a certain maturity; it was a kind, knowing quality, he sometimes thought, rare. She wore simple white Capri slacks and a simple white blouse, and the blue canvas rope-soled espadrilles were comfortable for their walk this warm, sunny spring afternoon. And if she was thinking anything, it was maybe how it had broken her heart even more, what she thought about often, the way that he, her husband, had maintained his hope for so long. It wasn't a hope that he had expressed anywhere else in life before that, she knew, and for at least the last few years he'd admitted that granting he was supposedly as successful as he was in the old and respected Texas law firm in Austin, the youngest full partner, the work had come to attract him less and less; he often said, good-naturedly, that he probably should have forgotten completely about law

school when young, dared early on to try something more interesting. But this past year, as the doctors kept gently lying to
the two of them—all those doctors inevitably with diplomas
neatly framed and from the very best universities on their office
walls, doctors inevitably wearing horn-rimmed glasses and blue
button-down shirts, or it sometimes seemed to her, they were all
interchangeable—true, as the cheery doctors all talked only of
more options, the new experimental treatments for Owen and
rates of possible success, she knew deep down the situation to
be otherwise, she knew that the blood tests and the marrow
samples told another story altogether; doctors had to convince
themselves of their cures, that was their daily business, understandably, and you couldn't blame them, they meant well and it
justified who they were. She had to admit how in the course of
that—his keeping up his hope as he did, believing the optimis-
tic doctors and refusing to do otherwise, repeatedly becoming
excited at what he saw as the slightest hint of a good turn for
Owen—could have been the saddest thing of all.

But maybe they weren't thinking of such matters. They were
just a couple, still young enough, both attractive, educated people—they had strolled across the bridge spanning the weedy riv-
erbed, and they had simply come to the restaurant for lunch and
weren't thinking of much whatsoever, or saying much, besides
the small talk concerning how good the meal was, how good
even the wine was at this restaurant, Arandas.

The waiters were attentive yet unobtrusive, maintaining full
dignity, like European waiters, and the food, touted as "interior
Mexican cuisine," was actually exceptional; without question,
the place deserved its reputation.

"It's very good," he said.

"Yes," she said, "and I'm glad we came for the weekend."

After a few minutes she said it was also good that they had decided to take the walk over to Nuevo Laredo for lunch, instead of coming in the evening, as they had originally planned.

"Yes," he said.

The news reports would later say that it had to do with a public appearance, to make a point. That meant asserting power and announcing, so there would be no mistake, that Paco Villarreal was out of the Mexican federal prison in Zacatecas at last. The escape, in all likelihood, had been not so much a scenario of any adventurous derring-do as it was large payoffs to the prison guards. And free again, Paco Villarreal was in Nuevo Laredo again to let the opposing cartel know where he physically was, tell them boldly that he had no fear and they couldn't ignore the Helios cartel—headed while he was away by his brother Esteban—in the ongoing Mexican drug wars currently playing themselves out in Nuevo Laredo; the local police would leave him alone, of course—they were easily paid off. The city itself was strategically important because the Pan-American Highway passed right through Nuevo Laredo and then Laredo. The highway, which became Interstate 35 clear up to Minnesota, was a main conduit for drug transport into U.S. markets.

But it wasn't like anything in the movies, the way they took over the restaurant that afternoon. And how it happened was that nobody seemed to have noticed the two young men, neatly groomed and dressed in good casual clothes, who came in to look around, politely so, and then leave for a few moments. They returned with three other young men accompanying a rather short man of about fifty in a loose-tailed light-blue guayabera shirt, with a pockmarked face and aviator sunglasses, who the couple dining would later learn was indeed the man named Paco Villarreal. And nobody eating seemed to have noticed that the twin large carved wooden doors leading to the outside courtyard, the entrance to the restaurant, had been latched, and that there was another young man posted to stand watch there. A middle-aged woman had been called over to the table, where the older man in the guayabera—having removed the sunglasses—was now seated with several of the younger men. She must have been the manager or perhaps the owner, and as she sat down at the table with the men, that, too, probably didn't seem to be anything out of the ordinary, if anybody in the restaurant did, in fact, notice her doing so; it could have been but a greeting to a regular customer, let's say. It was only then, when she stood up from the table, remaining very calm—a petite, dignified woman in a crisp linen suit, she had substantial makeup and carefully coiffed hennaed hair—did people look that way, and she had already motioned for two of the waiters to come to the table. She spoke to them in low tones, and then one waiter made the announcement to the room in Spanish and the other in English, obviously for the benefit of Americans, of which the couple might have been the only ones there. The people eating were told that Señor Villarreal would like all of them to be his good friends for the moment in celebration of his return to Nuevo Laredo after a long absence; a round of drinks for everybody—wine or a cocktail—would all be paid for by Señor Villarreal.

The couple looked around, and everybody was raising

glasses in a toast, there was even some applause; people probably didn't recognize the name—or didn't do so at first, anyway, there in the restaurant, it was later noted—and they were now certainly appreciative of the magnanimous gesture of this man, whoever he was.

The couple smiled to each other. She reached over and put her long slim fingers on his atop the table.

They continued with their meal. The waiter came with a bottle and refilled their wineglasses without their asking him, and they both nodded, smiled. If a table of people who'd finished their own meal had gotten up to leave and had been deterred from doing so, discreetly spoken to at the door by the muscular young man in the pink polo shirt and gray slacks and soft leather slip-ons, politely advised maybe to have an after-dinner drink or a dessert, even enjoy some dessert champagne, compliments of Señor Villarreal, as the reports later would say—and such details were included in the extensive coverage the next day in the big Laredo Sunday newspaper—the couple didn't notice that. And if some of the other people eating gradually understood, or suspected, that what was going on was that nobody, in fact, was being allowed to leave the restaurant before the group of men at the table had finished what probably were just drinks and appetizers—the men were in the restaurant for no more than a relaxed twenty minutes—the couple didn't notice that either. All of which is to say, there was never any commotion whatsoever. And the reports would also explain that some observers passing on the street had seen several armored black Toyota Land Cruisers, a convoy of sorts, parked outside the wrought-iron gates to Arandas on its side street, and while nobody in the restaurant who was later interviewed had seen any arms being carried, there surely must have been armed men, a contingent of them, in those gleaming black Land Cruisers parked outside. Still, for the locals, customized armored vehicles were rather routine in Nuevo Laredo.

After the men had left the restaurant the check came, and the couple out of politeness tried to pay the waiter for the extra glasses of expensive wine, but the waiter said it was entirely out of the question: all drinks had already been paid for by Señor Villarreal.

In the balmy late afternoon, the couple walked around Nuevo Laredo for a while before they crossed the bridge to return to Laredo. They strolled through the two squares of Nuevo Laredo, first the older one with its fine baroque church and big, leafily green trees with trunks whitewashed lower down and handsome statues, bronze gone to black, of honored heroes of the Republic. And then they strolled through the larger square, which served as a terminal where sooty local buses pulled up around its periphery, a tall, ornate clock tower exactly in its center; with its precise Bavarian workings from the nineteenth century, the clock, they knew, had always been a landmark for the city.

They lingered over coffee at a sidewalk place. Music played from a vendor's cart selling tapes and CDs across the street, *norteño* and pleasantly scuffling *cumbia*. The smell of exhaust from those rattling buses hung rich and nearly tangible in the air, yet it was somehow appreciated, too, because it became almost a fragrance that had always seemed to define Mexico.

By the time they did head back toward the bridge—the older silver-painted one, a long trestle with a pedestrian walkway and without the traffic of the sleek new multilaned international span for the highway—the lights were already coming on in the places along Nuevo Laredo's main street leading up to it, a soft, buttery illumination in the string of tacky gift and souvenir shops with their clutter of rugs, pottery, T-shirts, and countless swivel racks of faded postcards. And, of course, there were also the many open-fronted *farmacias,* each identified by a glowing first-aid cross and completely clinically white within; in the *farmacias* stood the pharmacists themselves, men and women, dressed in white lab coats and always silently waiting for business behind the long, very white counters, like just so many mannequins staring out, perpetually, at those strolling by.

The couple entered the empty U.S. customs and immigration terminal, and a uniformed agent asked them the usual question or two, then politely waved them through. They returned to the hotel, an especially well-appointed older one, with Spanish architecture and located right on the river and not far from the customs concourse on that side of the bridge in the currently deserted downtown of Laredo; they would start on the drive of several hours back to Austin the next morning.

Yes, as odd as it may sound, it would only be when they were in the lobby the next morning, waiting to check out, their bags packed and sitting around in the oversize yellow-upholstered easy chairs and paging through the Laredo Sunday paper taken from one of the polished mahogany coffee tables in that spacious lobby, that they learned what had transpired; they indeed learned in detail and realized how—as the paper emphasized in a prominent front-page editorial right beside the detailed news article and with no shortage of dramatic rhetoric—it was a wonder that the situation in the restaurant hadn't turned into "yet another bloodbath in the current, never-ending tragedy of senseless violence plaguing our sister city." Paco Villarreal certainly had announced to his enemies that he was out of prison and back in Nuevo Laredo. If nothing else, he had provided the full public confirmation of his presence needed, and such presence had already become newsworthy; word would travel fast—and then some.

They even heard two other couples—very loud and garish and, well, very Texan—talking about it in the lobby, also the violence in general in Nuevo Laredo. One of the overweight men told the other some story about how he had been in Nuevo Laredo just the year before and shopping for silver jewelry with his wife on the very day when the new police chief was gunned down outside the central police station only three hours after being sworn in. The other man, not to be outdone, told his own story about how one time, returning from a beach vacation in Mazatlán, he and his wife had been driving straight through in an attempt to get back to Houston by the next day, and they actually witnessed a fiery, full-fledged shoot-out—in the middle of the night at the newer international bridge for the Nuevo Laredo-Laredo crossing—involving one group of *narcotraficantes* in a large semi truck defending it from assault by another group, with the U.S. agents stationed there soon caught up in the heavy automatic gunfire themselves.

But, to repeat yet again, the couple, he and she, wouldn't know *any* of exactly what had happened in the restaurant until they read about it in the paper in the hotel lobby the next morning, well after they had been over to Nuevo Laredo for the late lunch. Actually, they had simply gone up to their room once they returned to the hotel that evening and remained there, not needing any dinner.

o o o

AND THEY HAD MADE LOVE THAT NIGHT after the walk across the bridge, there in their room in the hotel—lovemaking with its own kind of sadness to it, really, because they hadn't made love for so long—and afterward they lay in bed side by side. All blue shadows, the room was large, and they had turned off the air conditioner and opened up the row of big French doors to the balcony overlooking the river and the sparkling blanket of lights beyond, which was Nuevo Laredo, and then the silhouetted low hills of Mexico proper; there was a slice of an ivory moon. It was then, as they lay in bed in the darkness, that she told him something that she said she'd been thinking about; she spoke slowly and softly, almost more to herself than him, it seemed. It concerned something that had happened after their son, Owen, had gone through the long summer of intense radiation and chemotherapy and then transferred to the private school in the fall, St. Andrew's Episcopal Academy in Austin, doing so because, unlike the public junior high, St. Andrew's would let him make up what he had missed the year before without having to lose a grade standing. She told him how Owen came home one afternoon and Owen was smiling, gently so, telling her about how a kid from his eighth-grade class had come up to him after school let out for the day, introducing himself to Owen, and the kid told him that his, Owen's, hair was wonderful—the kid said that he personally envied somebody with a head of hair like his, which was, in fact, Owen's wig.

"We were in the kitchen at home," she said, "he was having an after-school snack at the table and even laughing quietly a bit about it, how the boy said he was sure that he himself was destined for early baldness, his father was bald, all his uncles. The boy said to Owen that he, the boy, would be lucky if he ever had a girlfriend, that he'd always wished he had a full, thick head of hair like Owen's. Owen said he couldn't believe that the kid couldn't see that it was a wig."

Lying there on the bed, he didn't say anything and he just listened to her speaking—somewhat vacantly, very softly—in the darkness. In truth, after she told the story, neither of them said anything for a while.

He finally got up from the bed, and in the dappled shadows, he walked across the room's cool terra-cotta tile floor and to the bathroom, to take a glass tumbler from the vanity and let the water run, let it get very cold, before filling the glass. Back in the bedroom, sitting on the edge of the bed, naked, he asked her if she would like a drink, and, naked, she nodded. She hoisted herself to her elbows, her hair still mussed from the lovemaking, her dark eyes wide open, and he held the glass as she sipped and swallowed some, then she nodded to indicate she'd had enough.

He then removed the tumbler from her lips, sipped some of the water himself, and placed the tumbler on the night table, next to the telephone there, its lit dial faintly green in the dark.

It was warm with the windows open like that, but comfortable. He looked at her. He reached out to lift a ribbon of her hair that had fallen across her damp forehead and slowly put it back in place, saying nothing.

"We walked an awful lot today," she finally said, smiling tentatively, "though, didn't we?"

"Yes," he assured her.

THE ABSENT PAINTER

HE WAS GONE.

Or, he hadn't been around the bar lately, and usually he was always around the bar at night, we knew. It went on for a week, then two weeks. At first it wasn't strange. Which is to say, the totally off-the-sheetrock stuff hadn't happened yet (the voice we heard, almost right out of the watery shimmer of our moonlit dreaming itself), and it was simply a matter of his not being at the bar. No, he hadn't been seen there for a while.

○ ○ ○

THIS WASN'T LIKE HIM, and what the hell, his studio was in the old warehouse building just across the street in what supposedly is our East Coast city.

And he had even worked out some deal with the bar owner to get his drinks in exchange for a painting or two. The owner, a rather crass blockhead who knew nothing about art, had gone to one of his gallery openings (was it the one with the beautiful young women, art students, in sort of courtiers' dress, topless in embroidered corsets and wearing costume-ball masks, oh, that was something, the gallery's idea to have them serve the usual stale canapés and the usual cheap white wine, not the painter's idea?); maybe the bar owner was impressed by that or just the look of him, the painter. The painter had worked shitty temp and labor jobs to support himself for years, but now that he was a painter, now that the critics were writing about him, he wore the same outfit every day: pegged black jeans, a blue-and-white striped sailor's shirt, a ratty black suit jacket over that, and a faded red baseball cap. But the outfit wasn't worn out of any affectation to look like a painter, and in truth he was a skinny, soft-spoken, and gently nervous man, hollow-eyed. Though it should be stressed that it was the *exact* same outfit every day, the painter never changing the package. And it *was* as if you had flipped open a big *American Heritage Unabridged* smelling of its pulpy pages to see an illustration and below that the noun *painter,* or gone into some undulatingly lit fine arts Web site where it said if you wanted to continue, click the button of an icon figure in the lower right-hand corner wearing, yes, black jeans, a blue-and-white striped sailor's shirt, a ratty black suit jacket, and a baseball cap, faded grubbily red.

o o o

A PAINTER, ALL RIGHT, and now where *was* he?

o o o

EVERYBODY WHO SAT WITH US at our usual corner table at night wondered. Of course, that wasn't all we talked about, but there would come a time in every session when everybody did wonder about it, as if it were a group exercise, something we had to do.

The blue-blooded guy with inherited money who dressed like one of the Kennedys relaxing; he wondered. The lawyer who didn't practice law anymore and just took an easy accounting job or whatever here and there to pay off his bills and keep his ex-wife and kid quiet while he chased twenty-five-year-old girls; he wondered. The writer with his mussed gray hair and boxer's broken nose, with all his railing about the greatness of Fitzgerald, the greatness of Faulkner, how those were the kind of literary citizens he was in competition with, even if the couple of novels he'd published were pretty flat and he was saddled to an underpaid college job teaching creative writing; he wondered. The too-understanding, too-kind, too-handsome guy whose father had been a Methodist preacher in some sane place like Missouri or Oklahoma, and who fantasized about leaving his job at the library one day to open a rare books store (there was something about the blue-blooded guy becoming his partner on this, bankrolling him, but, naturally, it never happened); he wondered, more sympathetic than the others about it, saying:

"He must be busy, you know, and he does have a show coming up in San Francisco, even one in Amsterdam or something, doesn't he? I mean, everybody gets busy sometimes"—he smiled, showing two dimples, an early-middle-aged bachelor who had the way of a concerned preacher himself, despite the fact that he, like all the rest of us, drank too much—"I mean, he's probably over there working right now. You know how he gets when he works."

But nobody was buying into logic like that, and it wasn't something with the neat deductive geometry that is any logic.

The new, especially cute and especially hip young waitress came over to our table one night.

She was studying theater. Lithe, she had bobbed red hair, genuinely green eyes, and a splash of freckles across her snub nose that only reminded you how goddamn sexy freckles can be on any female past the age of fourteen. She set down her tray on the empty table next to ours, there in the bar's corner; she removed the empty glasses, then leaned over to slowly wipe the black formica of our table with overlapping arcs of her damp cloth, before lifting from the tray the full glasses for our next round. She was wearing low-slung jeans that had almost forgotten about trying to keep in touch with her glowing, sculpted hip bones and a neon-green tube top that was perfect for her small breasts and hip in itself because tube tops today were sort of retro, with the miles of flesh—in between the jeans and the top—peachy and punctuated by a smiley-face tattoo the size of a quarter hovering over the fully visible, shadowy split of her behind. She continued in the slow arcing passes of the rag, and the tattoo was almost the ultimate in that aforementioned hipness—to have a little stemmed rose there or even the standard splash of weird new-age calligraphy would have been predictable, but how much more original, more *hip*, to have a smiley face looking at the world from its perch above that split of her (no scarlet thong panties, imagined or otherwise), a face that could have been saying in her own sexily slow rasp, "Have a Nice Day, OK?"

After she set down the drinks, she simply looked around to all of us seated there and said through her naturally pouty full lips, "Where's Bud? I haven't seen him lately."

That was his name, Bud, a stupid name for a painter, admittedly.

Everybody at the table said nobody had any goddamn idea where he was, told her that we were just talking about it. And as soon as she left, the boyish minister's son, having taken his first sip, abandoned his own earlier argument defending the absence, interrogating himself out loud:

"Yeah, where the hell *is* Bud?"

o   o   o

BEFORE LONG IT WAS A MONTH, and the sucker still wasn't there. The owner of the bar came in one night and in his block-headed way said to us that now that he thought of it, he hadn't seen him around either.

Again, it wasn't all we talked about, and, again, it would be a while before the stranger stuff started happening, but it came up at least once in the course of every night.

To be frank, for a couple of weeks the big news seemed to be that the guy who worked in the library and the blue-blooded guy were about to go in together on that rare books and first editions shop at long last. They had found a perfect storefront in the Warehouse District, and they were negotiating on the rent; it would be the kind of shop sorely needed, a place dedicated to worthwhile rare books, primarily good first editions of modern and contemporary literary works, not just the junk that becomes valuable for collectors because it's popular.

"There's popular and there's popular," the writer told them.

We all listened.

"Take Cormac McCarthy," he said. "Everybody is reading him now, or everybody literary, anyway, but that's good popular. A book like *Blood Meridian* with its half-hallucinatory quest for, yeah, blood in the orange desert down there in Mexico echoing the whole mad need of any civilization for empire, plus the pure muscle of the language, that's good popular. Though now that I think of it, that was never one of his really popular books, and probably the only popular one was *All the Pretty Horses*, which isn't as solid as *Blood Meridian*, nowhere near close to *Suttree*, McCarthy's overlooked masterpiece."

"No, I know what you mean." The ex-lawyer, African American, said that, and he gave it an African-American angle: "Take two sisters, for instance. Toni Morrison, she's good popular, Alice Walker, sort of bad popular."

"There you go," the writer said.

Every night it seemed they were getting closer to the deal on the bookshop. The handsome minister's son consulted the human resources department at his current librarian's job to see how he might get at some of his pension money early. Then, to really boost the viability of the project, the blue-blooded guy talked long-distance to his adult sister in Connecticut about selling off the summer house on Nantucket they had inherited from their parents years ago and which they had only been using for rentals, anyway; he explained to us that the family ski house in Aspen had already been disposed of. They started thinking of names for the store, but in the end it never happened, of course—the store, that is—and all it really took was the speech from a guy who sat down with us at the table one night. He was as big as Marlon Brando was before he died and he knew the book business, and in his mumbling, almost creepy Marlon Brando fashion (his hands were enormous, yet you could picture them gently handling a first edition of Hemingway's *For Whom the Bell Tolls,* let's say, dust jacket in mint condition, as if cradling a cooing dove), he told the pair of them:

"You might make it work, but it's a long shot today. The Net changed everything. You heard of Huey Long saying something like 'Every man his own king,' well it's gotten to the point, I'll be honest with you, it's gotten to the sad point that because of the Net you now might say, 'Every man his own rare books dealer.' You don't need a store today, you don't need anything physical, except for the books. A buyer can now view editions for sale all over the world on the Net, doesn't have to go anywhere. The business has all changed, and it changed fast."

Not that the two of them ever would, as we knew, actually get that store, but the prospect of it, which could have kept them excited for months, was cut short by the appearance of the hefty guy—cut *very* short.

Then there was what happened to the ex-lawyer with his sports gambling. He knew college sports, fancied himself an expert, and he started betting a little more than usual with the Italian guy who always drank alone standing at the bar and was a reliable bookie, guaranteeing much better payoffs than anything online. What the former lawyer ("defrocked lawyer"?—nobody really knew) did was bet on games that nobody else bet on, games where you could make some big money if you knew what you were doing, he claimed, because the line was always better, often wide open.

"I did well on a South Carolina game last week, the old Fighting Gamecocks, and got some good action going this week on San Diego State, those Fighting Aztecs."

"Gamecocks? Aztecs? You got to be kidding."

Any of us could have said that.

"Don't worry, I'm not kidding," he knowingly answered, "I'm more like *counting*—the loot, that is."

He himself was a good-looking guy in early middle age, usually wearing another tasteful dark shirt that you might describe as "dressy casual," with a sheen to it and the tails hanging out; he had melodic low voice that exuded only sexual confidence when around what he inevitably called "the ladies."

After another solid payday on the gambling, he always seemed to be noticing more than ever the many attractive young women in the bar. He would already be planning how he might try to lure this one or that out to a good French restaurant with the extra cash he now wielded. He'd see a tall girl with a true cascade of honey hair, pushing it back in raking shoves in imitation of the way models and legitimate movie stars do, and he'd say to us with a sigh, slow and low and, decidedly, assured, "My, that looks tasty." Or, he'd see a petite brunette with the kind of a figure that petite girls can have, what made them favorites for centerfolds in the old days because of their exaggerated proportions and because you couldn't really tell how short they were when displayed in a magazine on the usual shimmering satin sheets, yes, he'd see a very petite girl with a group of other young women at another table, and he'd say to us, "My, that looks *ultra*tasty."

But by and large he seldom got very far with much of that, more in the realm of braggadocio and daydreaming than anything else, considering his age. And he really had very little gambling success lately, his windfalls gone. Apparently, the Italian guy was playing him along, began reeling him in once he had him securely hooked, letting him make riskier and riskier wagers as his luck turned worse and worse. In time it was a situation with the Italian guy cutting him off completely on new bets and working out a schedule of payment (the Italian guy arranged it with fixed dates and fixed amounts as if he were setting up an installment plan for buying a used car), while the ex-lawyer had to log more OT hours on his current routine accounting job, no chance of spotting financial daylight soon, with the depth of the debt he'd thoroughly spelunkered himself into, certainly no extra cash to spend on women.

o o o

SUCH EPISODES CAME AND WENT, kept us very occupied in talk there at the table, until one night the writer (he had been canned by his old literary agent but had found a new, less-established one who he thought might be OK), he said outright what we ourselves seemed to have temporarily forgotten:

"It's been an awful long time, hasn't it, like *forever*, since we've seen Bud."

o o o

BUT MAYBE THE STORY on the painter and his background hasn't been suitably established here. Maybe you don't get the idea. We knew that he hadn't taken the normal route to becoming a painter, and lately a very successful one at that (even if the success seemed to spook him, as did so much else); he'd followed a different course, completely.

He'd bounced around after dropping out of a small state college, for a while played bass in a local rock band. When he did go back to another college after his first marriage flopped, he applied himself with the kind of conviction that only a reformed dropout could. He graduated Phi Beta Kappa (honestly, he was proud of that), then took a master's in art history. He never enrolled in a single studio art course, and therein lay the rationale for his success, possibly: he studied the confirmed greats in that major of art history while others in studio art routinely worked in college classes under the tutelage of the local ne'er-do-well faculty "artiste." For years he painted at night and worked every sort of shitty day job imaginable. He once sold red fire extinguishers on commission door-to-door in the burnt-out ghetto. Worse, he once worked as an assistant secretary to a real secretary in a law firm, a plight right out of the tale of the guy endlessly copying more pages in squiggly black ink, "Bartleby, the Scrivener," or that was our writer's allusion concerning it. With his second wife generating a steady income—she was a selfless woman who worked as a practical nurse, somebody who dreamed of a future life of volunteering her medical services on Indian reservations, even though there were no Indian reservations anywhere near here—he finally took a chance and started painting full-time. As those tons of graduates with studio art degrees cosied up to sleazy gallery owners (why do gallery owners always have such luridly orange man-made tans, both male and female?) and loudly bragged of their own talents, what they would someday produce, how famous they would be, he, Bud, just *painted*. He had no shows at first. He did the kind of things only hicks would do, like entering any contest he got word of, making slides of his work and sending them in—there was one contest in some unheard-of city in Spain he found out about on the Net, another in poky Peoria itself, no kidding, their municipal art museum there—and he kept winning, then winning some more.

One critic noticed him, then it seemed many critics did. The strange thing was that nobody knew exactly how to describe his work, which was so steeped in the full panorama of art history that none of the critics were truly able to say with any measure of precision what he was doing, but only get close to the *idea* of it, talk about it in more roundabout ways.

A girl named Celeste who was an artists' groupie kept a lot of the clippings and showed them to us one night. The clippings offered as good a proof as any of the vagaries of the so-called critics (who are critics, anyway? does anybody want to grow up to become a critic, like wanting to be an astronaut or a bona fide athlete? does anybody *aspire* to be a critic, and the word itself, if you say it often enough, soon sounding harsh and like something rock-hard you bit into and that broke one of your back molars?), anyway, the commentary in the clips about him was so hemming and hawing, always with much prefacing, that it was tough to know what in the wide world each *critic* was really blabbing about even when praising. The clippings became just so many indecipherable messages.

Like:

> "According to Plotinus, the eye is a microcosmic sun. This concept inspired John the Evangelist to identify Logos with light. Hence, the medieval artist depicted the divine world in the form of a ray of light traveling toward the recipient of the Logos—the Virgin of the Annunciation or Saul, blinded by a luminous ray,

falling off his horse. Today, in the painting of Bud Hardesty we see . . ." etc.

Or:

"As does any painting of any period, post–World War II art has necessarily concerned itself with the depiction of luminosity, but not to the degree that it can be said to be a unifying concern, and to a much lesser degree than many other movements and styles. Nevertheless, with the painting of Bud Hardesty there is . . ." etc.

Or:

"To enter the cathedral at Chartres on a sunny day is an unforgettable experience. At first one encounters only darkness, which is confusing, as the large windows indicate a wish to let in as much light as possible; definitely, the interior light is very different from that of the square outside, until we adjust to it, start to fathom its secrets. Which leads us to the painting of Bud Hardesty, in which one encounters . . ." etc.

Or:

"We have been witnessing of late attempts to effect a dematerialization of art. Advanced art is advanced by virtue of its concern with process, concepts, systems, and energy. To speak of a new art in terms of art objects that maintain a foothold in materiality and that achieve their effects by way of some measurable objects has become increasingly difficult. The most obvious and most visible kind of energy we are familiar with is, of course, light. Who as a child has not used a prism to break up light into rainbows, or a magnifying glass to start a fire, or a pocket mirror as a 'ray gun' to wage war against interplanetary interlopers? What Bud Hardesty's painting is saying is that to be a . . ." etc.

Or:

"The era of the nineteenth century in painting was supremely a . . ." etc.

But why go on?

The girl Celeste—the artists' groupie in her bib-front overalls and brand-new, too-big yellow work boots looking like clown shoes, her hair in an old-fashioned bun, Celeste smilingly chomping fragrant pink bubble gum with a soothing rhythmic click—she admitted that she herself wasn't sure "what the heck" all that "brainy stuff" the critics wrote meant. Sitting with us at our table, she fingered through the stack of clips she kept filed in an emerald-green folder of the sort a kid might tug out of a book bag on a first day of junior high civics class. She said that an understanding of the critics didn't really matter to her:

"Look at these articles, look at how *many* of them there are! He's broken out of the *pack!*"

She gathered them up as if a dealer raking in cards, carefully placed them in set order back in the emerald-green folder. (They sounded like something out of a book on painting—or probably they *were* out of an actual book on painting, virtually verbatim, and critics were known to pilfer and then doctor most anything in a pinch.) She stood, left our table. The ex-lawyer watched the upside-down valentine of her plump behind jello-jiggling in the bib-fronts as she walked away from us and back toward the bar, noting in his smooth, deep voice, "My, that looks *intriguingly* tasty."

But the painter never fooled around with any groupies, he wasn't that kind of guy. He seemed happy with his wife, the practical nurse who dreamed of helping Native Americans. She let him lead his own life, go to the bar every night and stay there with us till closing time. And it shouldn't be concluded that he was rolling in money either, and what did come in from the shows all over—plenty here in this country, and one in Hamburg already and another in Mexico City—was used to whittle down his own enormous debt that he had racked up in those years of abandoning the shitty jobs altogether and trying to make a go of it *just* painting. That he was provided free booze, and even food if he wanted it, compliments of the owner of the bar (the gallery opening with the topless young women in Venetian costume-ball masks was indeed the gallery's own scheme to attract publicity for the event, something the painter really didn't like—but if nothing else, it did impress that blockheaded bar owner enormously, as mentioned, did make him decide that maybe he himself should be thinking more about art and the "action" surrounding it), true, the painter even now needing occasional help when it came to food and drink illustrated that he wasn't quite economically liberated, though he was getting there. Not that he cared—he only wanted to paint.

With his studio just across the street, most of us had been given a tour of it at one time or another, knew what it was like: a little windowless room with black walls; whatever painting he was working on at the moment set up on an easel with track lighting above illuminating it; finished paintings stacked upright on the floor along the walls; a tiny refrigerator; a CD boom box for classical music while he worked; the bookcase that contained his art history texts from his time in graduate school as well as a lot of those somehow stupidly oversize coffee-table volumes that most people do just let sit on coffee tables, the expensive, glossy-paged things always printed in Japan or Italy and never the good old U.S., the painter *pored* over them; and, above all, the tangible smell of turpentine and linseed oil, because the painter knew what he liked and didn't like, and he liked oil and he hated acrylic. However, none of us ever went there to the studio uninvited, on our own. That was his territory, that was his own world. But he had *another* world, too, coming over to the bar at night and just shooting the breeze with us, talking about politics or sports or women or whatever. In any case, the studio's proximity made it all the more strange that such very strange stuff did happen when we started, one by one, going over there, each trying to rouse him at last.

We knew he was there. One of the pot-dizzy busboys from the bar's kitchen said that during his "smoking breaks" outside he regularly saw the painter heading into the old warehouse with its brick the color of kidney beans, on his way to his studio upstairs, but the busboy, who worked both the day and night shifts, said he personally never spotted the painter coming anywhere near the bar anymore.

o o o

NOT THAT IT DIDN'T GET DANGEROUS, or close to that with some "other hours" episodes for us.

We saw each other only at night, and, of course, there were all those so-called other hours for all of us. (The waking up groggy in the morning, telling yourself while sipping black coffee made in a painfully yellow galley kitchen of a one-bedroom bachelor's apartment that the booze didn't do the REM sleep much good, that's for goddamn sure; or the working of a job that never did add up to much, except a clock on the wall grazing away on the hours, as you found yourself whispering half aloud to the dead oxygen there in that office one midafternoon, the gray sky streaked with black clouds like an enormous feather outside, "How, oh, fucking how, did it all ever turn out like this?") It wasn't as if we ever spoke that much of our time outside the bar, and at night the hours together imbibing were for guys our age to just relax and talk "in general" over a few drinks, often laugh about something ridiculous in the newspaper or as seen on the television set high up above the long mahogany bar proper, turned on without the sound. The "other hours" weren't to be confused with the time at the bar at night.

But the ex-lawyer went through one extremely rocky afternoon in those "other hours" when his thirteen-year-old son from his failed marriage visited him one Saturday, and he was so set back by it that he had to tell us.

"You know, I'll be honest, I miss the hell out of the kid. I love him so much that it tears up my heart sometimes like a piece of steak you toss to the lions in the zoo and, you know, have the big gold lions just tear it up. Anyway, he's not into sports, and I can accept that, and not every kid is into sports, so my kid doesn't have to be. He's into music, not playing it, but listening to it. And there's this thing now where all these kids want to get this old stereo equipment like people used to have, or like we used to have, I guess, vintage stuff. Not so they can do any disco or rap routines, squawking vinyl records on turntables like a DJ, but just so they can have what seems to them the real thing, at last. I say it's better than him being hooked on mindless Nintendo or something like that at his age, right? So I told him I would buy him a set of speakers when he came for his regular Saturday visit, and we were in this shop that sells a ton of that old stuff, and I was kind of getting into it myself. They were authentic KLH speakers. Remember KLH? Speakers not that big but with prime sound, in that very cool teak casing that everybody wanted back when we were listening to Motown or the Stones, you know, and I was haggling with the guy on price. My kid, who's skinny and looks like his mom, was standing over by the speakers, kind of patting them. I don't know how it happened, or I don't know why I said what I eventually did say, except that it's possibly because I do feel guilty as all hell deep down that I don't spend enough time with him, my only kid, except on the occasional weekend like that, you know, and I'm not raising him as a man. Anyway, when the haggling on the price was done—some old hippie with a gray ponytail running the place, a reasonable, laid-back sort you could do business with—I went over and saw that my son was still patting the smallish speakers, saying, 'They're so cute.' I suppose it would have been different if we were alone, but I didn't like this ex-hippie with a gray ponytail hearing him say that, another man, and I told my kid, my son, 'Don't say *cute*, you sound like a girl.' It crushed him, and he simply walked out of the place and then sat in the car crying, and even when I loaded the speakers into the trunk, got back in the car myself, he told me he didn't care about the speakers. He said he didn't ever want to see them again. They're in my corridor storage closet now. I acted like a certified A-number-one jerk is what I did."

Then the blue-blooded guy, lean and patrician in his usual chinos and rumpled seersucker or tweed sport coat, an open-necked button-down shirt and casual leather boat shoes, Kennedyish, or, better, looking as if he were right out of gothic-spired Yale or even more heavily gothic-spired Princeton circa the Age of KLH Stereo Equipment and being fixed up on dates with lovely, soft-voiced girls from good women's colleges like Bennington or Sarah Lawrence or Vassar, he was pulled over after leaving the bar for the night; because it was his second DWI, this one could get tricky when his court appearance came. Another "other hours" happening. He told us about it:

"I had been on the phone with my sister that day, or for an hour of what passes for my day." He was very intelligent, extremely well read, could have had a fine career in any number of fields, but with substantial inherited money, he didn't have to work; we all knew that, hungover, he never got up before one in the afternoon, living alone. "It was beyond a mess," he said. "The whole thing started with something about how she held it against me that I hadn't gone along with her original plan to scatter our mother's ashes in Newport. I don't know what made her think of that, but that's what started it on the phone. You see, the ashes were scattered when we were both out at Aspen, trying to clean out the family ski house to sell it, which we did, and my sister had brought the ashes to Colorado to scatter them there, seeing that the two of us would then be together for once, which we weren't very often otherwise. I guess she had earlier mentioned something about possibly scattering them in Newport, on its Bailey's Beach. She'd maybe mentioned it as just an aside, but I didn't remember that ever being an issue. Ashes don't mean much to me, what's done is done when you number is up, if you get my drift. So I thought that in Aspen we had done what my sister wanted, an attempt at a family ceremony with the two of us on hand, tramping around and tossing the falling ashes on a green hill with some wildflowers behind Aspen, where it's hilly before the real mountains, and that was that. Or so I thought. Then she calls me up now from Connecticut, there in Cos Cob, five years later, and blames me for everything. She said I always knew our mother wanted her ashes scattered in Newport, where our mother's own family had had a summer place when she was a girl, and just because I was too busy with my boozing—that's what she said, too busy with my *boozing*—I didn't want to take the time to fly up to Newport and scatter them there in a proper ceremony, she said I only wanted to get rid of the ashes as conveniently as possible when we were out there selling the place in Colorado. She went on and on, saying things like, 'Did you even notice where we scattered them? It was so horrible, there was a bunch of condo complexes, and you were even too lazy to drive farther out, up to the mountains. My mother's ashes are sitting over some tacky condo complex's septic tank is where they are. Thanks.' It threw me for a loop, ruined the day. And I was drinking most of that day before I came over here, if you want to know the truth, and it was almost inevitable that I got nailed by the cop on the short hop back home to my apartment later, after leaving the bunch of you. They always get you late at night, when there is no traffic. The old standard cop's lie of seeing me crossing the road's yellow center line, the tried-and-true reason for probable cause and stopping you. I never fucking crossed any yellow line, and everybody knows cops are patent liars, it's a given. That's the way fucking cops work." And we nodded, definitely knowing how cops did work, cops also not hesitant, we agreed, to routinely rig a breathalyzer test and the like.

Those were "other hours" in our lives, all right.

o o o

MAYBE THE ULTIMATE ABSURDITY would come from one of us when very drunk. It was tough to remember who said it, the cigarette smoke clouding like yellow marble right before closing time, the place emptying out. We began talking about the painter again, that it was starting to be an unbelievably long, long time since he had last shown up, even if he was possibly trying to churn out a supply of new stuff for the show in San Francisco, or wherever his latest upcoming show, in fact, was. It seems whoever spoke it (again, it was tough to remember exactly who) must have had a particularly hard time on something himself that day, and he said directly what he had to now say:

"Maybe there is no painter, did you ever think of that? Maybe he never did drink with us, maybe it's just our *idea* of the painter, or our need for there to be a painter, Bud Hardesty."

o o o

HONESTLY, THAT'S HOW FAR-FETCHED IT GOT. And granting that most of us perhaps sometimes secretly suspected that such might be the case, that there was no painter, to actually hear it said aloud was pretty crazy. The painter *had* been drinking with us for years, we all *knew* him. The blockheaded owner of the bar knew him, the girl who was the artists' groupie knew him, everybody knew him. We all took turns answering that most far-fetched of far-fetched propositions.

"Not a chance," the guy whose father had been a Methodist minister said.

The writer became even more emphatic concerning it:

"No painter, eh? Well, there's a Bud Hardesty, I tell you. And I've got a good mind one of these nights to just walk over there on my own, go to the studio. I don't care about this unwritten rule that nobody ever bothers him when he's working, and this is all starting to turn preposterous. Something could have happened to him."

To that it was pointed out again that the kitchen busboy, Frankie, had more than once seen him going into and also coming out of the studio building, but it didn't convince the writer. (The writer himself had just been canned by his new agent in close to record time for being canned by an agent. The agent took the writer's supposedly recently completed novel manuscript to only three publishers and quickly gave up on it after the three rejections. Apparently, many editors at publishing houses, interested only in making a fast greenback nowadays, just logged into an online service they subscribed to, run by some slick business outfit—maybe like Nielsen, which does the TV-audience-rating thing—and checked your past sales before they even read a manuscript: they could smell remainder fodder five city blocks away, and the writer's agent flatly told the writer as much. The writer raved to us about how no *real* literature was being published in this country anymore, and we listened, let him rave, yet we suspected that the "new" manuscript he spoke of was probably quite poor, something older he'd salvaged from a drawer and tried to recycle.) The writer now said that everybody knew the busboy was stoned most of the time, everybody knew about Frankie's dope habit, one worse than that of any other kid in the kitchen—what he supposedly saw didn't amount to anything.

"And even if Frankie has seen him and Bud is fine," the writer said, "we deserve some answers for ourselves. How would he feel if one of us didn't show up for a couple of months?"

It was also pointed out to the writer that there were a number of guys who used to sit with us and now didn't show up anymore—they came, and in time they stopped coming—but he didn't go for that argument either.

"Will you listen to yourselves"—he held his ground— "we're talking about a friend, we're talking about goddamn Bud Hardesty. Oh, I'm going over there, oh, I'm going to get to the bottom of this before much longer, investigate and see what's really going on."

Others seemed energized by his conviction.

"I'm with you on that," the blue-blooded guy said, "there's a Bud Hardesty, no question about it."

"A-men to that, brother," the African-American ex-lawyer said, "but of course you're not really a brother." He laughed at his own joke.

Even the gum-chomping girl who just wanted to meet and be around successful artists, she realized it, and the lithe waitress, the would-be actress with the smiley face riding up and down atop her butt as she moved around the dark bar, she was sure of it. There *was* a Bud Hardesty.

And so, some of us did eventually wander over there to the studio, each on our own, to see what the hell was up.

o o o

IT WAS GOOD TO BE OUT IN THE NIGHT AIR, away from the smoke in the bar, away from the low noise and the clattering laughter from strangers at another table, the way there always seemed to be annoying clattering laughter from too-loud strangers at another table.

The side street was empty, except for the lumpy shadows of parked cars glistening with dew, and up above you the stars looked exaggeratedly large, as you asked yourself when you last had really looked at and fully appreciated the stars in the sky. *Ah,* the smell of autumn, the lingering aroma of burning leaves, though in reality our congested city was too distant from places where they actually raked and then burned heaped piles of bright fallen leaves. Or, *ah,* the smell of spring, the sheer perfume of the blossoms of so many flowering trees and bushes—forsythia and dogwoods and, strongest, the twisted-trunk lilacs in utter purple detonation, species also only found, admittedly, far away from the city. (But no contradiction there on seasons, and to be out of the bar at last, alone and looking for the painter, was to be in a realm where things were defined at last in the purity of the hope-filled abstractions you knew when you yourself had been twelve or twenty, when you could deeply inhale the out-of-doors air to the very tips of your socks, to say, aptly enough, "*Ah,* what a beautiful night!" In other words, it was all as good as *both* spring and fall.) Across the street rose the warehouse with its brick the color of kidney beans, a warren of cramped "studios" within the building for who knows what. (Somebody had gotten busted there the year before when it turned out that one studio was being used as storage for hot laptops, and another was reportedly a front for something shabbier, a "film school" that everybody knew was a cover for activities quite kinky—come on, who had a *film school* in a box little more than the size of a walk-in closet? And it also would be busted soon enough.) To get into the building was merely a matter of jiggling the doorknob of the bulky metal door enameled recently a glossy royal blue; the buzzer-and-lock apparatus apparently hadn't worked for years. The painter's studio, as we all knew, was at the top of three flights of stairs leading up from the makeshift lobby of sorts, with a sagging sofa and a perpetually empty security desk there under dull, flickering fluorescent lights. As said, at one time or another each of us had been there, and now it was as if each of us made his way up the creaky stairs slowly, alone and excited, but apprehensive, too.

Apprehensive and then some, because (one flight of the stairs taken) what if the painter was, in fact, madly working, and (another flight taken) what if he was totally caught up in the rhapsody of transposing the strange dreams he certainly had onto the strange canvases he inevitably produced, the aroma of linseed oil and turpentine strong, and (seven steps taken on the third flight and then a creaky nine) what if to get to the hallway of his floor and the cheap old indoor-outdoor carpeting there, a filthy, frayed aqua-and-blue tweed, was to hear his CD stereo boom box playing low something like spooky Brahms or spookier Chopin while he worked, that aroma of his painting decidedly gamy now, for you to dare to knock, even pound on the door, and be met with something like this, his shouting voice, which we swore we had heard:

"Don't bother me!"

Or:

"Go away!"

Or:

"Piss off or I'll call the cops!"

On the other hand, what if there came some other message, such as this and the kind of thing that he also might shout:

"Do something now, at long last, with what could turn out to be your wonderful life, you're not all that old!"

Or:

"Find the love in your heart, the glowing light, the luminescence of the ages that you know is there! The light, the light! Follow it while there's still some time! Know the healing, feel the very balm in repeating over and over that most soothing of all ultimately soothing words—*change!*"

Or most succinctly, but most powerfully:

"*Save yourself!*"

o o o

BUT, IN TRUTH, MAYBE NONE OF US ever did knock and there was no voice. In the end, we agreed that if the painter was working, we had no right to bother him. That was only fair—the bar was one territory, but his studio in the warehouse, that was another territory, surely, *his* territory.

○ ○ ○

MEANWHILE, WE KEPT DRINKING, kept joking, kept shooting the breeze (perhaps it was true, there never was a painter), and it was good to have our group of guys together every night at our table in the bar (but of course there was a painter).

○ ○ ○

OR TO PUT IT YET ANOTHER WAY, the painter himself didn't know what he was missing, we assured each other. It was his loss, and we heartily agreed that we had expended altogether too much concern and effort thinking about him.

It even got so that we almost wished him ill. Every now and then we each possibly hoped that the critics, insightful minds that they could be, would really chew the painter up on his next show, and who did he think he was to start snubbing us this way? To repeat, it was so good to have our group of guys at the bar, and, forget about Bud Hardesty, because what was currently more important was the new young waitress. She was even *more* beautiful than the lithe one with the smiley-face tattoo, a whitely blond number with a sexy Nordic overbite and amazing cheekbones who also was a theater student, but the kind of theater student shockingly beautiful enough that you knew was going to make it; she was that rare. True, it was really good to have this bar and our bunch of guys there at night.

But, needless to add, any of us, all of us, would have welcomed him wholeheartedly if he had suddenly appeared, the painter in his ratty black suit jacket and the faded red baseball cap and the black jeans and the goofy striped sailor's shirt (we affectionately reminisced about how he'd once claimed he owned a dozen such shirts when we teased him about wearing the same one every day, the gentle painter shyly and smilingly embarrassed, the way he could be), good old Bud Hardesty, in the bar again at last and at last back from the dead, as they say.

o o o

OR, DON'T THEY SAY THAT? Back from the dead? Or *something* like that?

SOUTHERN MAJESTIC ZONE

Fascism is not defined by its number of victims,
but by the way it kills them.

—Sartre

1. Estela believes. There is no denying that.

2. She goes to the embassy every day.

She believes that we will eventually get the visas, and I suppose it breaks what is left of my heart to see the doggedness, the intense fervor, of her belief. Beautiful, willowy Estela, just twenty-five, in her rumpled blouse and miniskirt; her long hair is glossy ebony, her eyes a veritable amber. She stood for hours this afternoon in a queue outside that foreign embassy here in the capital in this our faraway hemisphere. She finally gave up when they locked the iron lattice gates to that frillingly baroque building at seven. Estela in the honeyed light of a sun setting on the once stately boulevards lined with leafy, puzzle-barked plane trees, walking through the building traffic of taxis and so many buses with ridiculous whitewall tires, the clouds of grainy exhaust, walking past more slogans about government money (who stole it, who needs it, how it should be divided, the argument never-ending) spray-painted everywhere on the crumbling and, again, *once* stately buildings (more of that trademark baroque); she worked her way back to our cubbyhole apartment, arriving absolutely exhausted.

She was sweating. The couple of top buttons of her beige blouse were undone, showing the fleshy sheen of her small breasts. She simply sat on one of the straight-backed chairs, pushed the limp strands of hair back from her damp forehead, and felt around in her shoulder bag for the application papers, which she placed back on the table. Her voice was soft, whispery.

"The line was better today," she said.

I pretended I was interested in the big blue-bound book I was reading (a nineteenth-century treatise on metaphysics, where a dreamt chessboard is used to explain the liquidity of time, and where the parable of the race between Achilles and the tortoise given a head start shows you that even if Achilles is moving faster, the mossy green tortoise is nevertheless always moving, so the space between them gets infinitesimally smaller, but the key word here is *infinitesimally,* meaning that no matter how fast Achilles' thumping sandals carry him, he will never, in a day or several smoky eternities, catch up—space itself, like time, is questionable), yes, I sat at the table and pretended I was engulfed in the book. I tried not to look at weary Estela sitting there.

I tried not to admit to the foolishness of her unflappable belief. But I suppose that wasn't really the issue, and the issue that obsessed me then and that had been obsessing me for the last few weeks—as Estela returned *still* believing every day— was whether, if only in the name of supporting the two of us for two or three months more, I would have to perform the hack work and write that guidebook for the Museum of the Federal Police. It was the job that Colonel Hekht had, well, "proposed" to me.

And Estela kept coming back at twilight—just as weary, just as believing.

3. Indeed, this is the Southern Majestic Zone. And this is the capital of said Zone according to the rumored revised global configuration in what is called the Federation of Three. (Are you already laughing?) At least we are a capital in the global triumvirate, our politicians tell us; they boast we can finally hold our own with Bombay of the Eastern Mysterious Zone or the ascendant, booming Chicago that edged out Paris for the seat of what used to be a United States as lumped together with an even more vaguely remembered Consolidation of Grand Europe. (Are you *really* laughing?)

4. One afternoon in the bookstore, I got to talking with De Posada.

De Posada's store is on the especially broad avenue that stretches for kilometers between the Presidential Palace and the Senate.

De Posada deals mostly in rare books and old first editions. Or, as the authorities who don't even bother to try to shut him down say, "The man sells junk." I guess when the jackbooted Federal Police come in for an inspection, they see only the clutter of stacked copies, also the certifiably ancient calf-bound volumes with covers flaking to one step short of mummies' wrappings; they see the moth-eaten red-and-blue Oriental rugs worn to the straw core, the framed photograph on the dirty yellow wall of the country's one internationally known modern author (the idea of him doesn't particularly threaten the police—there remain rumors of the writer, now deceased, not having been entirely "manly"). When they visit, the police observe De Posada himself, from an old family and, therefore, somewhat part of the hated Oligarchy of the past, De Posada sitting at his tiny desk in the corner—a middle-aged man with mussed thinning hair and reading glasses halfway down his nose, a tattered tweed jacket—and for the Federal Police the very look of De Posada more than anything must convince them they definitely have nothing to worry about there. (Why, to them De Posada is probably even less manly than that quiet-mannered world-renowned writer, wearing a good Savile Row suit in the photograph perpetually staring down from the wall.) Even the stink of the mildewed pages, much like the dead something of the wide, muddy river that made our metropolis the important port it is (supposedly), signifies that everything in the place is dead, out of date, which, naturally, is the *whole idea* of a rare books store—still, a foolish pastime to run such an enterprise, the way the Federal Police see it.

All of which is to say, granting that troublemakers have been known to congregate in De Posada's shop, the Federal Police apparently don't care.

I like De Posada. I like how he loves books. I like how he puts aside volumes that he knows will interest me, how he never presses me to straighten out all the bills I owe him. And in the early evening, the dark cut by the buttery low lamplight in there, I told him about what I had been reading, and thinking about, in that last book he had supplied me. I was telling him of the conundrum of Achilles and the tortoise, how it had been haunting me, and then he was asking me about Estela.

"She's fine," I told him.

"She is a lovely young woman," he said in his even-toned, scholarly voice. "I have seen her going back and forth on the Avenue here lately. I see her almost every day."

"She goes to the embassy of that country we will emigrate to, she's working on getting us visas."

De Posada nodded.

"Then you will be leaving after all?" he asked.

"I suppose."

Nobody else in the place, he didn't say anything to that. I looked out to the Avenue. The shop had a single large window in front, a slab of glass framed in an old green casing of swirly cast iron, rather art nouveau, and plastered with announcements of poetry readings and new small-press editions. I could hear the bass drums and the chattering firecrackers of another demonstration coming from one of the side streets, or possibly a couple of demonstrations, banners with slogans unfurled. How it worked was that they gathered additional marchers in the side streets, then proceeded to the Avenue, probably with no more sense of direction than a jumpily malfunctioning compass needle, not knowing whether to pivot and head to the Senate, to shout their demands, or turn the opposite way and head to the Presidential Palace, to do the same, always just somehow ending up going one way or the other. Yes, I was looking out the window, the leaves of the plane trees beyond the glass flickering in the streetlights' glare, then De Posada was speaking to me again, asking me about the commission to work on the book about the Museum of the Federal Police.

"Surely nobody would blame you," he said. "It would be a lucrative commission, and they seem to have decided on you as the one to give it to."

I told him there would be no need for that; I said:

"We should have our visas soon."

"Of course," De Posada said, looking down to some tome he was pricing, pencil in hand; I guess he didn't want to look directly at me. "Of course you will get them. Why not."

Then two days later, Estela said the embassy had closed for a week. They needed to make decisions on the mountain of applications they already had (she still hadn't been able to submit ours), so it might be a good chance for us to visit her grandmother, the kind woman who had raised her at the large ranch in the country.

5. We walked to the grand old railway station in the morning's spilling sunshine. We took a train to the port.

At the port, we boarded the big white river ferry that plowed through the silvery water, which for once—the bright light hitting it directly that way—didn't appear its usual rust-tinged hue; the ferry sailed upriver for several hours, and let us off at the dock for the village in the province where Estela had grown up. We took a rattling country bus to the village, all pastel stucco and crumbling red terra-cotta, bony dogs dozing in the shade of the siesta hour; there was a rock song popular in the city playing on a boom box, floating from the open window of one tiny house, which was reassuring in a way—it suggested that there was still at least one kid longing for what the capital supposedly promised, a kid young and hopeful and, ultimately, innocent enough to believe that there *was* a more exciting, and much better, life in the city (the original lie). Estela's grandmother had sent a leathery old ranch hand to pick us up in a sputtering sedan. The ranch proper was in serious disrepair, and the sole remaining Indian servant who took care of her grandmother seemed to be in about as serious disrepair as the old guy who had picked us up. Nevertheless, her grandmother insisted that the best family china—a pattern of pale blue on white, gilt-edged, bearing the family crest—be used for all meals while we were there, the heirloom silver tea service after dinner, too.

During the meals her powdered elderly grandmother rambled, sometimes talking about her ancestors who had been honored patriots in the Great Civil Wars a couple of centuries ago, sometimes talking endlessly about her tiger-striped cat, Beppo, who had passed away the previous summer.

I liked the woman. And how very good it was to be out of the city, I assured myself on the second day there.

After her grandmother had retired that night, the servant finally done banging around in the kitchen, Estela and I relaxed in the spacious bedroom with its three balconies, a room that had been her own bedroom as a child. With the cicadas buzzing and the cattle in the fields lowing, also the wonderful "country aroma" of pure, pure chlorophyll as maybe cut with gamy manure pervasive, it was balmily warm, the long sheer curtains breathing in and out in the huge magenta night, the tall palms softly rattling like castanets; there was a perfect sickle of a yellow moon. We made love beneath the ceiling fan, indulgent, half-savage love, and sometime in the middle of the night we woke again, to make love like that again, our bodies glazed with sweat afterward, lying there, the ceiling fan continuing to chug around. I not only realized that it was good to be out of the capital, if just for a while, but I found myself on the verge of believing that we *would* get those visas. And I told Estela so.

"I know," she said, confident, never having doubted that herself.

I kissed her on the forehead, my Estela.

However, back in the city, the line even longer at that embassy once it opened its consular section again, I felt slightly ashamed for having told her—in what suddenly seemed like some other world (some other lifetime?) far up the silvery river in another province—that I believed it would all work out.

I had no right to do that to her, I knew.

6. What is history?

Or the history of an Invisible Republic such as ours (not even as discernible as some of the vaguely discernible entities on the map that you can be reasonably sure of, like Brazil or Argentina or Chile, even tiny Uruguay and matching, rhyming Paraguay, for that matter), our Invisible Republic that is presently the seat of administration for the Southern Majestic Zone?

I seem to see a land of untouched beauty, all emerald jungles and blue mountains and, of course, the sub-Antarctic of ghostly, wind-howling wastes far down south, then I seem to see hearty colonizers with polished armor and red-eyed horses confronting the indigenous peoples, carrying the flapping pennants of a religion as well as a hunger for gold and silver that gnawed like a rodent somewhere deep in their entrails. (So that would be an easy solution to it in the mind, that all was just greed, hunger for the materialistic, and that the world sends us only one message every day, with the largest law of things material—or corporeal, anyway—that you can pathetically bank on being "dust to dust," therefore why not acquire as much as you can for the moment; but that would be too easy a way to figure it out, and in the paintings of the martyred black-robed priests from that time, you discern something otherworldly in the eyes, a radiating, transcendent depth that has nothing to do with the materialistic whatsoever.) I seem to see next a silent slaughter of the indigenous by way of their slow dying from diseases that had hidden in the dank stone sewers of corrupt Europe for centuries, waiting for the pristine blood of strong, luminescently bronze bodies to feed on, and I seem to see an eventual independence from the colonizing homeland, then the nineteenth-century Civil Wars, with generals under feathered Bonaparte hats, atop fine steeds, marching their armies in phalanxes across the smoking plains, to confront other countrymen who simply did not have the right way of thinking about what a nation could and should be, which meant their way of thinking, what they were willing to risk having themselves slaughtered for, thousands under their command slaughtered for as well. (But the odd element about any of those Civil Wars, the two sides, is that there was nothing really to believe in; you could hold up a mirror to the large chauvinistic oil paintings from that era and see everything reflected in reverse, so the generals with the epaulets and brass-buttoned jackets and, indeed, that imposing headgear, such generals from one army were now on the other side, and possibly if you could hold the history books themselves up to a mirror and read like that the simple black marks that constitute the letters that constitute the words that constitute the language that is printed on a page, then you might read exactly the opposite story altogether.) Yes, in this history, I eventually seem to see a supposed Golden Age of prosperity and cultural enlightenment, as the fabled Twentieth Century began, our city itself assuming its distinctive demeanor, the wide boulevards and ornate imperial architecture, as more hard-working, blindly believing immigrants poured in from abroad, with our good railway lines the envy of the world, our enormous Centennial Opera House the envy of the world, the degree of our sheer civilization achieved through the wisdom of successive dignified, thoroughly democratically elected leaders, true, such an epitome of progress reportedly once reached here, more than the envy of the world, the goods and abundant agricultural produce from our legendary land exported everywhere . . . until that era, too, became but an illusion, and a currency that was at one moment enviable was at the next moment worthless, because the rest of the world was too far away from us, it had its own concerns and surely myriad matters closer to home and much more pressing in mind. And at that stage if others elsewhere seemed to be submitting to nationalists barking hate into oversize microphones, we were the ones who then stopped leading and followed suit on that front quickly and exaggeratedly enough, an ascendant lieutenant general emerging to rally the crowds of thousands in front of the lavender-stone Presidential Palace and shout his own entirely appealing hate through the loudspeakers, the cheering of the immense throngs deafening. (With repeated coups, however, and more generals betraying other generals, before long nobody remembered which leader had convinced us of which hate; the old black-and-white film clips from that time documenting the rallies could easily be the same if playing a sound track of the actual speeches or just dubbed with *congas* or *milongas* or hissingly happy *merengues*, absurd dance music—it was all equally meaningless—while the gruff men in the barrio bars bragged that one particular ultimate El Jefe was the *very* strongest, because besides fathering seven healthy sons, he kept a dazzlingly blond movie-star mistress whom, reliable word had it, he regularly and hungrily mounted from behind, and those same men in the bars, slapping down dominoes and drinking their dull beer, bragged . . . but everybody knows about that.) History . . . history . . .

I start to lose sense of any of it.

It could be that there is *no* history, when everything is said in done. History is something that is only possible if there is a present, so history can have nothing in the least to do with what the past was really like, because the present is what defines it and the ruling element of it, what they tell us is *now*—when we are the capital of the Southern Majestic Zone, when the talk of money and world banks and getting or not getting more international loans is played out in sloppy, enraged graffiti on the downtown buildings. And, now that I do consider this, the parable of Achilles and the tortoise (Zeno of Elea's musing, the thorn in Bergson's side) itself destroys the concept of the future, as any time future is constantly turning into a time present, as proven by the theory's reducing the alleged progression of time (the famous writer in his dignified Savile Row suit had something to say on this himself), true, by constantly slicing it into increments, then still smaller and smaller increments, to whisper in the end only the unwhisperable concept of infinity, so time never really does progress—the future, like the past, never does extricate itself from the present.

And once more there is, as said, just that power they tell us our nation wields in the world today, granting our currency is presently as insignificant as the puff of a dead jacaranda blossom, and also granting that within the last twenty months we have had five well-groomed businessman Presidents with smooth, resort-town tans and fashion-model wives (they come, then resigning in scandal, they go, interchangeable; they gracefully lie to us from the television everywhere), so who can blame the protestors in the streets for sometimes not knowing at all exactly which way to turn?

I suppose that history may be able to teach some lessons, and from the Roman Legionnaires to the Samurai Palace Guard to the heartily laughing NYPD members who brutally raped a man with a mop handle just because his skin was another color there in the windowless back room of a precinct station on a sweltering and forgotten afternoon somewhere in the seedier far reaches of a place maybe called Brooklyn, in the course of the entirety of that, history tells that the *sole* constant in the world is the Police—the Police are History, and the Police are Now, and the Police are the Future. Or, maybe the only constant for me at the moment is how I know could solve the bulk of this quite easily, by quickly cranking out that book on the Museum of the Federal Police, a task that I appear to have been officially chosen (anointed?) to do.

De Posada now tells me that lately, in the past several days, Colonel Hekht himself has been coming into his shop often. Colonel Hekht has been asking about me.

7. "It was before I knew you," Estela says to me.

"That's OK," I say to her, "I don't have to be in every dream you have. Just some of them."

We are talking, or we *were* talking.

We were in bed in the morning, at the cramped cubbyhole apartment in the city. I smiled. She smiled, beautifully so, the top lip flattening on just a hint of an overbite, in that Estela way.

"You know I dream of you a lot," she said. "And you do know, as I've told you, I dream of you writing there at the table and me coming out from the kitchen, with a cup of tea cradled in my hands, and quietly watching you write. The pen in your hand, the big yellow sheets you use for your stories, your poems."

"That's not a very complicated dream."

"It's the best dream. I can have that dream a million times."

"I hope you do," I told her.

"I *really* hope I do," she said. "But this was different. I guess I was there at the ranch, and I was looking for Beppo."

"Beppo was your grandmother's cat, right? I mean, your grandmother was talking about Beppo. Beppo died, right?"

"But in the dream I was younger. And Beppo wasn't dead, he was just lost. I suppose I was a girl again, a kid, but I had to find Beppo. It was as if the only thing important in the world *was* finding Beppo."

"It must have been your grandmother's going on about him, when we were there at the ranch, that made you think of that."

"No, dreams don't need anything like that. It was just that I *had* to find Beppo, it was just that and nothing else mattered."

"Sure."

She said she asked Rodríguez, the ranch hand who had picked us up in the rattling old sedan, and he told her to look under the big pink-flowering palo borracho tree out on the sunny Second West Pasture, but Beppo wasn't there. Next she asked different servants, because there had been many of them when she was a girl, not just the ancient woman, Yenny, who labored to take care of her feeble grandmother now, and they sent her to various spots throughout the main house—into wine cellars, dark, and into forgotten sleeping chambers, darker, in the rambling old place— and still she couldn't find Beppo, who in the narration was beginning to take on a distinct character of his own—not your generic tiger-striped feline, but a sort of daft customer, tubby and prone to rolling around on his back and madly boxing the air, even if there wasn't any fluttering yellow butterfly to attempt to snatch.

"I simply had to find Beppo, everything depended on it."

"And?" I asked her.

I tried to tell her that the dream must have gone somewhere, there must have been some conclusion, even meaning, to it, and, naked, she raised herself to her elbows, leaned over to now peck a kiss on the top of my head; she told me I was hopelessly shackled to being a writer.

"So caught up with essentiality of narrative," she said, "things like that. This was just my dream, nothing more than that. I was just looking for Beppo."

I looked at her, the true amber eyes, her lustrous hair tangled. I realized then that I loved Estela more than it was fair to love anybody. There was not only Estela's beauty, there was also her regal simplicity of thought, or maybe it was her genuinely knowing depth.

And with that she noticed how late it was, said that she should start moving and hurry over to wait in the motionless queue at that embassy once again. It was two days afterward that I admitted I couldn't dodge Colonel Hekht anymore. If I had talked my way out of his repeated phone calls and remained adamant with the uniformed thugs he sent over to the apartment during the day, I walked into De Posada's shop that afternoon to find the place completely ransacked, and I knew I had no choice but to contact Hekht myself.

"It's nothing," De Posada told me.

A bruise swelled like a rotten plum under his left eye.

"It was Hekht, wasn't it," I said, "he wants to put some pressure on me."

"It's really nothing."

De Posada strained to be brave.

As always, the framed sepia photograph of the nation's great modern writer—maybe its *only* great writer—stared down on us, definitely listened in on us.

I phoned Hekht at his private quarters in the barracks behind the Presidential Palace that evening. A half-hour later, Estela not back yet from her tireless standing in line for another day, I slid into the rear seat of the waiting unmarked black car and saw Hekht's face with its scars from burns he'd apparently suffered as a child. That face almost hovered in the darkness there, like a mask; he told the driver to get going.

We sped through the downtown's boulevards, then into the dim suburbs of low one-story houses and packs of ragged urchins in vacant lots kicking a soccer ball in the repeated half-ghostly and strangely silent pantomime of a game, the stench of open sewage heavy in such barrios; we kept going southward, along the river coast. We were heading to Real de los Nublados.

8. There was moonlight out at Real de los Nublados, or the ruins of it that existed as proof of the total folly of the entire original idea of such an enterprise.

Apparently, around the turn of the previous century, a daring, perhaps crazed financier, from Serbia, of all places, came to the country and first saw this spot of land where the river's muddiness becomes the aqua expanse of the sea; he decided to build a fine resort, world-class, as they might say today. He constructed a hotel and a fronton amphitheater and an especially massive bullring; he constructed a handsome and well-appointed horse-racing track, the spectator boxes luxurious. For the first bullfights three of the most famous names from the Spanish circuit were on hand to do battle, and King Edward himself was said to have once stayed in the posh hotel, but not long after that—two or three brief years—the financing collapsed, and the whole of it, everything, soon was abandoned.

Rising among the shaggy palms, the bullring with its colonnades and weed-infested Roman steps was illuminated by that milky moonlight casting long shadows, a scene right out of de Chirico or Magritte. With Hekht in his brown commandant's uniform, the officer's hat, we strolled the flats of worn, hard-packed cinnamon dirt, the two of us maybe stepping through the tangible Devastation of Time, while he continued to make

SOUTHERN MAJESTIC ZONE   149

his case, as interspersed with his seemingly knowing altogether too much about me, things he should *never* have known.

"You were comfortable," he said, "there at the ranch up the river, that estate of your lady friend's people."

"What are you talking about?"

I stopped, looked right at him.

He was a sturdy man, from the rural provinces himself; the facial scars were like rippled satin, his small dark eyes all but hidden under the hat's patent-leather visor.

"You were not comfortable there"—he posed it as a question now—"content and glad to be away from the city?"

There was no telling what the police knew, how they knew it.

"Yes, I suppose I was."

I had ridden out there with one intention, that of telling him outright that the way he had treated De Posada, a broken-down bookseller, was despicable and mindlessly bullying, but, of course, I didn't. We kept walking. The waves whispered from the beach with its scattered mangrove patches, and in the crumbling remains of the fronton courts, you noticed the cooking fires of vagabonds whose own ancestors most likely had first started setting up households there generations ago. A dog barked in four raspy shouts; the taillights of the long black car with the police chauffeur parked back on the road glowed intensely like twin red jewels. Hekht tightened his case. He said I was the writer who could do justice to the job, I could make what might be only a perfunctory guidebook in the hands of another writer into something much more than that, a meaningful and convincing and most necessary essay, so that the populace would know the true significance of the Museum of the Federal Police as it should be known; he had asked around the university, he said, consulted literary groups, too, gathering advice from many people concerning to whom the commission should go, and everybody told him—he was flattering me—that I, without question, was the writer who could execute this properly, the only one in my generation with some hint of promise. And he emphasized that the money involved was not to be overlooked, would actually make life very easy for me for quite a long time, not just a matter of months. I guess he also spoke in vague terms of the glory of our capital, the superiority of our way of life to that anywhere else on the planet, the wonders of the Southern Majestic Zone itself, all propagandistic clichés.

"I'm a poet," I muttered, "some short stories, too."

"A fine writer, as I'm assured by everybody," he said.

I didn't want to directly express my distaste, so I attempted claiming lack of expertise:

"I've never done anything like that."

"You're the only one," he said.

There was a hard and stubborn authority about Hekht, and in his stark uniform and showing the facial scars as almost a badge of defiance solidly separating him from the hollow promises of the jet-setting politicians with their sleekly elegant wives fresh from runway modeling, also the clamor in red and black graffiti about world finances shouting from downtown buildings everywhere as the street demonstrations thumped on, I sensed that Hekht would not be deterred. We kept walking. He said he had already arranged to have the museum closed to the public (who seldom ventured there lately, I suspect) and open to only me for the entirety of the next afternoon. I could stroll around and acquire a better feel for the place, decide if I hadn't changed my mind, he suggested.

Then something I didn't expect happened.

9. We had reached the garbage-strewn white sands of the beach, and swimming out into the waves were a dozen or so horses. Pudgy, swaybacked horses, unkempt and also rather small, it appeared, some chestnut and some piebald, at least one a velvet ebony. They were rearing, with their front hooves madly paddling into the spewing surf, and their whinnying echoed, loud and excited in the swimming; there were yellow puddles of moonlight the size of islands there on the water's glassy black farther out. Hekht explained that the horses were a herd that had propagated by itself, in the wild, descended from the ponies of the original Real de los Nublados racetrack. He said they fed off scrub grass along the beach, often bathed themselves and swam out to sea like this, always at night.

He next spoke of how the twentieth-century Scottish poet Edwin Muir once wrote that there was a time when horses were revered in Muir's native Orkney Islands, worshipped by the Druids because of what they literally were according to the apt verbal construction—*night-mares*—with the capacity to run away with our own phantasmagoric worst fears, our darkest imaginings every night while sleeping.

I stared at Hekht.

"How did you know that?" I asked—or, more so, *demanded* of him.

"But you know that," he said, "it's something you've come across in your extensive reading, isn't it? Something you once thought about when you read it, even if you didn't jot down a note on it, during all your time there in your little garret, with your books, with your carefully sharpened pencils and the big yellows pads of paper, no?"

"But how did *you* know about that, I only *thought* it!"

I was shouting.

10. Did Hekht take me all the way out there just to tell me that?

11. As I said before, *never* underestimate the Police.

12. The horses kept madly swimming out into the moonlit sea.

13. And then the rain was falling the next afternoon, the hosing, end-of-the-summer thunderstorms of late March, on and off, in this part of the world. But you really couldn't hear the storms once inside the stilled museum, which oddly took up two floors of the squat high-rise in the Financial District, just up from the Presidential Palace. The narrow streets of the Financial District were clogged with lines of people trying to change money; such lines were the only ones longer, surely, than those at the foreign embassies, where visas were near impossible to secure.

To find the Museum of the Federal Police you have to know where it is. There is no marking on the building, inconspicuous among the many international banks. And on this afternoon a svelte, heavily made-up woman at the reception desk in the building's lobby, with its good broadloom and potted palms, simply nodded to the row of brass-doored elevators, told me, as she might tell any tourist, to proceed to the Seventh Floor. But she obviously knew who I was, as did another woman—far from svelte, yet equally made-up and with close to an overdosing of lipstick, middle-aged and wearing a muted floral print, baggy, to cover her girth—who met me at the elevator, informing me straightaway that Colonel Hekht had said I would be making a visit. I remembered her from the other times I had come to the museum, and she usually instructed people to browse around the first few rooms on that floor while waiting for more visitors to show, enough to constitute a group, so that she—gushing and animated, the rich voice of an opera diva, suitably dramatic— would have a decent-size audience for her guided spiel. Not that she didn't have a couple of solid narrative tricks. In her introduction, I knew, she always reminded everybody beforehand that after this floor, Seven, the group would go up to the next, Eight, where she said "you might have heard" of the torn-apart coffin on display from when the Monto Terrorists broke into the cemetery vault some years ago to steal the hands of the corpse of the powerful dictator, and she said "you also might have heard" (what schoolchild in our nation, terrified in the night, *hadn't*?) of Room "Y" on that Eighth Floor, containing the notorious forensic displays. But with me she now played no narrative games, gave no tease to the plot of the story of my being there (how pure and admirably naïve my Estela was—with such haunting depth, too—in her knowing that essentiality of narrative was, in fact, but watery deception, a fool's game); the woman quickly disappeared into an office where, through the half-open door, I could see a roomful of uniformed men silently working away at computer terminals, heads kept low and probably not daring to look up.

I was now on my own in the place that had been left empty for me.

The rooms of the museum had white walls; the floor was painted a dark red, glossy and functional, what you might find in a military barracks; the outside world on the other side of the high-rise's windows was blocked out, the glass slabs blanketed by long, heavy, very gold drapes. Or to put it another way, there was a strength of basic color in that museum—white, red, gold. The displays in the rooms on the Seventh Floor were predictable, one offering a row of wax figures dressed in the complete progression of police uniforms in the nation over the years, beginning with sort of a plains cowboy look of maybe Basque peasant's gear from early on after the Independence, through the nineteenth-century gendarme style (cape and kepi), right up to even the functional dark-blue attire with trim white cap of a modern meter maid; there were framed photographs on the walls of commissariats throughout the city and various provinces, built or leveled or rebuilt over the years, and portraits of mustachioed police chiefs, also actual artifacts removed from torn-down installations, like an ancient dispatch board with its spaghetti of wires and a bulky old-fashioned teletype machine. I must admit I lingered in these rooms, stalling, and this introductory floor was easy enough, it even devoted some rooms to firefighters, seeing that the *bomberos* were under the police administration as well; the wax figures here wore heavy rubber slickers and complicated helmets with mirroring, spade-shaped brass shields on the crown announcing in detail brigade and station numbers. (I was already wishing I was anywhere but the Museum of the Federal Police. Or, more exactly, I was consciously trying to will myself elsewhere, maybe waiting out the thunderstorms in De Posada's cosy shop, thumbing through a volume's yellowing pages, or, better, making love with Estela in the country—the night cicadas buzzing, the ceiling fan chugging—at the ranch where I had been so relaxed, if only for a couple of days, though the fact that Colonel Hekht knew of my contentment there soon ruined any imagined projection of it now.) I started up the narrow stairs off in the corner, heading to the next floor, Eight.

The rooms continued with their lettering, nearly exhausting the alphabet in leading toward the ultimate Room "Y" (proof that there is no closure, after all, as "Z" would have had it?). Each room was devoted to a specific illegality, usually with more of the lurid, staring, incredibly realistic wax figures to illustrate the topic. It began rather innocuously with "Prohibited Games," where a rural type was shown leaning over a cockfighting ring, energetically goading on two feathery stuffed birds bearing spurs on the claws, frozen that way forever; there were displays of marked cards, antique slot machines. And always the essence of the white walls and the red floor and the long gold drapes, room after room. "Toxomania" (wax reproductions under glass of the human arm as jabbed with an assortment of medical syringes, also a suitcase with a false bottom spilling white powder); "Theft and Robbery" (a tall safe with two wax figures in suit vests and felt borsalinos drilling at it, plus photos taken at crime scenes showing successful endeavors in major bank-vault heists); "Fraud and Swindling" (confiscated counterfeit-bill presses and spread fans of salad-green U.S. dollars not the real thing, yet noticeably no counterfeit examples of our own currency, funny-book bright, probably because considering its record of wild fluctuation lately, it was by definition *not* the real thing); "Supernaturalism and Cruelty" (the two placed together, as if they were intrinsically linked, so you had a fiery-eyed wax figure in a cape confiscated off the back of the priest from a Black Mass cult, much Kabalistic heraldry, and under glass a matched set of small rusty knives to be planted in the flesh during the ritual ceremonies of some thoroughly bizarre sect, that kind of thing). So many rooms, until the ante was upped in Room "X," right before the infamous Room "Y."

Room "X" was devoted to "Civil Order." If there had been any touting of police public service in the earlier rooms, it pretty much got undermined here, not with what was, in fact, on display, but with the subtext to it that definitely existed as the frightening territory (I picture it a horribly iridescent morass, dank and shimmering) of the collective unconscious of the citizenry of our Invisible Republic, their knowing the truth they do about the Federal Police. You were greeted by a wax figure decked out in full riot gear—jumpsuit, plexiglass shield, helmet, jackboots, a fat-barreled rubber-bullet rifle in hand. The main attraction here concerned what the melodious heavy woman who had spoken to me at the elevator usually tossed out as a narrative tease for an upcoming tour, the defiled coffin already alluded to (sans corpse, surprisingly) of the infamous dictator (the one whose mistress had been the popular blond movie star). The box was set on a sturdy carpeted stand. You could see how the terrorists must have entered the burial vault and first smashed repeatedly at the coffin's lid made of what looked like greenish car safety glass, a good half-meter thick, in an attempt to break through its lamination (layers alternating the tempered glass with a gummily tough clear plastic, the resilient sheet of it not giving way); the coffin proper was heavy steel with a bronze finish, the elongated handles intricately tooled silver, and on one side the Montos subsequently had cut a gaping hole with a power implement, jaggedly ripping it open as if using some surreal can opener. They probably employed long knives to poke past the pleated cream-colored satin within and sever the Big Man's murderous hands. The hands wielded the utmost power, the Monto Terrorists knew, and when they themselves put on their ski masks and kidnapped political bigwigs, they often brought the hostages to a secret warehouse who knows where for detention and interrogation, slapped them around with the huge, hairy-backed hands, embalmed rock-hard. Soon the inevitable happened, and in the provinces any toothless old man in a straw campesino hat, let's say, who seemed to have exceptionally large hands was attacked, his own hands bloodily chopped off, too, until all sorts of terrorist cells for all sorts of causes claimed that they possessed the True Hands, while more toothless octogenarians stumbled around villages at siesta time holding up just elbow stumps healed over with bulging pink scars, dozens of amputees. (But that was then, and today they tell us we are an international success story, our city is the capital of the Southern Majestic Zone. We are mighty Chicago! We are mightier Bombay! We are civilization itself in this new world order, the Federation of Three!) In truth, that coffin never jarred me as much as the other displays here, not of the defused bombs found in public places, but the graphic enlarged photographs of the bodies of generals—and also proud admirals—blown to only the shreds of their spangled uniforms and wet, dripping innards more fit for a butcher counter, murdered in the series of urban car bombings during that period; such activity ended abruptly when the Montos made the major mistake of an attempt on the life of not simply another military notable but the Chief of the Federal Police himself, the subsequent revenge predictably brutal. I was already turning a little nauseous, and it is tough to explain what happened to me in Room "Y," where the holdings were supposedly forensic, though the placard above the door more directly announced what was to come—just one word, the all-inclusive showstopper: "Crimes."

Because with the rain showering heavily outside, and with me there amidst the sizable showcases of dismembered naked bodies molded in wax (real bodies?) from ax- and carpenter-saw murders, amidst the glass-encased display of fifteen wax vaginas, mounted like shriveled butterflies on black velvet, illustrating the shredding effects of violent rape on the soft tissues and membranes therein (were they wax vaginas? real vaginas?), amidst the . . . but, really, why go on—I at last knew without any doubt that to write the story of the Museum of the Federal Police would be to write of the ultimate Truth, perpetrate the ultimate literary triumph, too, because, History, Time, any of it, is no more than a set of severed hands, the knot of a wax vagina, complete with fuzzy mound of Venus and torn apart like a mutilated spring rose. This was a subject fitting for, and maybe beyond, Chaucer or Dante, also Milton or Cervantes or Goethe, even Shakespeare himself— Hekht knew this, every one of the Federal Police knew this, a writer could claim an unheard-of stature with such a staggering subject, and the rest of us were gullible schoolchildren, merely lost dreamers, to think otherwise, our nation's one unquestionably great modern author included.

I left Room "Y" and the museum, and, to be honest, I walked into the afternoon's thunder and lightning suddenly *wanting* to write that essay, a full-length book about the place. I suppose I would have eagerly, gratefully, marched to the Central Commissariat to see Colonel Hekht the very next day, thanked him for selecting me, if it hadn't been for returning to the apartment that evening and finding beautiful Estela, soaked by the rain in her miniskirt and blouse and sandals worn thin, her hair plastered with wet to her beautiful skull, Estela flushed, excited, laughing wildly:

"Look!"

She held up our passports in their textured light-blue covers. She held up the passport of her grandmother, for whom she had also obtained a visa. All miraculously.

After that, everything started to happen fast, De Posada generously lending me the money for the sky-high price of the tickets.

14. *We shall be delivered at last!*

15. The night flight would depart at midnight on the nose.

The futuristic expanse of the sprawling airport was thick with armed soldiers in camouflage fatigues, and I was jumpy. I was convinced Hekht had somehow gotten word of our leaving, that there was scant possibility that he wouldn't have had intelligence on it. But the visas were valid, I knew, they were solid and rare as three bars of gold bullion—and, as I nervously tried to joke to myself now, the pile of luggage that Estela's grandmother had me haul for her was maybe as heavy as at least *thirty,* never mind three, bars of gold bullion. I thought of everything that could go wrong. Seated in one of the orange scoop chairs in the main concourse with Estela and the old woman, I kept glancing up at the arrivals-and-departures board, its black cards constantly shuffling for changes and new announcements; I expected to blink and the next moment see that the flight was delayed, that even a whale-nosed, massive-winged 747, silver and softly hissing as the engines relaxed before takeoff, could be kept from going anywhere with the standard lie of "Maintenance Problem." But whenever I did look, there was no change: the little clear bulbs that formed the letters and digits on the panel's dull flat-black simply told of our airline's name along with the appropriate flight number, scheduled for exactly midnight; above all and most startlingly, the board continued to steadily announce "On Time." Estela held my hand, and together we looked over beside us and watched as her grandmother nodded off. By this point those battered suitcases and trunks of hers, some bound with rope by Rodríguez back at the family ranch (which was about to be foreclosed on, anyway), had already been checked in and taken away on the conveyor belt, to be loaded on board—I could only hope, trying my best to picture it in my ongoing nervousness—by the usual ghosts wearing plastic earmuffs who masqueraded as busy baggage handlers, everything now lifted from the motorized carts out there on the tarmac and heaped deep into the fat belly of the idling 747. Pleased to see that her grandmother was finally resting very peacefully, Estela smiled at me, held my sweating hand tighter on her lap.

As we sat there in the orange scoop chairs.

16. We made it through the security check of our personal items.

17. We approached the emigration section and the officers in their glass cubicles. The young crew-cut man flipped through all three passports sandwiched in that light-blue pebble grain—then as easy as that, like a confident kettle-drummer in a symphony orchestra coming in on cue, he stamped in a pounding flutter the open pages and then the corresponding official forms there in front of him.

He handed the three booklets back to me, wished us a good trip. We proceeded through the wheezing chrome turnstile, one by one. From the waiting area at Gate 24, I could finally see the jet beyond the tinted glass, evidence I needed. There were businessmen reading newspapers or fumbling with laptops, there were a few families with restless kids. In other words, already at Gate 24 there was some semblance of *normalcy*, the most treasured and absolutely precious of states of mind if you haven't possessed as much as a snatched echo of it for so long.

The three of us sat down in three more plastic scoop chairs, purple and not orange this time.

Which was when Estela, wearing a belted trench coat and heels for travel, she suddenly looked up and said, "Beppo!" She bounded out of her seat.

And with that everything inevitably unraveled, a gone universe disassembling and floating farther and farther apart through galaxies and forever nothingness, some kind of trumping cosmological drift, unruliness extant, powering it all.

Estela was shouting that we *couldn't* leave without Beppo the cat, and then she had her grandmother worked up about it as well. The sleepy old woman tapped some hidden jolt of electric energy deep in her being; she herself stood up and hurried around, peering under the scoop chairs for Beppo, asking people in that waiting area if they had seen Beppo. The call for boarding was announced, passengers were filing into the accordionized tunnel and onto the plane, showing boarding passes and passports (for any of them—despite their having looked quite relaxed in the waiting area—it must have been a most welcome relief just to be out of the Southern Majestic Zone at long last), and there I was with two women, both near hysterical about a cat.

I told Estela not to act crazy, and she only answered, "We have to find Beppo!" And when I said to her she was stuck in some deceiving nightmare, and "You're being duped by a fucking dream you had!"—it was the very dream she'd told me about earlier—that did no good either. I shouted to her grandmother that she herself *knew* Beppo was dead, she had talked at the ranch of missing him so, there was *no* finding of Beppo anywhere, Beppo had been gone for a year—actually, more than a year! But she could only repeat the exact words of her fragilely beautiful granddaughter, the old woman shrieking at me: *"We have to find Beppo!"*

And with that they were off, out of the waiting area, back through the emigration and security checkpoints, a roll of film in utter reverse development of what had transpired but moments earlier. Away from me forever.

When the attendant took my boarding pass, I pivoted to see Colonel Hekht with a few of his flunkies in the waiting area, the bunch of them standing there and grinning at me. I kept going, breathing hard, not even able to find much saving relief in the dead air of the cabin until after the flight attendants went through their miniature dream play with the orange life vests, until well after the bumpy taxiing was accomplished and the liftoff was at last complete, the wheels buzzingly cranked up and folded into the wings again with a dull final thump—and we were gone.

Where I am now, the engines droning.

18. The meal of a good, if small, steak with cheese scalloped potatoes and a crisp salad finished, the tray taken away, I sip red wine in a plastic glass now that the cabin is darkened, my fellow passengers having metamorphosed to only lumps under dark-blue blankets, tiny coffin-style white pillows wedged carefully under their heads—everybody hopes to pilfer some needed sleep on such a long flight. (Fifteen hours? Seventeen hours? Eternity? What's the difference?) Flying.

19. Occasionally, I look down and see the blackened, wave-chopped sea far below, very distant, though I *can* make out the wild horses surgingly swimming through it, pressing on and on.

Or sometimes I look out that scuffed plastic oval of the window, and in the aforementioned unraveling of the universe I see a pair of giant, severed Dictator's Hands as big as memory itself and holding up a blue-and-green globe, where if you look very closely, you surely can identify the Southern Majestic Zone, its glowing capital and also the glowing capitals of all those other Invisible Republics that will be my haunted, agonized, endlessly wandering lifetime from now on, too.

Yes, gone from my home, the Southern Majestic Zone.

A SHORT MANUAL
OF MIRRORS

The mirror is the problem of life that man must perpetually face.
—Rachilde (nom de plume—i.e., other persona—of
Marguerite Vallette-Eymery, 1860–1953)

1. Don't take one for granted, ever.

2. Be careful of mirrors in winter, which is when they seem to have the most to tell, especially in an empty house (a house in some Midwestern state perhaps) during the late afternoon of February sunshine spreading on a blanket of even snow outside; it can get tricky when they reflect each other, the one in the upstairs hallway in an oaken frame telling something to the one similarly framed at the other end of that hallway, across the stairwell and its honey-varnished steps carpeted with Axminster (worn carpet that is patterned, faded red, in spots showing the burlap backing), yes, telling something that has to do with the reflection of a blue jay alighting from the limb of a pine outside a twelve-paned window in the hallway—the blue jay perched there and then suddenly in full flight, a puff of dusty snow from the bobbing spruce limb lingering as the bird is gone in a squawking swoop, both mirrors

tossing the image back and forth, whispering about it there in the house, thoroughly empty.

3. Familiarize yourself with all the literary allusions you can concerning mirrors, just to be safe.

This includes any concerning Borges. And while Borges is often attributed with having said all there is to say on mirrors, Borges himself would always be the first to argue otherwise. Remember that Borges, who read *Don Quixote* when ten in English translation before he even approached it in Spanish, true, Borges in the span of his entire long life—from early manhood when he worked those long hours in the suburban library there in leafy Buenos Aires, wearily taking a yellow tram to the boring job every day, unknown then and his writing familiar only to those who followed the local Argentine literary magazines, to his very old age, when he was probably internationally celebrated more than any author had ever been celebrated, in person anyway, because with a new era of worldwide jet travel now established, there was Borges in a fine-cut British-tailored suit, blind, ever smiling, his companion/secretary, the gracious young María Kodama, leading him, Borges receiving honorary doctorates and orders of merit, Paris, Jerusalem, Mexico City, Cambridge (Mass.)—as said, Borges would always remind people that granting his lifelong fear/obsession when it came to mirrors and his own documentation of their ghostly doubling of us in so many of his stories, essays, and poems, he ultimately bowed to the essential truth about mirrors in literature: that everything that is to be said about them in literature had already been said in those few chapters about halfway through *Don Quixote* where noble Quixote himself, on horseback and with lance in hand, confronts the Knight of the Many Mirrors, whose armor itself is made of dangling reflectors, the Knight of the Many Mirrors also on horseback and with lance in hand.

4. And when it comes to literary allusions concerning mirrors, not only familiarize yourself with acknowledged masters like Borges and, indeed, Cervantes and their exploration of the subject, but don't overlook Delmore Schwartz. Or, at least don't overlook him physically, and it isn't because of any special working with mirrors in his poetry or allusions to them in the handful of superb short stories he wrote (of course, his signature story, "In Dreams Begin Responsibilities," is not a matter of mirrors, and the protagonist there is watching a movie of his doomed young parents' lives unfolding on a Coney Island boardwalk, so a mirror really has nothing to do with it despite what *anybody* will tell you); and when it comes to Delmore Schwartz, look specifically at the jacket photo taken when he was a young man, a black-and-white studio pose from the 1930s, so arresting, which certainly could contend for being the all-time best jacket photo, even the hands-down winner in that category (nearly the "ur-jacket photo," if you will, while allowing that the use of the rather pedantic *ur* isn't part of your normal working vocabulary).

It is a confident Delmore Schwartz, only in his twenties, already teaching at Harvard, already celebrated by the likes of T. S. Eliot, no less, and how handsome he is with such high cheekbones, the steady lips, the sweep of wavy dark blond hair, the gray eyes looking right at the reflected and hauntingly penetrating gray eyes looking back. In a way, the photograph suggests more about writing and who the author *really* is than anything by any master far greater than Schwartz and who might have had something major to say about exactly that (remember that Schwartz's output of work was comparatively small, he never did fully pay off on his promise; and with no eventual celebration of anything whatsoever later in life for Schwartz, he died at fifty-two in a dollar-a-day hotel room in Times Square, the Columbia Hotel to be exact; it happened one July night there in midtown Manhattan, the heat still wafting from the gummy asphalt streets, Schwartz—his wives and many girlfriends gone, his pres- tigious academic appoint- ments gone, his old close friends like Saul Bellow who once loudly champi- oned him gone, most of his sanity, in fact, gone, lonely Schwartz hallu- cinating that CIA agents were watching his every move, the man plagued with alcoholism and ongo- ing dementia by then in 1966—he suffered a mas- sive heart attack while tak- ing the garbage out to the

hotel's rickety iron fire escape, the broken, worry-ravaged body surrendering at last, though left unclaimed in the Bellevue Hos- pital morgue for three days, it has been noted): I mean, just *look* at that jacket photo, reprinted often over the years and recently turning up on the front cover of a collection of his journals.

5. But enough of that, and probably it is wiser to forget arming yourself with literary allusions relating to mirrors, because when everything is said and done, what is literature, anyway? What is it but something other than the real, which is to say, something other than what passes for our actual time on this planet, so brief and intangible, illusory, and everything, all of it, sometimes seems like just a, well . . . a . . . a . . .

But, to repeat, enough of that.

6. If you want to smash a mirror, do it at night, preferably on an empty beach, where as you slam the slab against a mica-sparkling rock set up for the purpose there, you will not hear the glassy crash of the shards, you will think it is just the sound of the waves, crested and rising black and veined with eerily white foam, as those waves roll and continually roll onto that beach.

7. And, if you want to smash a mirror, prove that it holds no dominion and convince yourself it's merely, well, silvery, back-blackened glass—just stuff, just material, etc.—be sure you go to that beach alone at night, in early spring or late autumn, when the sand itself has drifted in undulating boomerang patterns, when the moon is at least near full and achingly incandescent, so that the shards of reflected moonlight on the sand seem like only the shards of broken glass; that way, you will not even have to see, let alone hear, that you have, in fact, smashed a mirror, and you will just see those shards that are reflecting the moonlight as being only so much of the rest of the profusion of direct, unreflected moonlight scattered on the sand.

8. Personal anecdote can become useful as well.

9. Accordingly, if talk of mirrors comes up in company, when one is at a gathering with a drink in hand and there is the low clatter of conversation all around, people standing and talking, a gallery opening or during the intermission of a play, be ready to have something to tell the others standing there (*what if these people I don't know very well suspect who I really am? what if my lies are of no use whatsoever in the end and they know the truth, they realize everything about me, you ask yourself, and who am I kidding? it is a gathering with svelte women in cocktail sheaths smelling of perfume, men in fine slacks and blazers, men so sure of themselves, so able and triumphant in life, the way other men can be*), in such a gathering be able to recite like a memorized speech your own story of a mirror, or mirrors, to convince yourself you are in control, there's nothing to be scared of.

10. For example, let's say you are a man speaking:

"Mirrors? And now that you mention mirrors, here's something that's always stuck with me, what I will never forget. Young then, bounding around Europe with the mandatory backpack and youth hostel card, I was staying in a youth hostel in Madrid. Alas, what youth hostels in Spain were like back in those days, ancient Franco still in power and rigidly ruling in the assortment of almost comically spangled uniforms he wore, the *caudillo* and then some. Spain could seem uptight about everything then, including, and very emphatically, the sexual, being strictly Catholic. All the hostels were segregated as to sex, and staying there in the men's hostel, I don't know if any of us even knew where the women's hostel was, if there actually was one. All guys, and this was in the early seventies, and one very odd thing about this hostel in Madrid, or outside of Madrid by the new university complex and where the first low foothills of the jagged sierra begins, was that they didn't enforce the old rule saying you couldn't stay more than three consecutive days in any youth hostel. I suspect that was because they needed the business, wanted to keep the dorm pretty full until the summer again, when the place, a big old villa of a house, wasn't a hostel but a camp for Franco Youth or something—they brought in boys from all over the country for indoctrination, and there were formal portraits of grim, leering Franco everywhere in the place to remind you of that. Which meant that a lot of guys traveling got stuck there for weeks, settling in for a while, Americans and Canadians, guys who were tired of moving around, you know, tired of hitchhiking or taking lousy third-class trains, lugging a forty-pound backpack, even wondering what the hell they were doing in Europe to begin with and why they weren't back home getting on with their lives now that they had finished college. And it was raining all the time, the way I remember it *(speaking, you start to get nervous, you suspect that the people standing there and holding the drinks are already asking themselves where you are going with this, but you continue, you have no choice),* and before long nobody seemed to even want to go into the city. There was a big, cheap lunch they served at the hostel, it was the high point of the day, so everybody, the rain falling outside, just lay around on the dorm bunks in the room with the lights turned off, constructing the day around the event. We lay there dressed in the morning's dimness, reading, napping, waiting for that lunch they served, decent food and costing only a handful of pesetas or something, half a buck, and everybody, after lunch, just lay there on the dorm bunks some more, not saying much, napping, reading, just staring at the ceiling if you had the top bunk, just staring up at the mattress above you if you had the bottom one, thinking a lot—everybody was homesick, really, maybe missing pals, or missing more than ever a girlfriend, who now was probably dating another guy back in comfortable Chapel Hill or Ann Arbor or wherever, that sort of thing. Every afternoon this skinny guy wearing steel-rimmed glasses like two quarters shining would take out his guitar and sit on the edge of his bunk, he'd sing old Beatles songs and he'd sing them softly in his reedy voice, strumming the guitar, and all the songs, even the upbeat ones, were done real slow and real sad, songs like 'Michelle' and 'Yellow Submarine' and 'I'm Looking Through You.' In the dimness, the rain outside continuing to fall steadily and looking lavender, which rain sometimes can, dripping off the tile roof of the hostel as we all lay there, he'd tune up the strings in between numbers, then go right into another Beatles song, nobody saying anything, just getting sadder and sadder, surely, everybody there on the bunks more and more homesick. And I remember once when he did pause for a while, didn't start into a next song right away, he finally said, 'Anybody got a request?' but nobody said anything, we all quietly lay there with no lights on, dressed on the beds in the afternoon—a room not even properly heated, rather cold, dank—and he asked it again, 'A request?' And there was a big bearded guy, solid as a linebacker, a vet from the U.S. Army, actually, who once he was discharged from his base in Germany had apparently decided that he, too, would take the backpacking grand tour around Europe like other guys his age. His voice was deep, gravelly, and in the silence, the rain still dripping off the roof, gurgling along the gutters and into the downspouts, he simply and flatly said from his bunk, lying there wearing his army surplus jacket and with his hands behind his head, he said, 'Yeah I've got a request—will you just shut the fuck up before I kill myself.' It was perfect, that line of his *(but you notice there isn't any laughter at that, the anecdote is going all wrong, you were supposed to be talking about mirrors and you know that everybody else, their smiles frozen, they're all looking at you, staring, you'd better get moving if you hope to salvage this),* so, anyway, there were these two particular guys staying at the hostel, bona fide hippies, or stoners, even if we didn't use that word back then. They seemed to see Madrid as good a place as any to recuperate for a while after living in some commune way down south in Morocco, where they'd smoked themselves out of what was left of their mushy gourds, so much available kif in Morocco, guys who wore ratty djellabas they'd bought in Morocco and who didn't seem to care that all over Franco's Spain you'd see giant placards, red on white, announcing loudly that the possession of any illegal substance was punishable by sizable prison sentences. They just kept smoking, and unlike the rest of us they just kept going into the city every day, taking the Metro to the Prado specifically. And even more specifically, they headed straight to the one room where the museum displayed, on its own, *Las Meninas,* what could be Velásquez's greatest masterpiece *(no, this isn't going well at all, this relating of the anecdote, and then out of nervousness the man who is apparently telling the story, you, your stomach no more than a nest of slithering lime-green baby grass snakes, you try to make the point that you thought you were heading for, salvage the anecdote: you tell how the Velázquez painting shows the little princess, six years old or so, angelically blond, surrounded by her ladies in waiting, the* meninas, *as well as a female court dwarf in a frilled courtier's dress that's almost a parody of the attire of a lady in waiting, plus there's a sleepy brown German shepherd stretched out amid them; you tell how it is a large canvas easily ten feet high, in an ornate gold frame; you tell how when you were young and in Spain, it was considered so important by the museum that it was set prominently catty-corner in its own gallery and it was a gallery that had, for added effect, completely black walls; and in the painting there is so much else going on, with Velázquez himself depicted in the painting off to one side and at his large easel in this palace chamber with the assembled young court, the princess and her entourage, who are looking out at what he is painting in this painting; and a mirror on the far back wall of the enormous chamber—with its lofty ceiling and the whole place decorated with other canvases—reflects the faces of the king and queen themselves, the subjects posing for Velázquez and the painting he is working on; and right beside the mirror in back, very strangely, a man in courtier's garb of tights and jerkin and a complicated ruff collar is shown about to walk out and leave through a large carved mahogany door at the top of some steps, there always having been the argument on whether he is a royal deputy or possibly, again, Velázquez—as another self, now with shorter hair, a trimmed beard—and, therefore, it is the painter suggesting that while he is painting he can enter in and exit from his own painting, meaning his own imagination, anytime that he wants to, as you stoke up some courage now, try to work up to the punch line, or at least get to the point of the anecdote, keeping on with the story),* I had seen the painting, and in the opposite corner in that gallery in the Prado, across from the painting, also set catty-corner, was a full-length mirror. It was there supposedly to prove that the perspective of the painting was perfect, and that to view it reflected in the mirror was for the canvas itself—that life-size palace chamber depicted and those life-size people in it—to definitely appear alive, three-dimensional, even. But what these two stoners did was take it a step beyond that, and they actually found the equivalent of a five-and-ten, like a Woolworth's, in central Madrid, and they bought these cheap shaving mirrors, I guess that's what they were, and every day they went to the Prado, which was free back then. They went maybe to keep warm, or at least warmer than in the ill-heated hostel, but they also went to repeatedly carry out another mission more important. So, having first chemically primed themselves, some extensive quality time spent enjoying a few jumbo joints, they proceeded to the black-walled gallery, wearing their ridiculous djellabas—you know, the coarse, brown-and-white striped wool getups as long as droopy bathrobes and hooded, the kind they used to sell to all hippies for about five bucks all over Morocco, a mandatory purchase—and what they did in that gallery that was usually empty, seeing it was the tourist off-season, what they worked on every day, was positioning themselves for good reflection in the big mirror set catty-corner that way in the gallery, and then, that reflection achieved, they somehow put themselves, as reflected in that big mirror, into reflections in the shaving mirrors, turning the handheld things this way and that, to finally transport their own images right into the painting's scene of the palace chamber along with everybody else therein portrayed. I remember the guys once came back to the hostel at the end of the day and in their slow, hippie, soporifically relaxed style they told the rest of us how good a day indeed it had been, completely productive, saying to us things like, 'Man, I was right in there with the bunch of them, wild, I spent most of my time today talking to that little dwarf in her crazy party dress, a real trip she was.' To be honest, I guess I'll never forget those guys, they were something else."

(Still no laughter, the story turned out entirely wrong, you never should have told it, and you are more sure than ever now that the subject of mirrors is not one to raise in casual company, and what were you thinking, bringing up an anecdote about mirrors like that, trying to ward off the fact that mirrors do have the power they do, or your mocking such power?)

Actually, maybe avoid anecdotes about mirrors.

11. But once it has started, there's probably no stopping it.

Because there is a beautiful woman among those who have been listening, or, to put it another way, those others *pretending* to listen, as you went on—and on. And now you see, or imagine, that she is looking right at you while the group continues to stand there. She *has* been listening, and how captivatingly svelte she is in her black cocktail sheath, how lovely are her hazel eyes, fringed with incipient crow's-feet, her mane of mahogany hair, full yet admittedly not as lustrous as that of a college girl—she is no longer young, true, but a bit older now, she has entered into another, maybe more beautiful time in life, which makes that beauty especially riveting, very womanly and more alluring still. She starts talking. She doesn't seem bothered by the fact that the others were obviously bored by the anecdote you told, she doesn't seem to care about any of those others, the equally svelte (if not as strikingly beautiful) women around her, plus the successful-in-life, sure-of-themselves men, all with drinks in hand, and she just responds with an anecdote of her own, it seems, in order to try to render herself brave, to possibly ward off the power of mirrors, too, as she talks of mirrors.

Her voice is whispery, intense in its softness but whispery (breathy?), nevertheless.

"Mirrors," she says, as if the twin syllables, somehow hollow, have half hypnotized her, and all that is left is to let the other self that isn't her—but that is her—continue to speak: "Mirrors," she repeats it, with the same softness. And begins, stating the truth of the matter outright:

"My father, very handsome, very dignified, was a supremely rational man. He was a lawyer and then a judge, he was a presidential elector from our state three times, actually knew Kennedy on a first-name basis. There was little he couldn't do, and concerning his many talents it wasn't Kennedy that would come to mind, it was Jefferson himself, with the clichéd label of Renaissance man aptly applied at last, to describe my father, anyway. And when there was constitutional reform in our state right after World War Two, he close to single-handedly rewrote that document of governance almost as a philosophical tract, it later being hailed as a template for clear and logical thinking, lucid political insight, by those in other states when it came time for them to undertake constitutional reform as well. Also, my father had always promised my mother he would someday build her a summer house, my mother who as

a girl loved to swim in the ocean, and eventually he made good
on the promise. You have to understand that he didn't have
very much interest in a summer house himself. He never went
to the beach, his work was his sole genuine concern, and even
when the house did get built and we were all so happy there
during the sun-splashed ongoing dream that July and August
could inevitably be for our family, we knew that his idea of
weekend relaxing was simply to sit out on a lawn chair and
read maybe a biography of some significant world leader, with
his idea of casual clothes being his suit pants and mesh summer wingtips and a starched white dress shirt, the collar now
open and the sleeves carefully rolled up. Understandably
pleased that he had given his family the fine summer home, he
was nevertheless only waiting for Saturday to metamorphose
into Sunday, then Sunday to soon give way to Monday morning, when he could get back to the city, his law work and also
fighting the good fight of the Democratic State Committee.
But in true Jeffersonian spirit, he didn't employ an architect to
design the house out on the grassy point with a picture-perfect
view of a lighthouse on the peninsula across the bay—it was a
sizable plot of land, the several seaside lots he had bought up
quite reasonably, also right after the war—and he designed the
house entirely on his own. In the evening he worked on
sketches and made detailed plans on big sheets of crisp drafts-
man's paper spread out on the large dining room table in our
winter house in the city, marking exterior details and the layout of the rooms, then he constructed models of the successive
proposed designs. He worked his way through a half dozen,
made them out of shirt cards. He placed them one after another

on the folded-down music shelf of the grand piano in our living room, right next to the red John Thompson–method books we'd all learned to play from as children, leaving each model there for a week or so to get response from my mother and us kids, see what we thought. The final product was a fine balance of the new and the old—single-story and low-slung and wonderfully sprawling for the many rooms, but all of it with proper New England rooflines and good wood shingles that eventually weathered tastefully dark brown, and all of it with the two long porches and endless windows. You know, my brother and sisters and I used to laugh about that, his concern for windows, and he was forever talking 'fenestration' then, that was his big word, a delightful and suitably airy noun when you think of it, *fenestration,* definitely a favorite of his *(you are listening, you are looking right at her and she is looking right at you while she speaks, and who cares if the others do appear as bored by her slow-moving anecdote as they were by yours, perhaps the bunch of them hoping that the buzzing bell will sound for the next act, if it is during a play intermission, or that somebody will call those assembled in the gallery to move to the next room for some words by a preening, self-satisfied artist if it is an art opening, and suddenly you seem to sense that she, well, knows, and, more important, you know that she knows and that she knows that you know, and she continues, you could listen to her for a lifetime, or, better, a couple of lifetimes, even a spacious eternity as big as the ever-expanding, star-cluttered, resonatingly ebony unlimitedness that is the universe itself—get the idea?—as she keeps speaking),* but all that rationality abandoned my father when it came to mirrors. You see, it was well known in our family that my father could never sleep in a room from which he could see a mirror, he harbored an undeniable irrationality about that within him, lifelong. My mother didn't like to talk about it much, but she confided to me that it was true, always had been true, and in our house in the city the Chippendale furniture in their master bedroom had to be arranged a certain way, so that from where he slept there would be no glancing over at any point in the course of waking in the night and having himself reflected in the long mirror over the fine brass-handled dresser, a mirror somewhat tarnished with age, admittedly, the dresser and the mirror attached to it being a prized heirloom in my mother's family and the finish having gone iridescent in places, dull, like maybe silverware stored away in a drawer for years. The same went for hotels. My mother once told me, or again confided in me, that if my father had to travel to other cities and other states, for a meeting or to deliver a speech, he would always book into a good hotel in the city, and once escorted to the room he would always have the bellboys—in maybe green uniforms with gold epaulets, or maroon uniforms with gold epaulets, you know—he would have the bellboys work to tug and drag and tug some more all the furniture, until they had it positioned right, so during the night—horns sounding from the streets below in the strange city, people talking lowly outside the door as they moved down dimly lit halls in a hotel room in the course of a shadowy night in the strange city—so he could assure himself, now in the hotel room, that he was sleeping and also that there was no chance of him being reflected while he was sleeping (*you are enraptured, you have never met a woman like this before, the soft voice and those hazel eyes, flecked with darker brown like autumn leaves, the dab of lipstick on her front teeth that is exactly right in itself, perfect, a saving flaw, something you ask yourself if you might have encountered somewhere in a dream, and she continues speaking)*, which means that in the end it wasn't so much an issue of him seeing a mirror that spooked him, it was, of course, the mirror seeing him and doing so while he was *dreaming*, because what are dreams? In truth, are they only reflections of reflections, as the shuffled pack of cards that constitute the events of our daytime lives, it will be nothing more than a reshuffled pack of cards once the night and its darkness comes, once sleep with its many dreams also comes, no? And—now that I think of it, what I just said—do you ever wonder about something like those playing cards that we take for granted, how even in some entity simple and everyday like that, there is an ultimate conundrum, a telling futility, the usual playing cards showing a repeated red patterning of pudgy little angels, cherubic, on antique wide-tire bicycles happily riding along, the cards themselves absurd enough by definition to make you want to give up on everything if you dwell too much on them, admit that nothing adds up to anything, all is hopeless, which you've probably always realized and know deep down (*she suddenly looks quite scared herself, much more frightened than even you were when you were reciting your own anecdote about mirrors, an anecdote that seemed to be going nowhere, that seemed to cause those others to stare at you more, and she continues speaking*), and I suppose the more I think of it, and I do often think of it, I now know that for me (*she does try to force a laugh, a hesitant jangle in that whisperiness, she even tries to force a smile, but the*

left corner of her mouth isn't steady, it's twitching some, and there is that embarrassing speck of lurid ruby lipstick on her very white teeth, she is faltering, visibly straining), and I suppose that for me . . . I suppose . . . I . . ."
Her voice trails off.

12. Oh, how you long to tell this woman you have now encountered, by absolute chance, so *many* things.

13. Oh, how you want her to know what maybe nobody else knows, what you have never told anybody, including the two (or *three?*) wives along the way, the grown children off on their own somewhere on the West Coast (one of them now in Santa Cruz, or is it Santa *Barbara?*) who seldom as much as occasionally phone you lately.

You want to tell her how you were obsessed with Delmore Schwartz when you were in college, and while other English majors became predictably obsessed with Joyce or Faulkner or Virginia Woolf, for you, for some reason, it was always Delmore Schwartz. You must have read "In Dreams Begin Responsibilities" dozens of times, a moving, perfectly crafted short story, you kept thinking about a particular jacket photo of him, you studied it, dreamed of it (did the photo become more important than the writing?), as you hoped to someday be a writer yourself, fluent in allusions about other writers, triumphant with writing itself—yet none of that ever came close to working out, of course, it was inevitable you ended up in what is euphemistically, and somewhat very tragically, called the business *world*. And you long to tell her something else, tell her what you never have been able to tell anybody, how even this many years after your own mother died—it happened when you were a fragile fourteen, a happy enough kid before that with an old flap-hinged first baseman's glove you oiled with neat's-foot nightly, a kid who used on your brush cut back then a gunk they called Butch Wax that came in an orange push-up dispenser—you still have a recurrent dream of the mirrors trading reflectons with each other in the modest house where you grew up in the Midwest, where your mother showed only kindness to you, only unmitigated love; and in the dream it is winter, there is a blue jay on the limb of a tall pine outside the hallway window, from which it suddenly alights, a squawk, then a graceful, ascending swoop, and in the upstairs hallway of the house, empty, the mirrors seem to be saying to each other what couldn't be said outright in such emptiness of a long-forgotten winter day, and . . . and . . .

14. But what's the use, right? Because there is no lovely woman telling her anecdote, there is no exchange of anecdotes about mirrors at any gathering either, because . . .

15. . . . because. . . because . . . be . . .
    OK, let me try a different tack.

16. (also # 6.) If you want to smash a mirror, do it at night, preferably on an empty beach, where as you slam the slab against a mica-sparkling rock set up for the purpose there, you will not hear the glassy crash of the shards, you will think it is just the sound of the waves, crested and rising black and veined with eerily white foam, as those waves roll and continually onto that beach.

17. (also # 7.) And, if you want to smash a mirror, prove that it holds no dominion, convince yourself it's merely, well, silvery, back-blackened glass—just stuff, just material, etc.—be sure you go to that beach alone and at night, in early spring or late autumn, when the sand itself has drifted in undulating boomerang patterns, when the moon is at least near full and achingly incandescent, so that the shards of reflected moonlight on the sand seem like only the shards of broken glass; that way, you will not even have to see, let alone hear, that you have, in fact, smashed a mirror, and you will just see those shards that are reflecting the moonlight as being only so much of the rest of the profusion of direct, unreflected moonlight scattered on the sand.

18. In other words, be careful of mirrors. Very careful.

19. Don't *ever* take one for granted.

FOUND FRAGMENT FROM THE REPORT ON THE CADAVER DOGS OF NORTHERN MAINE, 1962

. . . needed for Trevor Oxnard's large dogs, inbred Labs they were, vicious dogs, glossy black fur, the truly haunting amber eyes that I still remember to this day, those eyes, and this would have been somewhere around 1962, though it is difficult to place an exact date on everything when it comes to the circumstances surrounding Trevor Oxnard's utter obsession with seeking out and doing what he did concerning the literary magazines of that time, his crazy scheme, he was rich, needless to say, old money, and there was the *Paris Review* and there was the *Antioch Review* and there was the *Carleton Miscellany,* the *Miscellany* being pretty respected, even avant-garde for its day, those were some of them, and what you have to understand is that there weren't as many literary magazines as there are today, by any means, and I suppose I should be honest, I will tell you that I was grateful to have any kind of sustenance then, and even if I would come to regret the night Trevor Oxnard found me there lost in the Portland bus station during the blizzard, with barely enough for the fare to get back to gritty Boston on one of those big-fendered

Trailways buses and with no idea of what I would do once I did get back there, a young man without any prospects might be a gentle way of putting it, broke, I was grateful indeed when he spotted me, a stranger, in the bleak waiting room, there among the fragile homeless people huddled on the old varnished wooden benches, lumps of so-called humanity just trying to hide for a while from the cold and thoroughly uncaring world of snowy Portland outside, but it was more than that, it wasn't merely a matter of no regular livelihood for me, and I was weary and I was tired and, to lift a line from a Saul Bellow novel, I was as worn out as a roller towel in a Mexican men's room, even if I was only twenty-seven, my whole life should have been ahead of me, but nothing was ahead of me, and if there was a touch of feverish delirium, it was perhaps understandable, too, I hadn't been eating right, and Trevor Oxnard did come into the waiting room there, wearing the fine navy-blue cashmere greatcoat over his shoulders like a cape, his features chiseled, all right, his longish gray hair swept back from his forehead, like on some bust of a composer or a known statesman, everything about the guy was theatrical, he nudged me awake as I dozed sitting up on the bench, working my way through who knows what manner of another phantasmagoric dream, and seated there on the bench I'd placed a copy of the *Paris Review* under my head as an impromptu pillow, against the back of the bench, and he later told me that he had just come into the station to see if the first editions of the next day's Boston papers had been tossed off the buses growling through Portland on yet another winter night, he later also told me that it was the fact that I was sleeping with the copy of the *Paris Review* under my head that caught his attention, my mouth flapping, I was probably snoring, and this was back when the *Paris Review* always had covers, every issue, featuring only abstract art, that was the code, I think, of the suave and sophisticated editor George Plimpton, and I can still see the cover of that issue, sort of a Rothko knockoff of a big pale-green block metamorphosing, softly, into a bigger pale-rose block for what I guess is the defining transcendence of Rothko's work, its essence, the softness that isn't at all definite or concrete, that transcendence, yes, a knockoff of a Rothko by some unknown artist was what was on the cover of those two hundred pages or so of poetry, fiction and, of course, the interview feature that were soaking up my dreams, you might say, under a head of hair that certainly needed a wash and cut that cold, cold night, the magazine provided an OK pillow, and woken by Trevor Oxnard standing loomingly above me I started mumbling something about the box of Good & Plentys I had on my lap, I had bought it from a vending machine with close to my last dime there in the waiting room, even Trevor Oxnard later would laugh, tell others the story of how, awakened, bleary-eyed, I simply started mumbling to him something thoroughly incoherent, and pretty crazy, about how the little Good & Plenty capsules were really all you needed for sustenance, I must have imagined they were vitamins, you know, the look of them, he would later tell the story of how I told him that night that the pink ones gave you certain necessary nutrients, the pearly white ones certain other necessary nutrients, and that's how it started, I forgot Boston, he said he had a job for me, he told me in his deep convincing voice that he could use a young man like me to help with the "project," that's what he called it, a project, on his estate and its extensive land on the craggy peninsula up by Bar Harbor, where we were soon heading together, we sped there that night in his sleek Jaguar coupe with the heater blasting, the headlamps of the Jaguar fanning this way and that on the plowed winding roads, the place near Bar Harbor had all once been the Oxnard family's swank summer residence, his grandfather's money was in steel manufacturing or something, the house was huge, a sprawling, weathered wood-shingle place in maybe the Queen Anne–revival style, all turrets and porches and gables, where he now lived alone, the rest of the extended family having long since forgotten about the place, or he lived there with just an elderly house-keeper and a caretaker/handyman, and there also were the different girlfriends a third his age who came from Montreal to spend a weekend now and then, talking their soft French like baby talk, pouty, smelling of perfume and powder, genuine sweater-girl figures and always quite chic, fashionably dressed, all of them pretty enough to be models or starlets, but most likely they were just expensive call girls from the Rue Crescent up there in Montreal, and before long I was set up in what had once must have been a guest cottage on the high cliff above the sea, the work Trevor Oxnard had me perform was easy enough, at first, anyway, and, oh, those dogs, those black Labs and those amber eyes that I still see to this day, the eyes that still look through me and somehow searingly penetrate to this day, there were a dozen of them, I guess, they were big, mean Labs, like I said, unusual temperment for Labs, and this part I never did get clear, I know they were what are called "cadaver dogs," meaning that they had been trained to sniff out the rotting flesh of corpses in wreckage after a disaster, an earthquake, for instance, but there were no earthquakes in Maine, and Larry, the leathery and laconic caretaker/handyman who himself was from a logging town farther inland, Larry, in one of his rare talkative moments, yes, he did explain to me in his slow, angular Down East syllables that some government agency in Augusta had bought and trained them several years before, that would have been 1957 or 1958, maybe, after the state had suffered not only bad spring flooding that wiped out a couple of smaller mill towns but also the odd tail end of a hurricane one September, the storm somehow veered off course from out in the open Atlantic and sucker punched the state, leaving a wide swath of destruction right up its middle, there were scores dead, bodies to be found, hence the dogs, until the next year, when somebody in the statehouse saw the expense of maintaining a kennel with dogs like that, a kennel somewhere far north in the state by Presque Isle, Larry told me, and the state official realized that it probably would be another hundred years before Maine incurred any kind of a hurricane or even spring flooding to such a ruinous extent, so the state put the dogs up for sale, Trevor Oxnard simply bought the dogs, and here's where it gets really tricky, here's where even I couldn't quite follow it, but I wasn't asking any questions, I had a place to live, I had three meals a day, brought to me in the drafty little guest cottage on the cliff by the housekeeper who came up the long path from the main house below, an ascending walkway through the scrub growth of bayberry and sea pine and bare wild-rose vines, she brought me the welcome and regular sustenance, and the work doing what Trevor Oxnard wanted done with the literary magazines took time, his project, but having any kind of real work was in itself welcome, at first, and it seemed that Trevor Oxnard had acted on a hunch in buying the dogs as he did from the state, figuring that if they could sniff out decaying flesh, they could also sniff out the dank, rottingly rich aroma of writing that was destined for obscurity, that would never last, he claimed, words aspiring to be literature that were written by a man or woman pounding away on a typewriter with hope and promise and excitement, those trappings of the creative act, writing that was printed in the handsome black lettering on fine creamy pages of literary magazines, and writing that would be completely forgotten, Trevor Oxnard would laugh, his voice now more of a sinister baritone than ever and the meanness tangible, with Trevor Oxnard for once abandoning his patrician vocabulary and summoning a suitable north-country metaphor to say exactly what he meant about such writing, "Stuff that in the end won't amount to a piss hole in the snow, if that," and at night as I sat at the desk high above the choppy black sea, all that Atlantic out there, all that sheer, hissingly wave-tormented nothingness out there, I started to hate the work, I could hear those dogs from Presque Isle in their pens down below by the once stately main house sometimes barking, sometimes chorally howling, and I doubt they even slept much, their sturdy haunches and dirty claws and their snarling dagger-sharp fangs encased in bared drooling lips as black as licorice, and, oh, need I say it again, those amber eyes, the dogs were just waiting to sniff out some more writing, find more quarterlies and journals, and I think the caretaker/handyman Larry fed them only the discarded carcasses of lobsters, and in another one of his rare moments of something resembling loquaciousness, Larry explained to me that lobsters were ancient bottom-feeders, and though their fleshy meat was a sweet delicacy to some, they basically fed on rotting carrion along the rocky ocean floor, so what better way was there to keep the dogs trained and accustomed to the stink of rotting than to feed them, in turn, what was left of creatures such as lobsters, which themselves were but made of carrion, and Larry would drive his rattling pickup truck over to the tourist restaurants on the coastal highway nearby and salvage from the dented garbage cans at the back of the parking lots the remnants of the tugged-apart carcasses after the tourists were done with them, once a week he would do that and fill maybe a dozen burlap sacks, then he would bring the dogs the rank, stinking refuse, with the stench from the yellow-greenish ooze in the body shell proper particularly powerful given a few days to ripen, serve the mess to the voracious beasts for them to masticate on the lobster carcasses hungrily, crunchingly, hard-boiled red shells and all, or, as Larry put it, speaking slow, looking right at me in the shadows but not looking at me, because you never could really see his eyes beneath the long visor of the filthy red-and-black checked wool cap, "Them dogs, e-ye-ah, with a taste of that, they only work up their appetite more, get themselves ready to sniff out and plant their teeth into what they really want, a crappy atonal attempt at free verse or a crappier, by-the-fucking-numbers short story, the usual flat-footed, predictable realism, maybe sandwiched between the light-blue covers of the *Sewanee Review*, e-ye-ah," and in his Down East elocution a simple "yeah" got stretched out for at least three syllables, "e-ye-ah," the dogs were let loose from the pens after midnight, and what happened in the course of that I really knew nothing about, they were let loose, barking and howling, and who knows how far away they loped, their lurid liverish tongues flopping, their paws the size of anvils rhythmically padding away the miles and miles in those endless, snout-to-the-ground nocturnal searches that could ensue once they got the powerful, uncut drug of a scent, you would think they would go no more than a couple of towns over in Maine at the most, but the way I pictured it, the way I clearly saw it and the way it must have been, yes, they traveled thousands of miles, the way any of us does travel in our dreams, the old business of bounding overnight to many distant cities, as they say, it might have taken them to a municipal library's periodical room in Cleveland, a hip bookstore in Berkeley, or even the piles of reading matter that included mostly newspapers and old large-circulation slick magazines but also other assorted publications, anything with pulp in it, left out and stacked on a moonlit sidewalk for a Boy Scout paper drive, let's say, beneath the clarity of stars bright in an indigo sky and the music of crickets chirping out secrets amid the dapple-trunked sycamores in any of who knows how many sleeping towns in this great republic of ours, good American towns with names that are little prayers in themselves, names like Middlebridge or Hillsboro or Plainfield, the kind of places that actually might have Boy Scout paper drives, all I know is that the dogs would go *somewhere* and return with plenty more of the literary magazines by dawn, some back numbers, some new issues, too, they would come back from *somewhere* after they had gathered as many of them as they could each night, tirelessly amassing more of them, retrieving them with jaws clenching the volumes tight, and in the morning I would look down the path leading up from the big house as I nervously tried to shed my own tossing and turning night of somnambulistic peregrinations, my aforementioned dreaming, in that ill-heated drafty cottage, my hands admittedly shaking a bit as I tried to keep them tight on the beige crockery mug of instant black coffee I prepared on a J. J. Newberry hot plate, and I looked out through the frosted panes to see again Larry struggling to push an old red wheelbarrow, rusty and with a single underinflated black tire as soft as a pillow, up the zigzagging path to the cottage, the bin of the thing overflowing with the literary magazines the dogs had gathered up the night before, gruff, stubbled Larry in the red-and-black wool peaked cap with dangling earflaps and having to set down that wobbly tripod he had been pushing when a couple of volumes slipped off the top of the high pile of them, yes, the load of what the dogs had surely brought back the night before, as Larry bent over to cursingly pick up the fallen copies and shove them back into the mound, the puffs of steam from his breath indicating more of the emphatic low cursing, and then he would lift the two handles of the wheelbarrow and lean into his grunting up the path again, to finally deliver another load of them to me in the cottage, where I would get down to the work I had to do for Trevor Oxnard for another day, I will admit that I had absolutely grown to hate it, I will admit that I myself had come to vocally curse that night of the blizzard when I just happened to have been dozing and waiting for a bus to Boston in the Trailways station and Trevor Oxnard just happened to pull off the highway in Portland and stroll in to look for the next day's newspapers as he drove in his smooth-humming Jaguar coupe, blacker than black, back from wherever he had been, heading to his place near Bar Harbor, it's the way you try to justify any misfortune, blame it on chance, but again as with any misfortune, it all ends up in nightmarish inevitability, stone-solid fate, and in a way I *had* to be there in the station that night, Trevor Oxnard *had* to stride in from the cold and head to the corner news kiosk in the station, spotting me with the *Paris Review* under my head propped against the back of the bench, and you have to understand that this was a time, then in the very early sixties, before electric paper shredders were in use, or in common use other than by CIA Cold Warriors and such, so my job was literally a manual one, and I would keep at the work for four hours before lunch and then for four or five hours more after lunch, again brought to me by the elderly housekeeper, usually just a lousy cold-cut sandwich with cheap French's yellow mustard on white bread and a glass of watery Kool-Aid, *sustenance,* and sometimes I labored six hours after lunch if the load was unusually large from the dogs roaming the night before, and what I would do was one by one rip apart the magazines, tear to something resembling confetti the pages of those journals like *Virginia Quarterly Review* and *Hudson Review* and *Antioch Review* and *Sewanee Review,* then take the peach baskets full of the shreds out of the cottage and to the edge of the cliff and begin once more the scooping up and tossing, letting the pieces float in the wind out over the Atlantic, and sometimes Trevor Oxnard would show to witness that final step in the travail, and sometimes if he saw the lamps lit at dusk inside the cottage on its seaside knoll as I finished up for the day, he would even forget about his current doe-eyed, pouty-lipped whispery twenty-year-old, the "company" from Montreal he was entertaining, and he would show up, hatless and the swept-back gray hair flowing, the cashmere greatcoat that did always seem like a villain's cape over his shoulders, to personally watch me grab another couple of handfuls of shreds from the peach baskets there as I stood atop the cliff and tossed the stuff into oblivion, more words lost forever in order to prove what Trevor Oxnard truly believed, or to quote his bellowing in that baritone of his, "Let them go! Let them all go!," the man excited, taking real satisfaction in the perversity of it all, and in a way I guess he was confirming what you knew deep in your darkest of dark moments, and it's that feeling you might get today when you somehow do come across an old issue of a literary magazine, a worn copy, the cover faded, and you let your eyes linger on the table of contents page, there in such sturdy Garamond or Baskerville or once futuristic Courier, and you see the names of all those poets and fiction writers, personal essayists, too, I suppose, who either you never have heard of or whose name, in the case of others, you do gradually recognize, remembering how often this writer or that writer had been a regular in the literary magazines at one time, long ago, 1961 or 1962, maybe, and you see that name, shake your head, and you can't help but sadly sigh and ask yourself, "I wonder whatever happened to . . . ," and when I found out later that Trevor Oxnard, after a privileged education, the kind that was fitting for a male of his generation from the very privileged family of a steel-manufacturing tycoon, not just the best prep schools but also private tutors and a degree in something from the Sorbonne, yes, when I found out that he had been a failed novelist when younger, somebody with scant talent who was never able to finish a manuscript long enough to even *submit* to a publisher, it suddenly made sense, he was making sure in his own way that nobody had any better luck than he did with their attempting to write anything significant and have it read by an audience, and his project confirmed his own warped conclusion that literature was ultimately a chump's game, but I knew deep down it wasn't such disdain that disgusted me, or it wasn't that easy, and as much as I hated the work, I myself knew already that most of what was in those magazines was probably destined to be forgotten, probably all of it that was in one magazine particularly, the *Sewanee Review*, was routinely bad and definitely destined to be forgotten, I had never really read much of that magazine before, it had never interested me, but now occasionally thumbing through it with the volumes that ended up at the cottage, I realized that even way back then, as today, the magazine had an unpleasant conservative tinge, sort of right-wing and tight-hearted, not just stuffy but something that didn't quite look you in the eye, why, Larry himself knew the score on the *Sewanee Review*, but that was just the *Sewanee Review*, that wasn't the other magazines, and often I would find something so good, so worth saving, that it would make me physically ill to have to get to work on it and grab the magazine in my hands pretty sore and chafed from the many hours and hours of tugging and ripping already, a poem in a magazine that whispered the metaphysical like graceful sunlight on a wide emerald lawn in warm August, a short story with characters very meaningful, a story so moving and so revelatory and so understanding of all the sadnesses and happinesses that do define us, a story that, indeed, stood as a valid evocation of our brief but oh-so-fragilely-hopeful, if nothing else, time on this blessed planet, the kind of short story that as soon as you got to the last page you found yourself half out of breath, smitten, immediately wanting to thumb back the few pages to the beginning and savor yet again the pure magic of the words in the wonderful sentences that yielded the accumulated satisfying paragraphs, to read it once more, and so it happened to me, it was a story in the *Carleton Miscellany,* a magazine that itself was once entirely admirable with a daring edge but now defunct, I couldn't destroy it, I hid the issue away, if nothing else I was making sure that there would be at least one copy of it somewhere, that this powerful short story somehow might have a chance of being read by somebody else who knows where or when, no, I couldn't bring myself to destroy even this *one* copy, which might be found by *one more* reader, and I know now it was like much of what I myself did read in those literary magazines when I was young, the quarterlies that I spent what little money I had on back in the late fifties and early sixties, after I'd finished four years at Amherst as a scholarship boy and obsessive English major, wishing so much to write great short stories or a great novel myself but getting nowhere with it myself, plenty of rejection slips to wallpaper my bedroom, all right, no better than Trevor Oxnard who came upon me at the moment when I did give up on trying to write, had finally sworn it off, when I found myself dumped by my old college girlfriend Molly from Mount Holyoke, and I'd visited Molly at her parents' place in Portland and there she told me I had to grow up, it was high time I did, and Molly said sternly that I had to stop daydreaming of some-day being a famous author, she had put up with my foolishness for several years now, she said, which was altogether too long, she wasn't getting any younger, plus she had now met another guy, an up-and-comer named Alexander who she'd known since her childhood growing up there in Portland, he had his own rapidly expanding law practice now, specializing in the new and very lucrative field of medical-malpractice litigation, and I barely had enough money to pay for the Trailways ticket back to Boston that snowy night in the bus station after she dumped me, and dumped me good, and Trevor Oxnard must have known I was a young guy trying to write, who else would be sleeping in a bus station with a copy of the *Paris Review* under his head, and even as I planned what you might call my escape now from Trevor Oxnard's place in Maine, even as I checked and rechecked what I had packed in the scuffed old russet leather suitcase with the gold monogram showing the initials of my boozing bachelor uncle who had been killed in the war, an implement of travel passed on to me in the family, I tried not to think about the dogs, their savage raspy barking, those amber eyes, the kind of eyes that saw right through you, that knew more about you than you knew yourself, and bundled up in my peacoat and long scarf and frayed knit watch cap, quietly shutting the door to the cottage that night, I knew Trevor Oxnard would come after me, I knew my chances were slim of even making it off the estate's vast property, with its hills and undulating sea-stone walls and thick forest of tall forbidding pines, his dogs would soon be after me, I might end up little more than the crunched stuff of those lobster shells in the dogs' ripping fangs, but I would *try,* and I just might get away from there with the issue of the *Carleton Miscellany* packed in the suitcase, Volume 17, Number 2, Spring 1961, the copy that contained the short story that had done such a number on me, pp. 57–71, I had packed it deep in the bag, and it doesn't matter now what the short story was about, all that matters is that I know that after reading it, it gave me the *very best* feeling of all when you do read something that knocks you out, I realized that it was so fucking good that I, broke, girl-friendless, I suddenly wanted to *write* again, it made me want to create something worthwhile myself despite whatever odds, and I made it down the steep path OK, I could see the silhouette of the massive house, that mansion looming large as a forbidding castle as I passed it, and the smell of the sea was heady and strong, and it was going OK until I stumbled against something, my worn-out suede desert boot tripping over a galvanized pail or even slapping flat into the rusted red wheelbarrow left by crazy Larry there, I'm not sure about this part either, exactly what I hit and that made the racket in the frigid and very still night, but after the noise, first there was only one of the dogs emitting a piercing yelp, then I could hear the whole kennel of them picking up on it in an off-key answer of collective echoing howls, and somebody was jangling with the big padlock and chain on the gate for the pens, too, somebody was letting the beasts loose, and as I began to run, awkwardly with the suitcase banging against my chinos, but running the best I could, I for some reason suddenly felt good, I did, I told myself that if I . . .

WHAT CAN'T NOT HAPPEN

THEY COULD SEE WHAT IT SAID UP THERE: Toulouse, Orléans, Poitiers, Bordeaux, and even Tours.

The Musée d'Orsay rose large in the moonlight. Tall window arches made a row, and topping each in the ornate nineteenth-century facade, bright buff stone, was the chiseled name of one of the faraway cities served when the museum had actually been a major railway terminal so long before—when travel was something half formal and thoroughly exotic, when it was very much the thing of a dream.

To gaze at the Orsay across the river that way was also to see it reflected twice as large on the mirroring black Seine; in the night's utter stillness, the long, blunt-nosed barges creaked rhythmically against their heavy sisal docking lines, as if whispering some important secret you really should know.

o o o

THE BUNCH OF THEM WALKING, they crossed the Pont Royal to the Left Bank. They were heading toward the museum in their sweatshirts and jeans and Reeboks or Adidas with soles worn low (lovely Claire also wore a wool cape, sort of a serape deal striped in the hues of the Spanish flag that other kids in the youth hostels often teased her about, though she didn't care), yes, walking like that across the Pont Royal now they could have been just another crew of American college kids, happily bounding around Europe after classes back home let out for the year. Except that it was the empty middle of the night, with that moonlight full and strong enough, in fact, to cast shadows.

And except for the truth that they were the young dead.

However, as they had convinced themselves, even if that was the case (a car accident on an icy road outside of Ithaca, maybe, or Hodgkin's disease discovered without warning in a chest X-ray, part of a routine physical required by the local health department for a summer kitchen job—there were so many hazards when young), somehow being dead didn't matter. And while they had never known one another before, they now had all agreed that with or without the usual Fine Arts 10 survey course or the like, they, too, deserved the chance to go to the great museums and see firsthand the famous pictures themselves.

There was little doubt that, foremost, it would have to be the Orsay.

Jimmy put on a mock thunderous voice when he said it again: "Orsay—the Mother of All Museums."

"I think you might be selling the Louvre a little short," Jennifer said, typically serious, "while I can see your point in saying that the Orsay is *the* place and that it is, admittedly, nineteenth-century French art, when sometimes the defining icon and ultimate achievement of graphic art itself, as opposed to plastic art, does seem to be nineteenth-century French art. Maybe just adding a footnote would do, OK, saying that the Louvre with its piles and piles of stuff from all the other centuries probably comes close."

"The Mother"—Jimmy put on more of the thunder, like an ad for a horror movie—"of All Museums."

Claire in the serape smiled, charmingly, and all night she had been smiling at just about anything Jimmy said.

o o o

KYLE AND TOM KEPT TOGETHER, talking sports the way they always seemed to be talking sports. Not that they didn't want to see the pictures as much as the rest of them, and not that they wouldn't be ready for it and would forget team standings and NBA play-off berths back home, even rumors of player trades—or at least occasionally forget about that—once they actually got into those rooms to look at everything that awaited them there.

o o o

AS IT TURNED OUT, IT WASN'T HARD TO GET INSIDE. It wasn't very hard at all. Kyle said a guy at his school, the University of Texas, had once told him about the trick. Apparently, his pal back in Austin had said that he discovered it quite by accident, on one of those sweltering August Sundays when the lines of people waiting outside to enter the museum stretched clear to the nearby purple trestling of the Eiffel Tower, or so you'd think; Kyle claimed that his buddy just went around the corner from the official front entrance and moseyed into the separate bookshop entrance there on the length of the building facing the river, and, "Voilà, as the man says," Kyle assured them, because inside the bookstore there were rear doors opening to the museum proper, you didn't even have to pay admission. While Jimmy himself was doubtful, saying it couldn't be *that* easy, Tom, the fellow sports nut, supported Kyle's idea whole-heartedly, and just when Jimmy was about to emphasize that there would be *no way* that the closed bookstore itself wouldn't be locked at this time of night, Kyle tugged the upright brass handles on the twin slabs of the doors, which gave way silkily and without the slightest resistance.

"Voilà, as the man says, all right," Jimmy conceded.

They passed the hodge-podge of tables bearing overpriced books aptly named "coffee-table" volumes, because outside of the rare party who actually was well-off enough to maybe have a luxurious sunken living room with a low-slung table in front of a sleek expensive sofa to spread such books out on, most every-body else simply flipped through them in the shop, reference room–style and without buying; they passed the racks of post-cards (five francs each, ten for forty francs) and the larger racks of videocassettes of the museum's holdings, with videos always an added staple in any museum bookstore lately. They passed through the bookstore's unlocked glass doors in back connect-ing to the museum as absolutely easy as that, too, and almost before they knew it they were, well, delivered smack into the ground-floor central concourse.

Elongated, the concourse was empty except for the sculp-tures, there in the midst of the decidedly startling conversion of what had once been a huge train station, clogged with huff-ing locomotives and *wagon-lits*, into what it was today, an art museum. Everything existed in that duality. There was the high skylight arch of the station, which must have once stretched the length of the platforms and tracks, with more of the translucent glass for towering fan windows at either end, illuminated well by the moonlight on this particular night. And you could still see some of the cast-iron pillars and beams supporting it all, now painted a tastefully soft olive green. Then there was the more recent work of the avant-garde architect, a postmodern Italian, which set up partitioning half walls of polished stone—black and real pink—that looked thickly solid and almost something out of an Egyptian temple, but streamlined as well, behind which were the ground-floor galleries; above in the open hall were two more levels of galleries on either side with balcony walkways, accessed by gleaming stainless-steel escalators. Here, while strolling around the sculptures that somehow made for a garden of ghostly company in this main concourse of the lowest level, maybe any of these five kids might have said what anybody inevitably would say in witnessing—beholding?—the place for the first time: "Wow, to think that this was once a *train* station."

o o o

JENNIFER HAD GONE DIRECTLY to the information desks at the official front entryway.

Though nobody was tending to any of the desks, she looked through the separate small stacks of brochures for the empty museum, first fingering the one in English, "Map of the Museum," with its little logo of the American and British flags on top, but then deciding on the one in French, topped with the tricolor, "Plan du Musée." Being a Harvard student, she was conscientious, as might be expected; she had gone to Harvard from a suburban high school outside of Cleveland, and she often tried to make everything a little education in itself—or, as she undoubtedly saw it now, why come all the way to France and go to the most special museum in that country of museums and not use your French to read the few paragraphs about the museum's history and look over the chart of its extensive galleries, as annotated in the language in which she herself had registered a near-perfect score on the advanced-placement SAT exam? That made *no* sense whatsoever, she knew.

Meanwhile, Tom, one of the sports nuts, had come up to her and told her there was little need for a map. Tom wasn't even in college at the moment, and he had been through enough junior colleges in and around Seattle that he'd decided he personally didn't require any of that to continue on with making the kind of solid money he was, programming in the high-tech industry; he thought he would probably never return to subjecting himself to more required political science and, worse, supremely boring "bonehead English." Unlike the tip on how to sneak into the museum that his new friend, the other sports nut Kyle, had gotten from a pal, it wasn't a matter of any pal who had given him the advice that he now offered to Jennifer—it was just something he had read in one of the usual airline magazines on the long flight to Charles de Gaulle, the engines hissing and it feeling like only minutes between a dinner they gave you that wasn't bad (a grilled chicken-breast filet, spicy, with sliced potatoes) in the falling darkness somewhere over the Atlantic and then the breakfast they gave you (croissants, wouldn't you know it, with coffee and a mixed-fruit cup) in the gaudily orange sunrise several hours later, somewhere over the same Atlantic.

"The whole place is laid out chronologically," Tom told Jennifer. "You really don't need a map, you just start here at this front entrance and go from room to room, first the early stuff, then work your way up. But I remember the article said this. It said be careful of spending too much time in the rooms on this floor, the earlier things, or you'll be tired by the time you do eventually make it to the top rooms with the big-ticket items, Monet and van Gogh and the boys. Honestly, there's no need for any sort of a map."

Jennifer was tempted to bark back to him that it was just what was done in a museum, you always got a map, to make sure you missed nothing, if for no other reason. And *of course* she already knew the basic layout of the museum from the extensive prep reading she'd done on it back home, and she asked herself why she was even listening to this oaf of a boy who only minutes before had been blabbing on and on about teams and players, now telling *her* what the etiquette of any museum was—but then she caught herself. She realized she had to be careful about putting people down with her—why not say it?—intelligence, especially boys. That had led to too many Friday and Saturday nights studying alone in the Lowell House library while her roommates were always off with dates for a movie or party somewhere.

"Can I keep it just for a souvenir?" she asked Tom, with put-on, exaggerated earnestness.

"OK," he said, "if you promise not to look."

"Right," she said flatly.

They caught up with the others, who had already "done" a few of those Pre-Impressionist rooms.

o o o

THERE WAS A ROOM FOR DELACROIX, with his color-saturated canvases of life in the Moroccan medinas and open desert, a sky always so blue, to the point that before you saw your first Delacroix you probably didn't know the absolute enormity of a perfectly blue sky. There was a room for Millet, with his noble peasants sowing the golden jewels of strewn seeds or praying their pious Angelus or, at last, trudging homeward in the bruised twilight with silver scythes over the shoulder, weary but somehow fully triumphant, nevertheless.

o o o

CLAIRE IN THE SERAPE WHISPERED to Jimmy:

"Do you know those clocks we saw outside? The giant clocks atop either end of the building that we saw when coming over the bridge, each of them up in a corner turret maybe?"

"Yeah."

"Did you see how the faces of them were glass," she said, "they looked at least a story high? And I keep thinking how big they seemed, how the face of each, with the big Roman numerals and the big iron hands going around and around, was crystal-clear glass like that, so you could see inside, meaning that each is a giant window that you can look out through, too."

"You could be right," Jimmy said. He was looking at Claire's gray eyes, her lustrous tawny hair, still tangled from the wind and the endless walking that the five of them had logged during so much sightseeing earlier, from Montmartre to Montparnasse; it was long hair spread out in almost silken flames on the serape that was, in truth, adolescently theatrical—and outright wonderful—as she stood there now in jeans and tennis sneakers. "They were clear glass," Jimmy confirmed it, "the faces off them."

But he didn't have much time to continue with any of that, because as the bunch now worked their way up the escalators to those "big-ticket" items on the top level, bypassing the rooms of mostly furniture on the second level (heavy on the flowing art nouveau—desks and armoires and sofas, all worth seeing but that surely could wait, there on that floor with its long balcony walkways), Kyle saw Jimmy and Claire whispering, spotted them lingering behind together more and more in the course of the viewing; Kyle called to the pair, sarcastically:

"Hey, no parking!"

Then his sports-nut buddy Tom picked up on it, as if the two had rehearsed it as a sitcom routine:

"Yeah, no parking"—he thumped out double resounding beats on the escalator's stainless-steel side panel, for the rhythm of the oldie disco song—"no parking on the dance floor."

They both snickered.

Admittedly a bit self-conscious to be caught like that by these other guys, Jimmy again bellowed, trying to appear casual even if he had been acting quite moony around Claire:

"The M-o-other of All Museums!"

The Vincent Price deep guttural roll was really overdone this time, gummily slow; everybody laughed, except for Jennifer, who was decidedly elsewhere.

Jennifer hadn't noticed when it happened, but somewhere downstairs, in one of those rooms, she had become almost vertiginous with excitement, overwhelmed.

It was one thing to have sat so many times in the cosy lecture hall in the basement of the Fogg Museum on Quincy Street at Harvard, to watch the prof up there in the darkness clicking on and off the projected slide images for a class lecture. But it was another thing altogether to finally be this *close* to the canvases. Actually, it maybe first struck her, she now decided, in that room labeled "Early Manet and Monet" on the first level; would you believe it, the holdings in the Orsay were such that something as major as Manet's *The Balcony* could simply be cataloged as "*early*"(!), and it nearly bowled her over to think that in *The Balcony* those fine, precise brushstrokes were close enough then so that her own breath caressed them: there was the green of the crisscrossing balcony railing, and there was the blue of the burst of flowers in the ceramic pot in front of the two women wearing very white summer dresses, and, most significantly, there was the profusion of black—though not just black, but the essence of black, in the haughty gentleman's imposing formal suit jacket and, more so, the dark, dark interior of the room in back that the trio seemingly had all just stepped out of to assemble for the portrait. What Jennifer decided right then and there was that Manet was the best painter of black. And while it was a given that Manet had learned everything he knew about black from the Spaniards of the Golden Age (and Jennifer was very familiar with them, she had done a long final paper on them for her own fine arts survey course that used the weighing-a-ton volume of Janson's *History of Art* for a text, those Spaniards like Velázquez and El Greco and above all—certainly above all—Zurbarán with his trademark swallowing black backgrounds for a simple Crucifixion, the same for his lovely early Christian female martyrs usually in the anachronistic Andalusian dress of his own day, beautiful Saint

Lucy carrying her carved-out eyes on a shimmering silver plate always Jennifer's favorite), true, granting that the Spaniards were Manet's teachers, Manet had transported their vision into another century, analyzed and refined and thoroughly perfected it, until he was exactly what he was—the *best* painter of black.

And she didn't care if the others might think her scholarly, an incorrigible bookworm, for what she had done next in that gallery with the rest of them there to witness it. She had taken out of her shoulder bag a little marbleized-cover composition notebook and a click-top Bic; she had written down what she believed without any doubt: *"Manet is the best painter of black."*

All of which is to say, Jennifer was beyond mere excitement, and this was proving to be *so much more* than even she had anticipated. A heart "thumping" wasn't just a cliché, she assured herself now on the escalator. Jennifer (she had died only two days after her twentieth birthday the year before, a very rare undiagnosed endocrine disorder) couldn't remember when she had been happier.

o o o

THE GALLERIES UP TOP WERE SOMETHING ELSE, and Tom knew that he himself had been right—or at least that article in the flight magazine had been right: nobody should spend too much time with the Pre-Impressionist works, downstairs, before this major stuff.

He and Kyle often weren't always really listening to Jennifer explaining to them the things she knew—like what a shame it was that so many of the paintings had sadly faded because of originally being displayed in what amounted to the bright

greenhouse of the old Jeu de Paume Gallery in the Jardins des
Tuileries, where most Impressionism had been housed for years
before being moved to the Orsay—yet Tom did admit to her
that it was damn interesting how she told them that a true triumph of the Orsay curators was the way they had managed to
assemble, through buying up and also national consolidation, a
full five of the maybe dozen particular Monets with the matching views of the stony gothic facade of the Rouen cathedral
in the dramatically changing light of different times of day,
displaying them beside one another here; that neatly provided
support of the definition of Impressionism as announced by
one early commentator, "the painting of light itself," Jennifer assured the sports nuts Kyle and Tom, and, like a teacher
indeed, she showed them that with the paintings now arranged
in a row, the "full and convincing vision" of what Monet was
really trying to say probably at last existed in a way that even
he himself didn't realize it could when he had painted and sold
the large canvasses individually over the years.

They nodded.

Jennifer did appreciate that Kyle and Tom finally seemed
to be listening to her, or doing so now and then. On the other
hand, she couldn't believe how it was nearly predictable that
while strolling through these many amazing rooms, the two
guys occasionally went back to talking about the supposedly
exciting play-offs they were missing in basketball (what were
people doing even playing basketball in June? wasn't that a
winter-season sport? yet just when Jennifer thought that, she
knew that she wasn't even sure it was June or any other month,
wasn't sure she was even here in Paris, to be honest); and what

was far more predictable, she told herself, was that their, Tom and Kyle's, own obvious enthusiasm inevitably had to be reserved for the van Goghs.

Not that Jennifer didn't like van Gogh, but *The Church at Auvers-sur-Oise* and *Van Gogh's Room at Arles* and, definitely, the *Self-Portrait of the Artist*, were just *too* well known, had almost become trite, and as soon as she saw Tom fumbling in his nylon Eastpak for his camera, she wanted to call out for them not to be that dumb, not to do what she knew they were going to do. But, sure enough, they were about to do exactly that.

o o o

"MAKE SURE YOU GET THE TWO OF US side by side, just the heads," Tom said.

Kyle, who had taken Tom's camera, a tiny canary-yellow plastic thing looking like a toy, told him not to worry.

"The viewfinder on it has a little target," Tom went on, positioning himself as he posed.

"Relax, man," Kyle said, "I know how to work it, and don't forget to say 'Chuck E. Cheese.'"

Jennifer stood away from them, watched.

Squinting and backing up a pace or two on the polished parquet floor, Kyle all but toppled over completely, Charlie Chaplin–style, when his legs hit one of the chrome-legged benches upholstered in black leatherette; after some mock brushing himself off for effect, twisting his head over his shoulder to give the bench a decidedly dirty look, he regained his composure and grinned widely, then resumed the squinting through the viewfinder. He told the posing Tom to tilt his own head a little bit closer.

Closer to what? What *else,* Jennifer answered her own question.

The *Self-Portrait of the Artist,* with van Gogh's spiky hair and beard that brilliant orange, his coat a startlingly lurid aqua, as Jennifer now said to herself, "Please, oh please, don't let one of them make a comment about the ear."

"And I want to see your *good* ear facing me," Kyle said.

"Extremely funny," Tom said to Kyle, who squinted through the viewfinder some more, "extremely sick, too."

"Chuck E. Chee-ese," Kyle repeated.

"This is going to be great," Tom told him.

Tom knew that a snapshot like this of his own head side by side with that of V. van Gogh would "rule" when he put it up in his cubicle back at the high-tech company where he worked in Seattle.

o o o

JENNIFER WAS GRATEFUL IF ONLY FOR THE FACT that nobody else was around in the halls and galleries now totally empty, that no other museumgoers were on hand to see her in the company of embarrassing fools like these two boys.

o o o

ALONE NOW, JIMMY FOUND HIMSELF in a rather odd large room of giant mirrors and baroque-bordering-on-rococo gilding; folding chairs, with purple velvet seats and more bright gilding for the frames, were lined up in rows. It was possibly a remnant, maybe the ballroom, of the posh upstairs hotel that had once been part of the railway terminal, and it was probably used now for museum lectures and the like. Also, it appeared that none of the others had any interest in it, or it seemed that Jimmy had just stumbled into it on his own, taking a wrong turn down a corridor darkened to protect some delicate watercolors in low-lit showcases, as the Impressionist rooms began to give way to those for the Post-Impressionists, Gauguin principally. Standing in this open room under the chandeliers lit and glistening like shattered ice, Jimmy gazed at a large billboard-size canvas set on a sturdy supporting easel:

LE COIN DE TABLE
Henri Fantin-Latour (1836–1904)
huile sur toile

It was a group portrait of ten or so late-nineteenth-century French writers and literary critics; some of them were sitting at the dining table with its white tablecloth and simple offerings (a decanter of brandy, coffee cups and a silver sugar bowl, a few half-eaten apples and pears, so it must have been after dinner), others stood behind. Most all wore black frock coats and floppy black cravats, the central, tallest figure in a formal silk top hat being somebody whose name Jimmy didn't recognize even when checking the little guide board; the guide board was a small rectangle showing a white-on-black outline of the painting, with numbers and names to correspond to each of the personages, and it was affixed to the easel under thick clear plastic, below the painting. However, Jimmy *surely* could identify without any key the two seated at the very end, *"le coin,"* of the table, which gave the painting its name—Verlaine and, more importantly, Rimbaud. (The fact that Jimmy, who had seemed to stare appreciatively but without any noticeably deep response to the other paintings he had seen so far, would now be lingering here was understandable. At Mankato State in Minnesota, before he fell through the ice and drowned one dim afternoon after playing choose-up pond hockey with some hometown pals during Christmas break only last year, yes, at Mankato his creative writing teacher Roger Rath had told him that as far as he was concerned, Jimmy had "the stuff"; and while Mankato was hopelessly off the map as an academic institution, Roger Rath, no more than thirty himself, was convinced that with the fine portfolio of poetry Jimmy could put together and with his, Roger Rath's, own bombarding of the admissions people at his alma mater of the University of Iowa with a *string* of glowing letters of recommendation, there was a good shot that Jimmy, despite his so-so grades, could crack that most prestigious of graduate creative writing schools.) Jimmy now assured himself it was fitting that the two poets, Verlaine and Rimbaud, should be paired together and obviously separated from the others in the painting by this artist Fantin-Latour, seeing that their stormy relationship—which had led to Verlaine at one point even shooting, yet luckily just wounding, Rimbaud and serving time in a bleak Brussels prison for it—was part of their legend. Balding and bearded, little Verlaine appeared uneasy in this setting, and Rimbaud beside him casually propped his own chin on one hand, gazing at his mentor Verlaine and completely ignoring the others at the table, as Rimbaud certainly looked more than ever like exactly who he was: curly-locked, snub-nosed, rosy-cheeked, he could have been a young rock star, albeit a rock star whose rapidly squandered innocence was a major part of his haunting appeal. Jimmy figured he was only about seventeen or eighteen then, the peak of his powers, without question, that produced the wild, half out-of-control poetry that his professor Roger Rath had first introduced Jimmy to and that Jimmy found better than the work of everybody else (Keats, Eliot, etc.) he was supposed to find better. Rimbaud's poetry was so alive in its youthful exuberance bordering on a visionary—no, *hallucinatory*—don't-give-a-damnism. Jimmy looked at the painting carefully, studied the other writers and critics depicted; he looked, too, at the surrounding details in the painted scene, the couple of canvases shown hung behind the group in the spacious gray-walled dining room there with its very large mahogany table for their meal, even examined quite closely the flowers set in a vase at the end of the table opposite that with the two special poets—and, still, he kept going back only to them, Verlaine and Rimbaud. Or, more specifically, to Rimbaud. Jimmy wasn't sure how long he was there.

It was one of those situations where you looked at a painting and a painting was so right that it could have been only minutes that you were gazing or it could have been a full and airily experienced long lifetime; or, to put it another way, it was what happened when a painting was no longer its colors and its figures and its essential satiny sheen on the canvas whatsoever, but it was a voice that spoke to you something you always suspected though were never quite sure of before. And this particular painting said to Jimmy, This is what poetry is all about.

Then something hit him.

He was *alone,* he had lost the others.

It scared him terribly (had that been his first thought when he was suddenly under the ice that afternoon in northern Minnesota, his heavy winter clothes soaked?— Jimmy pressing madly up against the frozen surface and unable to find the spot where he had crashed through, Jimmy with no chance of escape or rescue, because he had stayed to skate a little more on his own after the choose-up hockey game, his friends having already headed home and Jimmy resoundingly *alone*), and Jimmy now started wandering nervously through the Impressionist galleries, calling out a few times, nearly shouting, only to hear his own voice echoing:

"Hey, you guys, where are you?"

o o o

UNTIL, IN THE LONG HALL OF HONOR, a display of the museum's most important paintings regardless of chronology, featuring the most famous Monets and Renoirs and Cézannes, he stopped in close to a skid, staring now—again with all the leaden concentration that he had exercised on the group portrait of the literary men—at a picture by another painter whose name, like Fantin-Latour's, wasn't familiar, somebody who appeared to have found his way into this the most hallowed of galleries on the strength of one very great painting.

o o o

LE RÊVE
Pierre Puvis de Chavannes (1824–1898)
huile sur toile

○ ○ ○

The colors of the painting are soft, moonlit. There is a barren landscape, with a stretch of brownish earth in the foreground, then a wide gray lake going right up to blue mountains in the distance; there is the half-moon glowing above a scraggly pine tree of only a few limbs. Under the pine tree, in one corner near the foreground, is a young man sleeping, a sack on a pole set down beside him, to suggest he is a traveler. He is a very young man, with longish hair, though he seems somewhat troubled in his sleep, his eyes closed and his lips slightly agape, one hand clutching a coarse blanket to his shoulders, bare at the mussed neck of a loose white shirt. Above him in the sky float three suitably lovely goddesses, as if they are flying toward him; their hair is very golden, their white gowns flowing, and the one in the middle holds up a laurel wreath, while the two others are spreading things to the ground, as if seeds to be sown on the sleeper—flower petals from one, gold coins from another. (What did it mean? A dream of what life could offer, the laurel wreath of fame in the middle, the coins of riches on one side and the petals of love on the other?) There is an eerie quiet to the picture, the way the moon glows soft yellow like that, the way the long sky itself is a translucent Wedgwood blue. Actually, while the figure seems to be a young man, this sleeper with such red lips and such longish hair could just as easily be a beautiful young woman, an entirely and strikingly beautiful young woman.

Jimmy stared and stared.

This time there was no doubt what the painting was telling him; he spoke it aloud:

"Claire."

And with that, any worry about himself being alone vanished, because he knew he must find Claire—something was wrong, Claire was in trouble.

Panicking, his stomach a resonating pang, he didn't know which way to go; or, it was more so a moment of overwhelming confusion, a pivot with a squeak of his Reeboks on the polished floor like a basketball player cutting one way, then a pivot, an identical squeak, the other way.

Or maybe he couldn't run. His legs were no more than hopelessly overstuffed sandbags—suddenly Jimmy felt as if he had *never* moved, had no idea of what the very *notion* of movement, in fact, was.

Until he remembered how Claire had talked about the big clocks, the glass-faced ones they had seen from outside, studding either end of this imposing museum building facing the Seine.

o o o

THEN HE *WAS* JOGGING, out of breath and rushing through the rooms to what he knew was one end of the building, beyond that lecture hall of sorts, to where he was sure one of the clocks was. Though when he got there, he found that the clock was set in the far wall of the deserted museum café, on the other side of a locked glass door. He yanked on the chrome knob, nothing budging, then yanked harder, again to no avail; he could see the café's little round black marble tables and modernistic chrome chairs, he could see the glass-faced clock beyond that, making a giant window, as Claire had observed, and he was close . . . but it was no use, and Claire wasn't there, anyway. He was breathing hard, and he jogged through the empty rooms again, almost a frenziedly rewound film clip of his previous route, and after getting lost in the stairway ramps toward the end of the top floor, he finally arrived at the building's other front corner, so high up, which corresponded to the café's corner. He first spotted a canvas that looked like a huge aerial shot of Paris, old and possibly a painting composed from the vantage point of a hot-air balloon, and he knew that was a good sign—it only stood to reason that an aerial shot be displayed, because through the glass face of the other one of those big clocks, which he now saw, you also had what amounted to an aerial view, allowing you to peer down on an entire panorama of the city.

It was dim in that corner, like a utility room with no adornment, except for the single canvas. Just more of the old train station's cast-iron pillars and beams painted such soft olive green, and the clock's oversize glass face *easily* a story high, so all outside could read it from afar.

Claire was standing there alone, her back to him and looking out.

o o o

IT IN ITSELF WAS A PAINTING:

YOUNG WOMAN IN SPANISH CAPE LOOKING OUT THROUGH TIME

There was the silhouette of her; there was the giant clear-glass disk of the clock, a relatively small clutter of oiled gears and springs exactly in the center, and there were the long hands of it, the squared-off Roman numerals themselves inlaid deep in the thick glass; the minute hand now cocked back a bit, then inched forward.

And beyond it spread the fine vista of Paris, milkily moonlit. You could see the river, with the Place de la Concorde on one side of the scene and the Palais du Louvre on the other, the slate rooftops of the central city everywhere, and in the distance rose white, onion-domed Sacré-Coeur virtually incandescent atop the very steep hill of Montmartre. Claire must have heard him coming up behind her, and she slowly turned to face him, a beautiful girl with rare gray eyes, the looming clock face behind her.

"Hi," he said softly, relieved.

She smiled.

"Hi," she said to him.

o o o

THEY HAD BEEN SITTING THERE on the low riveted crossbeam, which provided a ready bench, for a while, no idea how long (they had forgotten the clock), and Claire was still talking, trying to tell this boy about it.

"Africa?" Jimmy asked her.

"That's where we lived the longest overseas, crazy as it may seem," she said. "It wasn't as if my father was any big shot in the foreign service. He was only AID, Agency for International Development, a lawyer for them handling legal issues, and his going into a whole new career that way, from a local practice in Baltimore to AID, was part of his big change in midlife, with a new wife and a new job. It got worse with the problems between me and my sister there in Africa, Côte d'Ivoire."

"Ivory Coast."

"Yes. You see, I always saw my sister as the smarter one, the sensitive one. I was an airhead, as far as I was concerned, and it didn't matter that everybody told me I was so pretty, and it didn't matter that I knew I could have my pick of the boys when I got to the prep school in Providence. I went there for my last two years, transferring from the school in Switzerland. And it was a really welcome change, I guess, after that all-girls boarding school in Switzerland, seeing that this school was coed and there were actual boys on the premises at last. I was instantly a celebrity with the other kids at the prep school in Providence—Moses Brown School was its name, originally a Quaker operation—a celebrity simply because I *had* gone to school in Switzerland, and I suppose they all saw that as making me exotic, what made me seem somehow prettier than I really was."

"You are pretty," Jimmy told her. "I mean, you are really pretty."

"Don't say that."

"It's true."

"But don't say it."

"OK."

"And, again, if it sounds like I was just a spoiled rich kid with those fancy schools," Claire continued, "that wasn't the case either. Working for AID, my father was given a more than generous allowance to send us to school where we wanted to go, because there wasn't any embassy school, any American school or anything like that, in dinky Abidjan. It was a perk that came with the job. Anyway, even if my sister was a year older, I think she was envious of me for having the wherewithal to pick the cool kind of schools, places offbeat and like the one in Switzerland, or Moses Brown, while she just automatically chose predictably top-notch Phillips Andover in Massachusetts. But after all that fancy education, the fact that I only got into a place like St. Lawrence in upstate New York, a party school, maybe really proved I was an airhead. My sister, Elizabeth, was even envious of that, I think, convinced I was enjoying something special there, while I suppose I would have loved to have gotten into a place like the University of Michigan. She was enrolled in their sort of elite honors program that was mostly out-of-state kids, Elizabeth accepted on early admission, no less.

"With all of the boyfriends, I don't know, but I guess with them I was trying to prove something to myself, something about how sad I felt all the time, even if I was popular. And I suppose that's the word for it—a stupid one, but that's it—*popular*. But it could have meant something else, if you know what I mean. And I did have a really lot of boyfriends, one after another, sleeping with them all. I slept with the school's acknowledged walking Adonis, captain of the soccer team, just because I knew I could sleep with him. I slept with the one really rich frat boy at St. Lawrence, a guy who drove around in a perfectly restored old Lincoln convertible like you see in the films about Jack Kennedy, just because I knew I could sleep with him, his father the CEO of some giant oil multinational. Every summer I spent a couple of months in Abidjan, which I really loved because there were great beaches and also such great African rock music everywhere, the electric guitar in the songs plink-plinking away, sort of meandering very happily, if that makes any sense. You even begin to appreciate, after a while, the smell of open sewage as mixed with that of the tons of perfumy flowers, sweet hibiscus especially, though admittedly most of the people are pretty poor. I just wanted to relax for the whole summer in that great sunshine of Abidjan, after barely squeaking by final exams again back in freezing Canton, New York. I know my sister hated me when I told her about the fun, all the crazy parties at St. Lawrence, and I know she hated me for heading off in my father's little government-issue Ford Escort every morning in Abidjan to go to the beach again for the day, just a T-shirt and camp shorts and flip-flops, my bikini under-neath, when she thought she didn't look good in any bathing suit, never mind a bikini, so she never went to the beach. Guys a lot older than me, European businessmen or whoever, would wander over from the private beach of the ritzy five-star hotel next door there and try to line up a date that night for dinner with me, and if I told my sister about accepting, or told her about what happened later on and during that date, back at the man's hotel room, she just stewed, said I had no control of myself. I don't know what it really was, and I know that my father divorcing our mother and marrying a woman half his age affected Elizabeth very badly, while I don't think it both-ered me—my father was happy, and from what I could tell my mother there in the Baltimore suburb never seemed at all bit-ter or anything like that, but maybe I didn't see her enough to know how she really felt about the whole thing one way or the other. Meanwhile, for no reason I could figure out, I kept get-ting sadder, and back at St. Lawrence, it turned worse."

She stopped.

"This is boring, isn't it?" she said to him, obviously convinced that it was.

"No, it's not," Jimmy said. "It's not boring at all."

"Anyway, there were more guys at school, but with each new boyfriend I got even sadder. The college health services thera-pist told me I hadn't come to terms with my parents' divorce, and I wanted to tell her that the divorce had nothing to do with it, that was my sister's problem but not mine. The thera-pist also told me that there was nothing out of the ordinary in leading a full sex life, and for the insomnia I complained about

she eventually prescribed Dalmane sleeping pills, thirty mil-
ligrams. The first thing I noticed on the prescription form even
before I was halfway across the campus that bright autumn
day, the leaves exploding in their colors—I remember that,
those fiery leaves—the first thing I noticed was that it was a
prescription for three refills of thirty pills each, or one for the
first order, plus two refills. I had plenty of time to think about
it, while I kept getting sadder and sadder, forgetting about
the boys and forgetting about most classes by the end of that
semester, too. And I suppose that before long all I did think
about was how soon I could get the little brown plastic vial of
the red-and-gray capsules filled again, because according to
the prescription you could only get a refill once a month for
another thirty-day supply. I stockpiled is what I did."

Jimmy remembered the Puvis de Chavannes painting, called
The Dream: *the sleeping young woman—he decided that for him
it would be a woman—with that little sack on a pole set down
beside her, and above were the lovely floating beauties in white
gowns sprinkling what life did offer, but what could just as well
have been sleeping pills, three full brown plastic vials of them,
stockpiled, onto her slumber like that. Maybe Jimmy knew what
had been Claire's fate from the moment he saw that painting, and
as much as he might hope against hope that he didn't know what
he did, the whole thing had taken on the irreversible momentum
of a nighttime imagining that you couldn't deter, an ultimate and
powerful inevitability.*

"Well," Claire continued, taking a deep breath as if to mus-
ter courage for the recounting, "to make a long and obvious
and pretty stupid story short, I did it over Christmas break

when nobody else was around. I had special permission to stay in the dormitory, when everything on campus closed for vacation, because my official home address was overseas, and one afternoon when the latest blizzard was almost beyond heavy, when I, alone, was way sadder than even I thought I ever could be, I just popped them all, like casually downing a few handfuls of those sort of old-fashioned Jujubes you get at a multiplex when seeing a movie. I looked at the snow falling outside, and I was totally relaxed on my bed, until I started to become groggy and it suddenly occurred to me—I *didn't* want to do this, I *shouldn't* have done this, I had so many things I hoped to do and I was still so young, and what did, you know, what did a stage of sleeping around with boys or any of the rest of my boarding school and college mess-ups matter? But here's the important part. Though I couldn't move, and though it was already too late, flat on my back by then, drowsier by the second, for some crazy reason I tried to will my way out of it by straining as hard as I could to *picture* in my mind my body somehow moving over to the telephone there on my dorm desk to somehow try to call my sister in Ann Arbor. I wanted to tell her that she should never blame herself for any of it, it had nothing to do with her—you see, she had called me a whore the summer before in a family fight right before each of us flew back to school in September from Abidjan, and I, too, had said things I shouldn't have said to her, so the last time we saw each other we hadn't been speaking. I knew she would blame herself, she cared about me deep down. I loved her so, Elizabeth, a special kid—I still love her so."

Jimmy didn't say anything at first, then finally spoke.

"What you said about being young," Jimmy said, quietly, "it's the hunger."

She looked right at him. Hell, she was beautiful, he thought, that tawny hair on the shoulders of the striped wool cape of a girl who *was* exotic, Jimmy knew, who had gone to a ritzy boarding school in Switzerland and who did spend her summers like some jet-setter on the palm-lined, powdery-sand beaches of West Africa. She lifted her hand and reached from where she was sitting, gently touched his cheekbone.

"You're really nice," she said.

But in a way Jimmy wasn't listening to that, and he simply had to tell this girl about how he himself had once tried to write a poem about it, the hunger of just being young; he told her he had titled it exactly that, "The Hunger."

"It's what makes you want to do everything in the world," he said, "like see for yourself all the great museums and everything else, what we're doing now, that makes you want to—"

She put her cool finger to his lips, told him, "Shhh, they're coming."

○ ○ ○

NEVERTHELESS, CLAIRE DID HAVE ENOUGH TIME to add, again whispering as she had whispered to him about the clocks themselves when they'd first arrived at the museum, "I knew you were something like that, a poet, and I knew it from the beginning, when we were first walking and talking."

Jimmy tried to tell her that he wasn't really a poet, not by any means; he was only somebody who took creative writing classes from a great teacher in poetry, a guy named Roger Rath at Mankato State, but it was a start if nothing else. And who knew what such a start could lead to, right?

o o o

JIMMY HAD TO RESORT TO the "Orsay, the Mother of All Museums" line yet another time to ward off the teasing from the other three, who found Jimmy and Claire sitting close that way in the shadows, the brainy girl Jennifer surprisingly having joined ranks with the sports-nut duo, Kyle and Tom, in the general goofing around.

They were all tired by this point, the way you do become exhausted in a museum after too many galleries—after too much walking over the creaking floors, after too many pauses, progressively longer, to rest for a while on the black leatherette benches with chrome legs; nobody had much energy for the final few rooms. Gauguin and his full-lipped bronze maidens with fleshy flowers like detonating stars in their shining black hair received rather short treatment, if truth be known, and Jennifer, worn-out herself and ready to move on, only halfheartedly said that she was hoping there would be more of Henri Rousseau, but, as she assured everybody, that sole Henri Rousseau on display was the *very* major canvas *The Snake Charmer,* showing the shadelike standing figure in an emerald nighttime jungle playing a flute, a black serpent frighteningly, yet lovingly, entwined about the darkened specter.

Kyle, from the University of Texas, was already thinking of something else, talking about what they might do next.

"Let's go over to Champs-Élysées," he said, "let's find the Planet Hollywood. I heard it's there. I want to get a Planet

Hollywood cap, you know, like a baseball cap, red maybe, that says *'Planet Hollywood, Paris'* on it."

And with that, Kyle and Tom, the happy sports nuts, did go there separate ways in opinion, Tom saying he couldn't believe what Kyle had just said, and that buying a Planet Hollywood cap was about the *corniest* thing that any *corny* tourist could ever do in Paris.

Jennifer laughed.

"Except," she said, "for maybe having your portrait sketched by one of those creepy guys, probably correspondence-school *artistes*, sitting around waiting for suckers under the Eiffel Tower. Remember them?"

"Yeah," Tom said, "I almost forgot that one, Jen, you're right, that's the *real* corniest, except if maybe you have the *artiste* do it *while* you're wearing a Planet Hollywood cap!"

Everybody was laughing, Kyle, the current butt of the banter, included.

o o o

AND SO THEY LEFT THE MUSEUM. Outside, they continued along the wide sidewalks, there beside the wall on the quay.

If you saw them that night, you might have watched them marching in a line over the Pont Alexandre III, its white arches, wedding-cake frilled, that spanned in graceful leaps the glassy black Seine, the city very quiet, thoroughly deserted in the moonlight. And what moonlight it was, because the full moon was glowing even brighter, if that was possible, each time you looked up to notice just how goddamn achingly bright it was.

The moving queue of them disappeared into the maze of

streets with the endless stately buildings of the Right Bank, their laughter growing softer in the distance, and then gone.

o o o

JUST MORE AMERICAN COLLEGE KIDS, surely, if you didn't know the truth, just the bunch of them off to the Champs-Élysées to find, yeah, the Planet Hollywood reportedly right beside the Ben and Jerry's—somewhere over there and far off from the Musée d'Orsay, where now the carved lettering in the fine buff-stone facade still announced to anyone willing to listen the names all those cities the station had once served, almost spoke them like a litany or a telling prayer: Toulouse, Orléans, Poitiers, Bordeaux.

Even the wonderfully distant, half-magical ancient royal city of Tours.

A LATE AFTERNOON SWIM

A mythology ravels and then it unravels.

— Louis Aragon

I AM ON THE BEACH IN FRONT of the Neesawquague Shores Beach Club in Rhode Island, but the beach itself is deserted. Or deserted the way it can be late on a weekday when only a few stragglers remain. It's late in the season, too, possibly August.

o o o

THE BEACH CLUB HAS A LONG BOARDWALK PAVILION. It has cabanas and a dining room and even a small ballroom, for the season's big dances. Built in the 1920s when this whole peninsula was first developed by a so-called visionary mogul as a hopefully ritzy resort (winding two-lanes along the high golden cliffs, the dreamy, movie-inspired concepts for the summer places, some Tudor and some Mediterranean and some Colonial), yes, built in the 1920s, the beach club faces the surfed crescent of a beach on one side of the peninsula, which rises like Gibraltar, and it seems to exist in essential colors: the white for the buildings that are the pavilion, the black for the planks of the boardwalk proper, and the red for what could be the miles of ship-style pipe railings.

I suppose I am about eleven years old, and somehow I have been poking around at the far end of the wide beach. I am heading back now to find my mother. She herself likes to linger like this, late in the day. It seems I told my mother I just wanted to take a walk down to the splashed rocks with their blankets of barnacles at that far end of the beach, look for what are maybe tiny fiddler crabs in the pools there—you crack open a nacreous blue mussel to its orange innards, plunk it in the pool, and they come scurrying out from hiding.

"OK, you take a walk and I'll continue reading," my mother has told me, "and when you come back, we'll take our dip."

My mother, a good swimmer, always refers to a swim as just that, "a dip."

And even though I am only eleven (possibly twelve), I already seem to have the insight of somebody much older and much more troubled, a middle-aged man like I am today. Even at that age I already seem to see myself here in a room an Arizona city removed from everything that was the first important years of my life, with the computer screen glowing and writing something like, "I am on the beach in front of the Neesawquague Shores Beach Club." I suppose the whole idea of my being on the beach and looking for my mother is tricky.

Which is to say, I also already have a sense that to return from those rocks to my mother, now long deceased, could mean some difficulty, and it could prove, to use that word again, *tricky* indeed.

But I have left my mother sitting in her low-slung canvas

beach chair. She is still relatively young and so beautiful, wearing a wide-brimmed white beach hat and a white beach jacket over her bathing suit, lipstick, too. She is reading a French novel, and she has also stuffed into her white beach bag, I know, the worn French dictionary I myself will take to Harvard a half dozen or so years later, because that's the way my mother is. If the other women who were sitting with her in a semicircle of beach chairs earlier in the day gossip or thumb through women's magazines, for my mother the best part of the day is after they have gone, when the beach has emptied out this way, and she can read. During the week my father stays up at our house in Providence, seeing that his law firm doesn't close for July and August, and I guess my sisters are off for dinner or stay-overs with friends at other houses in Neesawquague Shores. So there's no need for me and my mother to hurry back home. It is very much so just my mother and me.

We will have something like BLTs for dinner, with a lot of mayonnaise and, especially, a lot of sliced fat Rhode Island tomatoes, the way I like BLTs.

Nevertheless, I'm nervous about that swim with her.

o o o

BUT MAYBE I HAVEN'T SAID ENOUGH about what I just mentioned, now that I think of it, the dictionary, a French-to-French one. I mean, it is just like my mother to take it to the beach.

I still have it, of course. One of my sisters got it when she mustered the courage during boarding school to forgo for one season those dances at the beach club (and the boys in their British sport cars, all moonily hanging around our own house and pretending to be admiring their golf clubs or talking about Dartmouth or talking about Brown, all pining after my sisters, each a beauty in her own way), true, she decided to spend a summer studying in France. The dictionary is really more of a compact, one-volume dictionary/encyclopedia for students in France, hardbound with an orange-brown cover, glossy like you would get on a kids' storybook, and a yellow band on the front with black letters within:

NOUVEAU LAROUSSE ÉLÉMENTAIRE

It's about the size of the kind of world almanac of facts they used to sell in supermarkets, and looking at it now I see that it was printed in 1959. And the title page does tout it as more than an ordinary dictionary, saying right under the title, "*Un dictionnaire sans exemples est un squelette.*" I know that *squelette* can translate as "outline" but also literally as "skeleton." Nice. The dictionary promises "*43 700 articles*" and "*1 700 illustrations en noir,*" plus "*19 planches hors texte en couleurs.*" My mother was a librarian before she married, and she loved books, the challenge of them, the wonder, and she loved having a dictionary that was entirely in French for her reading of something like Flaubert's wild vision of ancient Carthage, *Salammbô*, let's say. She would read her favorite French novels over and over. There was no pretension to it, and, in fact, my mother would always wait until all the other bridge-club types had left before she took out her reading that way.

I would like to say that thumbing through the dictionary now I find specks of sand, sparkling with mica like some heavenly (metaphysical?) dust, but if such was there from those afternoons on the beach, it is long gone. The endpapers of the dictionary are great, both sets in full color, and the front set giving a history of the automobile in pictures, and the back set offering the same for the airplane. All with the usual pro-Gallic slant that was the essence of the haughty Republic in a time like 1959. The automobile spread begins with a depiction of a guy in a red jacket and tricornered Parisian hat driving a wagon powered by some sort of steam (1682), and then, after more inserts, it progresses to an open-topped yellow bone-shaker driven by a guy in goggles beside his fashionable lady friend in front of the Petit Palais exhibition hall (1900), and then right up to one of those sleek rocket-shaped Citroëns with no driver visible inside the silver sedan that has mirroring silver windows (1959). The airplane spread begins with some French soldiers in kepis in the middle of a field gazing at a parked white bat-wing contraption with propellers (1896), and then . . . but why go on, except to add that the spread ends with an oversize tin can of a contraption with a needle nose, looking as absurd as the earlier big bat-wing contraption, not quite any real satellite but perhaps a far-fetched French conception of one floating in a lurid pink sky (1959). To see either display you would be convinced that outside of France there was little that mattered in the development of these modes of transportation, and just when I am thinking there is nothing whatsoever on railways, probably because by that time in history, 1959, rail-ways obviously had been eclipsed by the other two, do I notice small black-ink handwriting along the outer edge of the air-plane endpapers; there are numbers with slashes:

#58/ 3:50
#103/ 4:45

It is my own handwriting. And after thinking and thinking, I conclude that it must have been the schedule times of the late Friday-afternoon trains that I would sometimes take while at Harvard from South Station in Boston down to Providence, using the old, thoroughly decrepit New York, New Haven, and Hartford line. The association is strange, and, as said, just when I was telling myself trains don't merit the endpaper treatment in the dictionary's history of transportation, I almost receive a message about trains, or that one railway line in particular. I used that dictionary for French lit classes all through college.

But what I am writing here is really not about the dictionary. This is about when I am walking back from the rocks at the far end of the beach, to take a late afternoon swim with my mother. And I am very nervous about that.

o o o

WHAT AM I WEARING?

Me, a bony kid and always tall for my age, I am wearing swim trunks with a pattern of chess pieces, black on white. I have let the trunks' tie strings dangle outside like limp spaghetti strands because I have seen the bronzed lifeguards do exactly that, and lifeguards are to be emulated; I myself am surely tanned nut brown this late in the season. The sand has cooled after the heat of day and I move softly over it, nearly moon-walking, and there are low waves on that crescent of the beach, a quarter mile across; they make for measured phalanxes, not heavy surf but good rolling surf, nevertheless, the kind you can get a long ride on. Indeed, they crest in blue arcs veined with foam, spewing spray at the top, then slap, one after another, to spread in layers like molten glass and eventually lap and ultimately expire up on the shore, where the wet sand is amber, not the powdery white it is here, much higher up.

I know if I do swim with my mother, I will ride some of the waves, while she will head farther out, beyond them, to where the surface is glassy in the stillness of the late afternoon doused with thick honey sunshine; she will float, do her slow backstroke, and float some more. I know that even though I am nervous about taking this swim, apprehensive, it has nothing to do with any fear of the water. I have always been completely at home in the wet, never resorting to gradual immersion but always just stomping my way in, taking that first dive into it with determination, to frog-leg a few pumps under the shampoo greenness of it, bob up, look around, and tell myself what I always do once the first contact of what should be the cold of a plunge is accomplished, "Boy, this is warm." To ride a wave takes some expertise, I realize, and though I can't bodysurf like maybe the muscular lifeguards do when the waves are truly big two or three times a year, after a storm, when the lifeguards themselves set up the snapping red pennants for the swimming area and they catch the crests that then break high and very far out, I am good at knowing when to jump into a smaller roller that is closer in, catch it right at the peak of its rise and before the collapse, to keep my arms outstretched like Superman, and, with the roar of it thumping in my ears, get that feeling, the fine assurance, that you *have* caught it, that you *are* skimming along the top rather than plowing through the water, to airily glide. Still, I know there might be none of that for me for the time being, because what I am fearing is that this swim with my mother this particular day could be dangerous on another level, a level that I at eleven or twelve am not supposed to know about.

I see my mother beyond one of the empty white lifeguard stands. I look up to the clock above the ballroom entrance on the beach club's pavilion and notice that it is past six. My mother is reading, turning the pages slowly, but I don't think she has even removed the dictionary from her beach bag, probably not hitting a word yet that she wants to check the meaning of; her French is very good. I do see a few other people here and there, packing up and leaving. There are no crew boys from the Umbrella House to help with such chores this late in the day, and a man and his wife, quite old, wrestle with a large canvas umbrella as if taking down a complicated boat sail, finally coaxing it to folding; a young mother with some very young kids has all of the tin pails and shovels and those little tin sand sifters gathered, and with the kids in tow she reaches the steps to the boardwalk pavilion at about the same time as the old couple. At the opposite end of the beach, toward the peninsula of Neesawquague Shores and where you can see our own house almost out at the Point, a man in what looks like a yachting getup is walking a skittish brown-and-white setter; another man, bald and flabby in his swim trunks, is at the water's edge, about to go in. And outside of them, the beach is definitely deserted now, and I tell myself I want it always to be like this: me in the chessboard swim trunks with my breathing from the chest a little tight—nicely so and what I've heard grown-ups call "the saltwater blues"—after my couple of swims already that day with my pals, and my mother sitting there with her white hat and white beach jacket. The sunshine has lost its glare of morning and then midday, and now is softened, that oozing honey of it that does prompt surreally long shadows from the little Towers of Babylon that are the lifeguard stands (my sisters used to joke about how when they were younger and had a crush on this lifeguard or that, they would *look forward* to a splinter in the foot picked up on the boardwalk, because it meant approaching one of those bronze specimens when you yourself were twelve or fourteen and having him take the white first-aid kit from the storage compartment built into the stand, while you sat there and he cradled your foot and manfully probed for the thing with tweezers to try to find and remove it, if it actually were there, for him to finally dab the wound with antiseptic mercurochrome, wonderfully stinging, before applying a white cloth band-aid, my sisters always laughed about that), yes, the sunshine that renders all the colors truer than true and almost in too-clear focus, not just the white, black, and red of the beach club, but the golden cliffs of the peninsula rising there, the cap of green atop the cliffs and the dots of the houses, some pastels, yellow or pink, and the sky cloudless and so blue that you think somebody is putting you on. That's what I want—to be on my way, closer but never any closer, safe and not having to confront this business of the swim with my mother.

But my mother spots me. She waves arcingly, slowly, the book in the other hand resting on the lap of her flower-print bathing suit.

o o o

THE DICTIONARY IS IN HER BEACH BAG, I know. The same dictionary I am holding here all these years later, today, when my mother has been dead so long.

I look up some words in that dictionary now as I sit here at my desk.

> **appréhension** n. f. Crainte vague, mal définie; *avoir de l'appréhension.*
> −Syn. Angoisse, crainte, inquiétude, peur. −Contr. Confiance, sérenité, tranquilité.

Vague fear, all right. And how about those painful synonyms supplied—anguish, inquietude, fear—while the antonyms soothingly whisper just the opposite.

> **regret** n. m. Chagrin causé par la mort d'une personne: *la perte de cet ami m'a laissé un grand regret.* Déplaisir d'avoir perdu un bien qu'on possédait ou de n'avoir pu obtenir celui qu'on desirait.

Interesting, that first definition of the word, more like *grief* in English, but the second different, displeasure at losing what one once had or—this is more exact—not having gotten what one desired. But how is anybody to know what he or she desires, until *after* you don't get it? The word has a built-in conundrum, a contradictory flaw.

> **tristesse** n. f. État naturel ou accidental de chagrin, de mélancolie: *sombrer dans a tristesse.*

Simple enough, a state either of the natural or the accidental variety, yet it comes down to the same thing, melancholy, and saying "*sombrer* in sadness" isn't redundant, because *sombrer* means sinking and not merely the English word *somber,* it gets at the throbbing ache of it, the sinking into sadness, which also does entail, when you think of it, a lot of the previously cited anguish and apprehension, too.

I go back to the title page and look at the address of Librairie Larousse given as "Paris VI," and "13 à 21, rue Montparnasse et boulevard Raspail, 114."

Hell, am I ever stalling. I mean, I'm killing time with the dictionary, and there is my mother beckoning me on the beach. She now places the novel on the spread towel beside the chair and stands up, lifting off the floppy beach hat and letting it drop to the chair; she takes off the white beach jacket and begins looking in the beach bag for her bathing cap, I suspect. I spot the dictionary, its orange-brown cover, which she lifts out as she probes deeper for the cap in the white woven-straw bag, and I want to shout out to her something like:

"That's the dictionary I'm now holding in my hand!"

Or:

"Do you remember that dictionary! Do you remember how Veronica got it in France one summer, how we all used it over the years, how I took it to college! I have it, I have it still!"

But I don't shout that, and I watch as my mother simply puts it back in the bag, now that she has found within the pink rubber cap with puffy rubber flowers decorating it. She is smiling in the sunshine, in the aforementioned stillness of it all, a late afternoon in front of the Neesawquague Shores Beach Club. It *is* 1957 or 1958, I know, but that leads to the *larger* question.

How can it be 1957 or 1958, when I was eleven and twelve,

respectively, but I have that dictionary right here on my desk beside
the computer and it says it was published in 1959? And, to skew the
chronology more, didn't my sister go to study in France the summer
before Kennedy was elected, in 1960?

I want to shout to my mother (which seems to remind me
now of some very well known short story where there is a similar
scenario, the title escaping me? *intertextualité française?*), I need
to tell her, "Something's wrong, something's terribly wrong!"
But I don't.

o   o   o

I WONDER WHY MY SISTERS are off with friends. My three sisters.

My oldest sister, the quietly assured and poised one, who will
play the harp at the posh Order of the Sacred Heart women's
college in the New York suburb, who will marry a fine young
man from Yale and he will go on to distinguish himself at a New
York law firm, they will have five children, though he will die of
cancer before fifty; my oldest sister is gone from the beach. The
middle sister who is a true beauty, something in the cascading
mahogany hair and wide white smile, the mile-high cheekbones
and the large pale-blue eyes, all tracing back to somewhere in
the Irish ancestry on my mother's side, who will get thrown out
of the same Order of the Sacred Heart college, though to her it
won't matter, her career is already beginning, first her landing
acting jobs in New York, then the several films as a legitimate
starlet in Hollywood, a succession of marriages in the course of
it, but that is what is to be expected of a legitimate starlet, as she
herself will later concede; she, my middle sister, is gone from the
beach. My youngest sister, the brainy one, who will constantly

astonish us with her own precociousness (we used to joke that all we needed for her to do was invent and patent "one little thing," put all of us on easy street forever), and she will attend Brown because my mother herself eventually gives up on her belief that the Order of the Scared Heart is the only training for a young woman (characters in F. Scott Fitzgerald novels attend Sacred Heart schools, why, even characters in Henry James novels attend Sacred Heart schools, all the Kennedy girls received such an education, of course), my youngest sister who will go on to law school and then teaching law at Stanford, married to a history professor there, and while unable to have kids themselves, they will "adopt" many of their students during troubled times in the students' own lives, an ever-changing family of sorts that she will eventually say she has always been grateful for; my youngest sister, she, too, is gone from the beach.

And as explained, during the week my father stays up at our house in Providence. He is not a fan of the shore, and even on weekends he seems half out of place there, his idea of casual wear simply meaning his suit trousers and one of his white dress shirts with the collar open and the sleeves rolled up, thin-soled summer wingtips (have I already used such details about our family summer house in a short story I have written about other people? have I foolishly *squandered* all the details of my life elsewhere?); he usually seems to be waiting to return to his work at the firm, also the continual good fight of state politics and his post on the Democratic state committee. He built the summer place only because he'd always promised my mother, who loves the ocean, who loves to swim, that he would give her a summer place one day. And though as a young attorney starting out in the Depression he couldn't manage to do that, right after the war he bought up the land far out on the Point, the scrub-growth lots thick with bayberry and wild rose and bounding rabbits; he made good on the pledge, building the sprawling one-story place that has such big picture windows that let into our lives the hugeness of what might be called the Essential Sea, where at night the bell buoys out there softly clank, the scanning green beam from Beavertail Lighthouse over on Jamestown Island floods through the rooms like some spilled grace, to maybe make our dreaming easier, to maybe make our dreaming that much more marvelous indeed. In Providence now for the entire week, my father is gone from the beach as well. Again, that leaves only my mother and me to linger, to not be in a hurry whatsoever, because there is nothing we have to get back to.

There will be the slow walk along the shore, then up the right-of-way path, with me carrying my mother's beach chair. At the house we will take turns using the outdoor shower.

o o o

FOR DINNER MY MOTHER WILL MAKE US BLTS, the bacon crisply frying.

o o o

WE WILL HAVE COFFEE MILK WITH THE SANDWICHES, maybe potato chips, too. We will have a slice of cake for desert. The rectangular cakes in boxes are bought from the "bakery men" who come in their small panel trucks to Neesawquague Shores, wearing uniforms with bow ties, to stroll up to the door with their hoop-handled trays and show the housewives their wares (many of the housewives do not drive, my mother included)—the Cushman's Bakery man in his black-and-white truck on Monday, Wednesday, and Friday mornings, the Arnold's Bakery man in his maroon truck on Tuesday and Thursday. They are like the Hood milkman, whose truck with its jangling glass bottles can be heard in the sunny summer mornings coming around the narrow, lumpy asphalt road there at the Point, or like the Loutitt Laundry man, who brings back in his truck my father's white shirts, wrapped and comfortably starched "medium." Sometimes Neesawquague Shores seems like its own distinct territory, even a separate and blessed kingdom, supplied by friendly outsiders who visit but then politely and understandingly leave, to let us get on with our lucky lives entirely on our own. The coffee milk will be just right, and I will stir into mine too much syrup to make it more than just right.

○ ○ ○

AND MY MOTHER WILL MAKE US BLTS, the bacon crisply frying in the big, bright kitchen with its museum of streamlined white appliances.

○ ○ ○

BUT I ALREADY SAID THAT, DIDN'T I, about her making the BLTs.

○ ○ ○

"BILLY, WHERE HAVE YOU BEEN?" my mother says to me on the beach.

I am standing beside her now. Some gulls hover above, pleasantly cawing; the air is salty, fragrant.

"I told you, I went down to the rocks. I fooled around there some. I was looking for crabs. They're fiddler crabs, I guess."

"Crabs? For bait? Is somebody taking you fishing, Ray's dad?"

"No, just to fool around with them, look at them, see them come out from under the rocks and ledges in the pools. Tiny green ones. Why do they call them fiddler crabs?"

About to lift the bathing cap up to her head, my mother stops, thinks about my question for a second or two. Her hair is still dark and her own features, the high cheekbones, are those of my middle sister, the true beauty.

"Well, it would seem they're called fiddler crabs because they have only one claw. Yes, they have only that one large claw, the poor little things, so it looks like they're, well, playing away at a fiddle all the time."

I want to talk with my mother about metaphor, but I realize that at eleven or twelve I know nothing about metaphor. Still, just their being called fiddler crabs is a metaphor, the representation of one thing in terms of another thing so that you will see the first thing better. But is that the trap of metaphor, and in seeing the first thing supposedly better, in making the association between the A and the B of it, is the inherent sense of the original thing, the actuality and substantiality of it, merely sacrificed to the airy pleasure of the mind jump, like the rush you get from a chrome nail puzzle untangled (metaphor describing metaphor), so that in the end you have only the words, representations themselves, and you realize that you missed the actuality and the substantiality—the *living*? But, of course, I don't have any of that knowledge then, or those questions, and when my mother offers the easy explanation concerning the name fiddler crab, which I myself probably knew but forgot, I only say:

"Oh yeah, that's right."

"Are you ready for our dip?"

She says that cheerily, and with an utterance that simple, that routine, there is so much love in her eyes, so much happiness. She tugs the cap onto her head, dark pink, with the lighter pink flowers blossoming all around it, tucking her curls under the edges; it matches her white bathing suit that has the pink flower print on it. As she continues tucking the curls at the edges, she says she lost track of time.

"I was reading. I was reading my book. Did you notice what time it was when you came by the club?"

"It's pretty late, almost half past six by now, I think."

"But we don't care, do we?" she says, still smiling, her lipstick very red, her teeth very even and white. "We don't care, because tonight it's just us."

Yet I don't answer that. I only say:

"Fiddler crab. That's perfect when you think of it, Mom. I mean, just the way they move around, the way that they bounce around, really, and that one claw seems to be bouncing, too, like some guy is really playing something and is really excited about what he is playing on a fiddle, like a jig." Then I wonder about that, asking her, "A jig would be something you play on a fiddle, right?"

"Certainly, a lovely Irish jig."

I nod. I am also fingering something in the back pocket of the swim trunks with their black-on-white chess-pieces patterning—a splatter of knights, rooks, pawns—and somewhere there is also a matching cabana-suit jacket lined with white terry cloth to wear with the trunks, to make a set. But at age eleven, or twelve, even if I in past summers wore without protest both a cabana suit's trunks and the jacket always lined with terry cloth, did so for years, this season I have refused to do it, thinking the jacket looks "fruity." *Fruity* is a big word that summer, the same summer that my older sisters are listening to Kingston Trio albums and there are exciting quiz shows on TV with studio accessories like "isolation booths" for the contestants, and *fruity* is the exact opposite of *cool*, the latter surely my all-time-favorite word that summer. I finger the back pocket again, and I remember that my best friend, Ray Rogers, has given me a baseball card. The card is nothing valuable like a Ted Williams or a Jimmy Piersall, but possibly one of that overweight right-handed pitcher, Awful Ike Delock of the beloved Red Sox, meaning that at least it is a Red Sox card, vaguely worthwhile.

"What's that?" my mother asks me.

"I almost forgot. A card, a baseball card Ray gave me. He had an extra. It's only Ike Delock."

"And what's wrong with Mr. Delock?"

"He's awful lately is what he is."

"You can put it in my bag."

"Good."

I look at the card—jowly, bulb-nosed Awful Ike with his scrunched blue cap bearing the red *B* pulled low—and I walk over the sand to the beach bag next to the wood-framed chair. I open up the mouth of the straw bag. I want to find a safe place for the card, deciding that I will slip it inside the front cover of the French-to-French dictionary—the sight of which suddenly frightens me more than anything, makes me more scared than ever. *Does my mother have any idea how that dictionary will someday end up with me in a room in an apartment in Arizona, that I will thumb through it and look for words to try to define how nothing did turn out the way I thought it would in my life, then how I will go back to typing on the black plastic keys of my computer, writing what I am writing here? Does my mother have any idea how the dictionary itself with all its definitions could almost be a metaphor for, or more exactly a perfect icon for, everything that did go wrong in my life? Or, how possibly everything in life is just airy insubstantiality, as attested to by the patent contradiction that if it isn't even 1959 yet, when the dictionary was published according to the title page, how can I as a kid be about to slip a baseball card under its front cover, meaning that nothing but nothing means anything, all as invisible as forgotten oxygen itself, all vanished before we even have a chance to define it as what we commonly and with naïve smugness call reality? Does my mother know all this? Well, does she?*

But I myself don't know then, at that age, any of that complexity suggested by the presence of the French dictionary either, and I simply put away the card for safekeeping. I decide not to place it within the dictionary's cover, but just flat beside it, then I look up to her, smiling myself, repeating for some reason:

"Fiddler crab."

"What?"

"Fiddler crab," I say. "That's a really, really good word for them, or two good words for them."

"You like words," my mother says, obviously not realizing the irony in that, how words will lead me to all of this convolution, the years and years of substituting for reality the syllables that become the words that become the sentences that become the paragraphs that become the *writing* that can only *suggest* reality, until for me there is no sense of my own failed marriage, my own dear three daughters I never see enough of there in faraway Seattle, in short, all the ongoing sadness I feel lately. "You've always liked words."

She says that and appears to be very appreciative of such a quality in me, and, after all, what *other* than that would a loving mother once a librarian wish to see in her only son?

"Yeah. I never thought of that, but I guess I do."

"Ready?" she asks.

"Ready?" I answer her question with a question.

"For our dip."

"Yeah."

But I know I am lying.

o o o

AT THE WATER'S EDGE SHE WALKS IN SLOWLY, reaching down to scoop up handfuls of wet and massage it on her arms, smiling, looking at me.

"Come on, Billy, the water is fine."

Which is not what I want to hear from her. I want to hear her kindness spoken from the heart, I want her to tell me soothing things there against the backdrop of the ocean's enormity—a long, red-hulled freighter moving but not moving out on the horizon—I want her to tell me things that always had such necessary understanding, even if I know she often fought her own sadnesses in life. For my mother there was depression that came in dim bouts. And even at the summer house it would cause her—when the fog set in, the horn moaning over at Beavertail Light—to stay in her bedroom for days, and if any of us kids, or even our father, went in to try to talk to her, she only whispered to any of us, blankly, "I can't help it, ever since I was a girl, the fog has always frightened me so." It was like the O'Neill play. But she would always eventually come out of it, manage to keep a brave face for us kids and my father, and now all I want to hear is for her to tell me that to see my own sadness as a grown man breaks her heart, that she only wanted the best for me. I want her to tell me how proud she was I did so well at Harvard, how proud she was when I dedicated my first novel (it garnered better reviews than the others, won a prize) to her and my father. I want her to say how even she detected a problem when I first brought Alison, golden-haired and elegantly tall, to spend weekends at the summer place when I was at Harvard and Alison was at Wellesley, yes, tell me that she, my mother, sensed that Alison wasn't the right one for me, that Alison had come from too much money out there in Lake Forest, with her father the shipping-company magnate he was—Alison would always expect more from a husband than anything that could be offered by the young aspiring writer I was, longing to be Joyce, especially longing to be Borges, my unapproachable heroes. I want her to tell me that the failure of the marriage wasn't my fault, and granting that I did render everything rotten with the affairs with my female grad students over the years, it was not right how Alison herself in time turned utterly cold, utterly mocking of me and my failure to do anything truly significant with literature, "a broken-down creative writing teacher at a second-rate Arizona college, that's a *major* laugh," to quote her, and I want my mother to tell me . . . But she isn't telling me anything. She is up to her waist now. No plunging in for her, she leans back against the surface to let the water gently catch her like that, cushioning, and she floats on her back for a while, her legs outstretched and her toes bobbing above the smooth blue beyond the waves now. Which is before she starts a slow backstroke, soon rolling over to begin sidestroking and then the overhand crawling out and away from me, her pink bathing cap bobbing.

This is totally unexpected, and here I am, an eleven-year-old kid, maybe twelve, and my mother is abandoning me! Doesn't the bald guy at the end of the beach who is toweling himself dry now after his own swim see it! Doesn't the other party in the goofy yachting getup who is walking the edgy brown-and-white setter on a leash at the other end of the beach see it! Here I am, having been so apprehensive of having to face this moment of taking a late afternoon swim with my mother, and now my mother doesn't even wait for me to take that swim with her, and she is slowly moving away from me, a deliberate flapping kick as she strokes, heading out farther and farther! No, I am not about to go *into the water* at this stage, but I do shout to her from the shore.

First, the things that any eleven-year-old would shout:
"Don't leave me!"
And:
"Mom!"
Then other things, cupping my hands, my face reddened in what is becoming my absolute anger, close to rage:
"It's this goddamn obsession with words that did it to me! This whole missing of the real at the expense of the goddamn unreal!"

She's farther out now, smaller to my sight and heading toward the horizon, going back to, returning with full conviction to, what is surely the Horizon of the Dead, where she rightfully belongs, of course. Nevertheless, I keep at it, the shouting: "You're to blame, you know! You're the one who got me like this! I mean, what other kid had a mother who read goddamn Flaubert on the beach!"

But I catch myself on that, know I shouldn't have said it as soon as I do say it.

I have always loved, and will always love, my kind, selfless mother so.

o o o

EXHAUSTED FROM THE YELLING, drained, heartbroken myself, I look at the computer, the monitor glowing with (how did that line go?) the syllables that become the words that become the sentences that become the paragraphs that become, as always, the writing before me, the machine lowly humming. The ceiling fan chugs. I assure myself that if nothing else I have committed some of it to prose, in a room in an apartment in Arizona. I glance around for the dictionary, the orange-brown volume with its band of yellow bearing the black titling, *Nouveau Larousse Élémentaire,* and I pick it up again while sitting at my desk here, opening randomly, hitting on page 511. I spot a small illustration beside a fine-print definition, showing a seated man in a tux, the bust of him, as seen from across the top of the grand piano he is playing, and on the piano rests a little pyramid with a waving arm:

254   Sleeping Mask

métronome n. m. Instrument employé pour indiquer
les divers degrés de vitesse du mouvement musical.

I like the idea of that, the diverse, or various, degrees of speed.
It's one of those words that in any language you hear so often
that you forget the innate beauty of it, in this case the solidly
hollow tick-tocking knock contained therein.

I flip a couple of pages, and my eye snags on another small
sketch illustration of two towers rising above domed roofs of an
old city, puffy clouds in the sky:

minaret n. m. Tour d'une mosquée, du haut de laquelle,
chez les musulmans, le muezzin appelle le peuple à la
prière.

I look some more at the detail of the illustration, which is
labeled "*Minarets*" in the scripted plural, the one on the left a
square block like those I myself have seen in fine Tunisian cities
such as handsome Tunis or, better, perfectly preserved ancient
Kairouan out toward the Sahara in Tunisia, the "Fourth Holiest
City in Islam," the other on the right cylindrical and slimmer,
airier, of the Ottoman variety, possibly.

"*Minaret.*" I whisper the word, try it on my palate.

I keep thumbing through the dictionary now, letting my eye
snag on random definitions. I like doing that.

I keep doing that.

o o o

AND MY MOTHER IN HER FLOWER-PRINT BATHING SUIT and
pink bathing cap keeps swimming farther out, to the enormous sparkling ocean, very, very blue.

ABOUT THE AUTHOR

PETER LaSALLE is the author of several short story collections, most recently *What I Found Out About Her*, and the novels *Strange Sunlight* and *Mariposa's Song*. His stories have appeared in magazines and anthologies such as *Tin House, Paris Review, New England Review, Yale Review, Zoetrope, Best American Short Stories, Best American Mystery Stories, Sports Best Short Stories*, and *Prize Stories: The O. Henry Awards*. A collection of essays on travel and literature, *The City at Three P.M.: Writing, Reading, and Traveling*, was published in 2015. Currently, he divides his time between Austin, Texas, where he is a member of the creative writing faculty at the University of Texas, and Narragansett in his native Rhode Island.

BELLEVUE LITERARY PRESS is devoted to publishing
literary fiction and nonfiction at the intersection of
the arts and sciences because we believe that science and the
humanities are natural companions for understanding the human
experience. With each book we publish, our goal is to foster a rich,
interdisciplinary dialogue that will forge new tools for thinking and
engaging with the world.

To support our press and its mission, and for our full catalogue of
published titles, please visit us at blpress.org.

BELLEVUE LITERARY PRESS
New York